THE SILENT GAVEL

AN ALEX HAYES LEGAL THRILLER

L.T. RYAN

WITH

LAURA CHASE

THE ALEX HAYES SERIES

CHAPTER
ONE

THE CARDBOARD BOX split along the seam as I lifted it, sending law books flying across the hardwood floor. Pages fluttered open, spines cracked against the baseboards of my new apartment. November sunlight filtered through the window behind me, tossing shadows across the titles. *Federal Criminal Procedure. Rules of Evidence. Texas v. Johnson.* The last one landed face-up. I stared at the case name for a beat too long.

Texas. Houston. Everything I'd left behind three days ago.

My phone buzzed against my thigh. Dad's name lit the screen.

"Hey," I said, wedging the phone between my ear and shoulder as I crouched to gather the books.

"How's the unpacking going?" I could hear the tinge of sadness in his voice. Even though he supported my moving to D.C., I knew he didn't want me to leave. Ever since we'd reconciled, I'd come to rely on him for support and guidance. It was hard for me to turn away from all of that and go back to living alone, to *feeling* alone.

"Books tried to stage a revolt just now." I stacked them against the wall, aligning the spines out of habit. "But I'm winning."

"That's my girl." Papers rustled on his end. He was probably sketching his next woodworking project. "You get that bookshelf assembled yet?"

I glanced at the pile of compressed wood and hardware near the kitchenette. "It's on the list."

"I could come up for a weekend, help you get settled."

The offer was more than just furniture assembly. We'd only had eighteen months together after his pardon—eighteen months to rebuild what years of wrongful imprisonment had stolen. Now I was seven hundred miles away again, choosing the fight over proximity to the one parent I had left.

"I'd like that," I said, and meant it. "Maybe in a few weeks, once I'm through the first trial by fire at the office."

"Speaking of, are you nervous?"

I straightened, rolling my shoulders against the stiffness from six hours of hauling boxes up three flights of stairs. The Metro Center apartment wasn't much. A one-bedroom, galley kitchen, a living room barely big enough for a couch, but the commute to the DOJ building was a straight shot on the Red Line and the rent wasn't terrible. Sort of made it worth it.

"No," I lied.

Dad's chuckle told me he didn't believe me. "Your mother used to do the same thing. Pretend she wasn't wound tight as a spring before a big case."

The mention of her had me going still. I'd grown used to him talking about her more freely since we'd pieced together her death in 2003, but each reference still brought up a lot of emotions on my end. She'd infiltrated a trafficking network, gathered evidence, and paid for it with her life.

"I talked to Erin yesterday," I said, changing the subject. "And Lisa. They promised to keep me updated on the Blake Costello situation."

"The retrial?"

"If there is one." I moved to the window, looking down at 7th Street where evening commuters streamed toward the Metro station. A homeless man camped on the corner shook a cup at passersby. Someone's car alarm bleated two blocks over. The city hummed with a different frequency than Houston. It felt faster here, colder in a way that had nothing to do with the temperature. "DA's office is still deciding whether to retry him after the appeal. Lisa thinks they'll drop it. Too much heat after everything with Leland."

"It's a tough situation."

I pressed my palm against the glass, cool against my skin. Down in Houston, the network that had destroyed my mother was still breathing. Judge Everett Leland awaited trial. Judge Henry Thatcher was dead, murdered before he could talk. And somewhere in the hierarchy, the king piece remained unnamed and for now, untouchable.

But I had the flash drive now. Melissa Thatcher's files. Her evidence.

And I had the DOJ's resources.

I just needed to use them.

"Alex?" Dad's voice pulled me back. "You still there?"

"Yeah, sorry. Just thinking."

"Don't think too much tonight. Get some rest. First day's always the hardest. Remember that."

"I will. Love you."

"Love you too, kiddo."

I ended the call and put the phone on the windowsill, watching the street below. This city held different dangers than Houston's sprawl, but the game was the same. Power mixed with corruption. People who believed themselves untouchable.

Three sharp knocks sounded at the door.

I crossed the apartment and checked the peephole. My boyfriend, James Holloway, stood in the hallway, takeout bags balanced in both hands, his tie loosened and top button undone.

I unlocked the deadbolt and chain, pulling the door open.

"Hey," he said, grinning. "Hungry?"

The smell of garlic, basil, and tomato sauce hit me first. My stomach clenched, reminding me I hadn't eaten since the gas station breakfast sandwich I'd grabbed on the last leg of the drive, somewhere in Virginia.

"Starving." I stepped aside to let him in, relocking the door behind him. "Is that—"

"Carmine's. The good Italian place near Judiciary Square." He set the bags on the kitchen counter, the only surface not buried under unpacking debris, and turned to give me a hug. "Figured you'd earned it after moving day."

I grabbed plates from the box I'd labeled *Kitchen* while James unpacked containers of pasta, bread, and salad. We worked in silence. Six months of long-distance calls and stolen weekends had taught us this rhythm. But all of that was over now. He was here. I was here. No more flights or goodbyes.

"So." He handed me a fork, leaning against the counter. "Ready for tomorrow?"

I twirled pasta around the fork, not eating yet. "As ready as I'll ever be. You've worked with Chambers before, right?"

"Rory? Yeah, for three years before he moved up to section chief." James's expression shifted into a rare one of reverence. "He's a legend in the Criminal Division. Ran the Enron prosecution task force back in the day, led the corruption cases after Hurricane Katrina, got convictions on half the Louisiana legislature. Smart, ruthless when he needs to be, but fair. If you're on his team, he'll go to war for you."

"And if you're not?"

"Then you better hope you transferred to Tax."

I managed a bite of pasta. It tasted like cardboard; my appetite strangled by nerves. In the living room, the TV murmured. I'd left it on for background noise while unpacking, some 24-hour news channel filling the silence.

"He doesn't suffer fools, but he values initiative," James said. "If you see something, take it to him. Don't sit on leads or second-guess your instincts."

"Come on, we both know that won't be a problem for me." I gave him a side-eye.

James smiled, the crooked one that had first caught my attention in a Houston conference room when I'd been drowning in Leland's corruption case. "I know."

The news anchor's voice sharpened, pulling my attention toward the living room. I caught the words *trafficking* and *dismissal*, and my heart rate kicked up.

"Hold on," I said, setting down my plate and moving to where the TV was against the half-unpacked boxes.

The chyron read: *Judge Dismisses Major Trafficking Case—Technical Grounds.*

A reporter stood outside a federal courthouse somewhere, wind whipping her hair across her face. Behind her, defense attorneys descended the steps, triumph poorly concealed behind professional masks.

"... Judge Lawrence Keller ruled this afternoon that federal prosecutors failed to properly establish chain of custody for key evidence in the case against Leo Brown and three co-defendants accused of running a labor trafficking operation across five states. The dismissal came as a shock to prosecutors, who argued the technical violation was minor and should not result in—"

"That's bullshit," I said, not realizing I'd spoken aloud until James appeared beside me.

"What is?"

I gestured at the screen, where they'd cut to footage of victims' advocates outside the courthouse. "Chain of custody issues don't warrant dismissal unless they're egregious. Any competent prosecutor can establish chain through testimony and documentation. Keller just handed those defendants a gift."

James's hand settled on my shoulder. "Maybe. Or maybe there really was a gap in the evidence. Sometimes judges' hands are tied by procedure."

I turned to look at him. "You believe that?"

"I believe in the rule of law. Even when it produces outcomes I don't like."

The principled answer. The DOJ answer. The one I'd given a thousand times myself before learning that sometimes the law was a weapon in the wrong hands.

The news anchor pivoted to a new story, and I caught the words *confirmation hearing* before the scene changed to the Capitol building's facade.

"... Senate Judiciary Committee will convene tomorrow ahead of the confirmation hearing scheduled for Judge Franklin Pearce, nominated to fill the vacancy on the Fifth Circuit Court of Appeals. Pearce, currently serving on the Eastern District of Texas bench, is expected to face questions about his record on criminal justice reform and environmental regulation ..."

They cut to footage of Pearce. He was in his late sixties with sandy brown hair graying at the temples.

"Good for Frankie," James said, the affection clear in his voice.

I glanced at him. "Frankie?"

"Franklin Pearce. He was one of my professors at Harvard before he went on the bench. Constitutional law and criminal procedure." James looked almost nostalgic. "Brilliant legal mind. Wrote half the textbooks we used in law school. If anyone deserves a circuit seat, it's him."

The name scratched at something in my memory. Judge. Texas. Fifth Circuit. The network operated primarily in Texas and Louisiana, using judicial protection to shield trafficking operations. Leland had been Harris County. Thatcher had ties to Dallas. And now, a judge from East Texas was ascending to a higher court.

"You know him well?" I asked, trying to keep my tone light.

"Well enough. We've kept in touch over the years. He actually called to congratulate me when I made section chief." James picked up the remote and clicked off the TV, cutting Pearce's face off mid-sentence. "Come on, let's eat before everything gets cold."

He moved back to the kitchen, but I stayed rooted in front of the dark screen, the afterimage of Pearce's face burned into my vision.

It was nothing, I told myself. First-day paranoia. The network had made me see threats in every shadow, connections in every coincidence. Franklin Pearce was James's mentor. A respected jurist. A man about to ascend to one of the most powerful courts in the country. Nothing more.

The pop of a champagne cork made me turn.

James stood by the counter, two mismatched glasses in hand. They were the only ones I'd managed to unpack today. Bubbles rose in golden streams, sparkling from the overhead light.

"To new beginnings," he said, offering me a glass. "Your first day at DOJ. Us, finally in the same city. No more flights or countdowns."

I crossed to him and took the glass. He raised his in a toast, and I matched the gesture.

"To new beginnings," I echoed.

The champagne fizzed against my tongue as I took a sip, dry and expensive. James watched me over the rim of his glass, and I forced a smile I didn't quite feel. Tomorrow, I'd walk into the DOJ building. Meet Rory Chambers, maybe find a new opportunity to dismantle the network from the inside.

Tonight, standing in this half-unpacked apartment with boxes stacked like walls and the man I loved pouring champagne, Judge Lawrence Keller's face stayed crisp in my memory. A trafficking case dismissed. Technical grounds.

And Franklin Pearce, ascending to the Fifth Circuit while James smiled and called him Frankie.

I drank, letting the bubbles mask the knot forming in my chest, and told myself it was just nerves.

CHAPTER TWO

THE DEPARTMENT OF JUSTICE building rose from Pennsylvania Avenue like a monument to power. Its Art Deco limestone stretched toward a late November sky gone pale with morning haze. I stood on the sidewalk across the street, coffee burning through the paper cup in my hand, and stared up at the words carved above the entrance: *Where Law Ends, Tyranny Begins.*

A Metro bus hissed past, diesel fumes mixing with the scent of roasting peanuts from a street vendor. Commuters streamed around me, briefcases swinging, shoes clicking against concrete. No one looked up at the building. To them, it was just a backdrop. Just another federal structure in a city built from them.

To me, it was everything.

Crossing against the light, I dodged a taxi that laid on its horn. The revolving doors spun me into a cavernous lobby where marble floors gleamed under fluorescent lights and security checkpoints funneled visitors through metal detectors. A guard waved me toward the left lane marked employees, and I pulled my brand-new DOJ credentials from my bag.

The laminated card felt flimsy in my palm. *Alexandra Hayes, Assistant United States Attorney, Criminal Division.* My photo stared back, taken three weeks ago in Houston before I'd boxed up my life. I looked tired in it.

"First day?" The security guard scanning my badge was in his fifties and had thinning gray hair.

"That obvious?"

"You're gripping that coffee like it owes you money." He handed back my card and gestured me through. "Good luck up there."

I cleared the metal detector and found myself in a second lobby, larger than the first. Elevator banks lined both walls. A directory mounted near the information desk listed departments in alphabetical order: Antitrust. Civil. Civil Rights. Criminal. Environment. My eyes snagged on Criminal Division—Fifth Floor.

"Ms. Hayes?"

I turned. A woman approached from the direction of the elevators. In her mid-thirties with dark hair pulled into a bun so tight it looked aerodynamic. she wore a navy pantsuit and carried a tablet in front of her chest like it was some sort of shield.

"That's me," I replied.

"Marina Meyers." She extended her hand. "I'm your assistant. Welcome to DOJ."

"Thanks." I shook her hand. In Houston, I'd shared an assistant with three other ADAs and considered myself lucky if she even remembered to route my calls. "I didn't realize I'd have—"

"Everyone gets one here. You'll need me, trust me. This place generates paperwork like a paper mill." Marina gestured toward the elevators. "Ready for the tour?"

We rode to the fifth floor in silence broken only by the mechanical sound of cables and Marina's fingers flying across her tablet screen. The doors opened onto a hallway lined with offices, names on placards, and carpet-muffled footsteps. Everything smelled of coffee and toner and ambition.

Marina led me past conference rooms and copy stations, narrating as we walked. "Mailroom's on three, IT help desk is extension 4400, kitchen's at the end of this hall but the coffee's terrible so most people hit the Starbucks on 9th. Your office is 512. Chambers pulled strings to get you a window."

We turned left, and Marina pushed open a door.

The office wasn't large, maybe twelve by ten, but it had a window overlooking Pennsylvania Avenue and a desk that wasn't particle-board. Empty bookshelves lined one wall. A computer sat dark on the desk with two monitors flanking a docking station.

"It's great," I said, and I meant it.

"Better than great. Associates usually get interior cubes for the first two years." Marina set her tablet on the desk and pulled up the blinds. I squinted against the sudden morning sunlight flooding the room. "Chambers likes you."

I looked down at the street below through the slightly streaked window.

"Oh, and speaking of the higher-ups—" Marina's voice dropped half an octave, as if she was about to share a conspiracy of her own. "Did you hear about the press conference?"

I turned from the window. "What press conference?"

"Deputy Attorney General Eleanor Vance called one for Friday. Just announced it an hour ago." Marina leaned against the desk, eyes bright. "Word is she's going to drop some serious dirt on Franklin Pearce."

"What kind of dirt?" I kept my voice level, trying to portray casual curiosity instead of the sudden spike of adrenaline pumping through my bloodstream.

Marina opened her mouth to answer, but a knock on the door frame cut her off.

Rory Chambers filled the doorway. I recognized him from his bio picture. He was easily six-two, broad-shouldered, and in his late fifties with silver threading through dark hair. He wore a charcoal suit and a maroon tie. His presence compressed the room's air, shrinking the office.

"Marina," he said in a warm voice. "Poisoning my new hire already?"

"Just giving her the tour, boss." Marina grabbed her tablet, grinning. "I'll let you two get acquainted."

Slipping past Chambers, she disappeared down the hall. He watched her go, then stepped inside and closed the door behind him.

"Fair warning." He settled into one of the chairs facing my desk, gesturing for me to take the other. "Marina's a fantastic assistant, but she loves gossip. Take everything she says with a grain of salt."

"Noted," I said as I sat in the leather chair behind my desk.

Chambers studied me for a beat. Up close, his eyes were dark gray, like storm clouds. "I'm glad you accepted the position. James spoke highly of your work in Houston."

There it was. The shadow of James's recommendation, the idea of arriving here because someone vouched for me instead of earning it myself. It was something I knew I would have to face when I decided to accept the offer in the first place.

"I hope I can prove myself," I said, "separate and apart from his recommendation."

Chambers's lips curved into a smile. "That's the spirit. And you'll have plenty of opportunity." He crossed one leg over the other, his ankle on his knee. I bit back a laugh as I noticed that his socks were designed with script from the Declaration of Independence. "I'm starting you off easy. A low-level fraud case that made its way into federal jurisdiction."

I waited, keeping my expression neutral even as my stomach clenched. *Easy* and *low-level* were words every ambitious prosecutor dreaded.

"Harris County, Texas," Chambers continued. "County commissioner named Gerald Stokes. Bribery and fraud tied to municipal bond allocations. Federal nexus came through interstate financial transactions—wire fraud under 18 U.S.C. § 1343. District court in Texas prosecuted it, got convictions on Stokes and two co-conspirators."

"So what's left?" I asked.

"One of the defendants cut a deal. Started talking." Chambers's expression shifted, his skepticism bleeding through. "Claims he can implicate Texas Senator Carla Redmond in the scheme."

My eyes widened. A sitting senator involved in wire fraud? That wasn't low level. That was political dynamite.

"Do you believe him?" I asked, trying to understand Chambers' metrics for this case.

"Honestly? Probably not. Guy's looking at twenty years and desperate to reduce his sentence. But we can't ignore it, either. We need to follow up and see if there's any substance to the allegation. If there is, we bring it to a grand jury. If not"—He spread his hands—"we close the book."

I nodded. "Where do I come in?"

"You're running second chair. I'm pairing you with Helen Banks. She's been here twenty-plus years, handled more public corruption cases than anyone in the division." Chambers leaned forward, placing his forearms on his knees. "This is pretty cut and dry, but you'll learn the ropes from Banks. Who knows? Maybe she'll take you under her wing, help you learn to fly."

The words pressed against my teeth—*I've flown plenty on my own*—but I swallowed them. This wasn't Houston. I wasn't a lead prosecutor here, wasn't the one who'd brought down judges and mayors and dirty cops. Here, I was the new hire. The transplant. *James's recommendation.*

"I appreciate the opportunity," I said instead.

"Good." Chambers stood, unfolding to his full height. "IT will be by shortly to walk you through policy stuff. By end of day, I'll have all the case files sent to Marina so you can take them home and start reviewing. Banks's in court today, but you'll meet her tomorrow."

He moved to the door, then paused with his hand on the knob.

"One more thing," he said. "The PIN—Public Integrity Section—has jurisdiction over this because of the corruption angle. You'll be working with them on the investigation side, but the prosecution runs through Criminal. It's a small case, high-profile in Texas because of Stokes's connections, but ultimately …" He trailed off, choosing his words. "Don't expect fireworks."

I nodded. "Understood."

Chambers left, pulling the door closed behind him.

I sat in the empty office, surrounded by bare shelves and dark computer screens. The city moved beneath the window. Somewhere in this building, Deputy Attorney General Eleanor Vance prepared to hold a press conference about Franklin Pearce.

And Marina's words echoed: *serious dirt.*

My phone buzzed. A text from James

How's day one?

Good. Meeting everyone. Talk tonight?

Absolutely. Dinner at mine? 7?

Perfect.

I set the phone face-down on the desk.

I powered up the laptop on the desk, waiting for the login screen to load. Outside, clouds gathered over the Capitol dome. Rain coming, maybe. The monitor flickered to life, the DOJ logo bright against a black background.

CHAPTER THREE

THE RED LINE platform at Metro Center smelled like brake dust and stale air. I wedged myself between a woman in scrubs and a teenager with headphones leaking tinny bass, clutching my messenger bag against my chest. Inside, case files pressed thick against my ribs. Three hundred pages of bond fraud documentation Marina had delivered at 4:47 p.m., just as I'd been eyeing the clock.

Take them home, she'd said. *Get familiar with the players.*

The train arrived in a rush of warm wind and screaming metal. Doors hissed open. Bodies surged forward, a choreographed crush of briefcases and backpacks and thrown elbows. I found a spot near the center doors, one hand wrapped around a pole still warm from the last person's grip, the other maintaining a death-hold on my bag.

The doors sealed, and the train lurched forward.

Welcome to Washington D.C.

I'd ridden the Metro twice before. Back when I was in high school and had gone on a school trip, but this was different. This was my commute now, twice a day, five days a week. The train swayed through the tunnel, lights flickering as we passed into darkness. Around me, passengers stared at phones or books or off into the distance, faces slack with commuter autopilot. A man in a suit dozed against the window, head bobbing with each jolt.

The recorded voice announced Judiciary Square as the next stop.

Doors opened. Bodies shuffled out, and new ones pushed in. A woman with a stroller fought against the tide, frustration carving lines around her mouth. The businessman sleeping against the window jerked awake and checked his phone before settling back into unconsciousness.

The doors closed, and we plunged back into the tunnel.

Houston had been all sprawl and highways, air-conditioned isolation in moving steel boxes at seventy miles per hour. This was proximity. Humanity compressed into metal tubes, breathing the same recycled air.

Gallery Place. More shuffling, more bodies. I lost my pole grip for three seconds during the exchange, caught myself against someone's shoulder, and mumbled an apology that got swallowed by track noise.

By Dupont Circle, the crowd had thinned. I found an empty seat near the doors and collapsed into it. My messenger bag sat heavy across my lap. My feet throbbed inside my heels. It had been a mistake to wear new shoes that I hadn't properly broken in yet. I just hadn't appreciated how much walking I would be doing in the city. Through the window, darkness rushed past, broken occasionally by maintenance lights or the ghost of our reflection in the glass.

The files in my bag seemed to gain weight with each stop.

Gerald Stokes. Harris County Commissioner. Wire fraud. Nothing special.

But I'd spent four years learning that nothing was ever as simple as it appeared on paper.

My stop came at Cleveland Park. I climbed the escalator toward street level, legs burning, and emerged into twilight. November air hit my face, cool and refreshing after the Metro's stale warmth. Streetlights flickered on as I walked the four blocks to my building, past rowhouses with lit-up windows and a corner store advertising two-for-one wine bottles in its window.

The apartment building's lobby was empty except for the mailboxes and a fake plant that needed dusting. I climbed three flights, each step an exercise in pure willpower, and fumbled my keys from my bag.

Inside, unopened boxes still lined the walls. I'd made no progress unpacking since last night. The bookshelf remained unassembled near the kitchen. My coffee cup from this morning sat in the sink, ringed with dried residue.

I dropped the messenger bag on the floor and slumped onto the couch James and I had assembled yesterday. The cushions exhaled beneath me, springs creaking. Through the window, the streetlight cast orange shadows across the ceiling.

Had I made the right decision?

Houston was home. Dad was there. Erin and Lisa were there. I knew that city's rhythms, its courtrooms, its corruption, even. Here, I was starting over. New office, new cases, new commute. Learning to navigate a subway system instead of I-10. Working fraud cases instead of murder and trafficking.

Build credibility, James had said when I'd wavered on accepting the offer. *Establish yourself in the division before you go after the network.*

He was right. I knew he was right.

But sitting alone in this half-unpacked apartment, exhaustion pressing against my skull, I was seven hundred miles from everything that mattered.

My phone rang.

Lisa's name lit the screen, and relief rushed through me.

"Hey," I said, cradling the phone against my shoulder.

"How was day one?" Her voice carried that perpetual optimism that somehow never grated on me. It made me miss home even more. "Did they give you an office with a view?"

"They did, actually. Window unit overlooking Pennsylvania Avenue." I kicked off my heels and drew my blistered feet up onto the couch. "Got to watch important people walk to important meetings all day long."

"See? Already living the dream. Though I have to say, you sound exhausted. You okay?"

"City travel's just different. Tiresome."

"You'll get used to it. Give it a few weeks and it'll be muscle memory. You won't even think about it."

I wanted to believe her. "Maybe."

"Did you get a case assignment yet?"

"Yeah, bond fraud out of Harris County. Running second chair with a veteran prosecutor named Helen Banks." I glanced at my messenger bag. The files were calling. "Low-level case. Nothing special, but maybe an opportunity to learn from someone seasoned."

Lisa laughed. "There's no such thing as a 'nothing special' case for you. Your track record proves that."

"Maybe for once I'd love straightforward. Walk in, present evidence, walk out with a conviction. No conspiracies, no chess pieces, no bodies, no bullets in my shoulder."

"Where's the fun in that?"

I smiled despite the exhaustion. "How are things at the DA's office?"

"Chaotic as always. Tom has me on a domestic violence case that's turning into a nightmare. Witness recanted twice, the defense is claiming coercion. I'm spending half my time doing damage control." Her tone shifted to something more serious. "Blake Costello's retrial got officially dropped, by the way. DA's office announced it this morning."

The news was bittersweet. Blake was an accessory after the fact to Melissa Thatcher's murder. But the more I thought about it, the more convinced I was that he was merely a victim of the network's machinations. Coerced into a situation that he had no control over. It was also a reminder of how many cases had been poisoned by Leland's corruption, the many lives twisted by judicial rot. In the chaos of my final Houston months, I'd uncovered his ledgers of bribes and fixed dockets, the raid on his home yielding that damning chessboard that mapped the network's bishops. His arrest had cracked open dozens of tainted indictments, but the fallout lingered, with appeals clogging courts and victims reliving nightmares in endless hearings. It was hard for me to leave all of that behind, but I still believed I could do more here, at Main Justice.

"Good," I said. "He deserves that much."

"Agreed." Lisa paused. "Oh, and before I forget—I'll check on your dad. Make sure he hasn't accidentally injured himself with whatever project he's working on this week."

The offer warmed something in my chest that the champagne last night hadn't touched. "You don't have to—"

"I want to. Plus, he promised to build me a bookshelf if I bring him lumber measurements. It's a win-win. I'm gonna slowly replace all my IKEA furniture through subtle project suggestions to him."

I chuckled. "He'll love that. Thank you."

"Anytime. Now go dive into those case files. Show Helen Banks what Houston prosecutors are made of."

We said our goodbyes, and the apartment settled back into silence.

I stared at my messenger bag for a full minute before forcing myself off the couch. The files could wait thirty more seconds while I changed into sweats and filled a glass of water from the tap. I gulped the water, refilled the glass, and carried it and the bag to the small table that doubled as my workspace.

The first file opened to Gerald Stokes's booking photo—late fifties and jowly. His expression looked resigned. Behind him, the Harris County Sheriff's Office logo stamped the wall.

My phone buzzed with a text from James.

Good time to call?

I dialed instead of texting back.

"Hey," he said, picking up on the first ring. "How'd it go?"

"Exhausting. Met everyone, got the tour, have a mountain of case files to review already." I flipped pages as we talked, scanning financial documents. "How's your day?"

"Still at the office, actually." Background noise filtered through the call. "I was supposed to make dinner, I know. Rain check?"

"It's fine. I've got reading to do anyway." I paused on a page detailing wire transfers between municipal accounts. "What's keeping you?"

"The Vance situation. Chambers wants me to get ahead of it before Friday, so we're prepared for whatever fallout comes."

My hand stilled on the page. "What do you mean, get ahead of it?"

He hesitated for a moment. "Can't really talk about it now. I need to finalize a memo first. But we can discuss it later when things aren't so … complicated."

"Okay," I said.

"Friday, though. Once the confirmation hearing dust settles, we'll do dinner properly. Somewhere nice. Celebrate your first week surviving DOJ."

I smiled softly. "Deal."

"Get some rest. Love you."

"You too."

The call ended, and I set the phone face-down beside the files. I pulled the next folder toward me, opened it, and started reading.

Gerald Stokes had been taking kickbacks for five years before anyone noticed. The scheme wasn't overly complicated. Award bond allocations to specific firms in exchange for cash payments disguised as consulting fees. His co-conspirator, Max Macdonald, had handled the financial paperwork. Their third partner, Michael Beard, had provided the infrastructure through his investment firm.

Beard was the one who'd started talking. Claimed Senator Carla Redmond had orchestrated the entire operation, that Stokes was just a middleman funneling money upward.

I flipped to Beard's deposition transcript, scanning his responses.

MR. BEARD: *Senator Redmond approached me in 2019. Said she needed a revenue stream for her campaign that couldn't be traced back to her. We built the structure specifically for her specifications.*

MS. SIMON: *How did you communicate with the senator?*

MR. BEARD: *Phone calls, mostly. Disposable cells. She was careful.*

MS. SIMON: *Do you have records of these communications?*

MR. BEARD: *No. She made us destroy everything after each transaction.*

I sat back, chewing my thumbnail.

A desperate man with no corroboration, pointing fingers at a sitting senator to reduce his sentence. Any defense attorney would shred this testimony in minutes.

But Chambers was right. We couldn't ignore it.

I read until my vision blurred, until the financial documents bled together into meaningless numbers. Outside, the streetlights flickered on.

My phone sat silent beside me, no new messages.

James was still at the office, preparing for whatever Friday would bring.

And I was here, learning the rhythms of federal prosecution one bond fraud case at a time.

I closed the file and rubbed my eyes.

Tomorrow, I'd meet Helen Banks. Start building the investigation into Beard's claims. Follow the evidence wherever it led, even if it led nowhere.

But tonight, in this half-unpacked apartment with case files spread across my table and exhaustion pressing against my bones, I let myself wonder what Deputy Attorney General Eleanor Vance would say on Friday.

And whether James's memo had anything to do with Franklin Pearce or the network I'd come here to investigate.

CHAPTER FOUR

I WAS three pages into Max MacDonald's financial affidavit when a knock rattled my door frame.

A woman stood in the doorway. She was in her early fifties, iron-gray hair cut sharp at her shoulders, and a navy suit that had probably seen a thousand courtrooms. She carried a leather portfolio under one arm and a coffee mug that read *Res Ipsa Loquitur* in faded lettering.

"Alex Hayes?" she asked in a voice that she most certainly used to talk over objections.

"That's me."

"Helen Banks." She stepped inside without an invitation and settled into the chair across from my desk. "Good time to talk about the case?"

I closed MacDonald's file and straightened in my chair. "Absolutely."

Banks set her portfolio on the desk between us and opened it, revealing handwritten notes in block letters. She took a sip from her mug, eyes assessing me over the rim.

"So," she said. "Tell me what you know about Carla Redmond."

Her tone was casual, but I caught the test underneath. She wanted to see if I'd done my homework, if I'd read past the surface of the files Marina had delivered yesterday.

"Texas senator, third term," I said. "Sits on the Appropriations

Committee. Made her name pushing infrastructure spending in Gulf Coast states after Hurricane Harvey."

"Good start. And why are we looking at her?"

"Robert Kline." Pullingd the relevant file from my stack, I flipped to Kline's plea agreement. "CFO of Bayou Builders. He testified during his deal in the Torres case that Gulf Coast Strategies was funneling bribes to Commissioner Torres as part of a larger operation. Said a senator—Redmond—secured federal appropriations for Houston's municipal bond project in exchange for kickbacks."

Banks's expression didn't shift, but something in her posture relaxed half an inch. "What was the Torres case?"

"United States v. Daniel Torres. Houston. Commissioner charged with bribery and wire fraud. Conviction came down last month."

"And Kline's testimony during that trial gave us Redmond." Banks made a note in her portfolio. "What else?"

"Anonymous FBI tip corroborates Kline's story. Mentions Gulf Coast Strategies making payments to Redmond and ties to judicial nominations." I paused, choosing my next words carefully. "We're tracking the tip's source."

"We are." Banks studied me across the desk. "What's our federal nexus?"

"Wire fraud, 18 U.S.C. § 1343. Federal appropriations money moved through interstate transactions. Redmond used her position on Appropriations to secure funding for bonds, then Gulf Coast Strategies kicked a percentage back to her through shell companies."

"Which brings us to Victor Ramsey." Banks flipped a page in her notes. "CEO of Gulf Coast Strategies. Tell me about him."

I reached for the file I'd read until two this morning, the one that had kept me awake long after I'd closed the folder. "Ramsey's the architect. Built Gulf Coast Strategies from a regional consulting firm into a major player in public infrastructure contracts. Connected to half the power brokers in Texas—state legislators, county commissioners, federal officials. His firm's been awarded over two hundred million in contracts across the last decade."

"And how many of those contracts came through legitimate channels?"

"Hard to say without subpoenaing his records." I met her eyes. "But Kline claims Ramsey ran the bribery scheme, that Redmond was his biggest investment."

Banks smiled briefly. "I'm drafting a wiretap request for Ramsey's phone. If he's still communicating with Redmond or anyone else in the network, we'll hear it." She tapped her pen against her notes. "What stage are we in?"

"Pre-indictment. Investigative phase. We're building probable cause before taking this to a grand jury."

"Which means?"

"We need more than Kline's testimony. We need documents, financial records, communications. We need probable cause that Redmond received payments and that she used her office to secure the federal appropriations in return."

"Exactly." Banks closed her portfolio and leaned back in her chair. "I want you drafting subpoenas for Redmond's emails and bank records. We'll build from Torres's financials. Trace the money backward from Gulf Coast Strategies through whatever shell companies they used, see where it lands in Redmond's accounts."

The corners of my lips began to lift as I processed that Banks was confirming my initial suspicion. This wasn't actually low level. This was a sitting senator, a corruption case that could crack open an entire infrastructure of bribery if we pulled the right threads.

"I'm on it," I said.

Banks stood, collecting her portfolio. "We'll meet twice a week to review progress. Tuesdays and Thursdays, nine a.m. Unless something urgent comes up, then find me immediately. I don't care if I'm in court or a meeting with the Attorney General himself."

Moving toward the door, she paused with one hand on the frame.

I took the opening before my courage failed. "Can I ask you about the Vance press conference?"

Banks turned, one eyebrow raised. "What about it?"

"What do you think she's going to say? About Pearce?" The words tumbled out faster than I intended. "Everyone's speculating, and I just—"

"In D.C., people come in and out like waves," Banks said, her voice flat. "Best thing you can do is try to be the dune. Stay away from the tide; be above it all." She adjusted her grip on her portfolio. "Focus on your work. Let the politics sort themselves out."

She left before I could respond, heels muffled against the carpet, down the hallway toward her office three doors down.

I sat in the sudden silence, staring at the empty doorway.

Be the dune.

Solid advice. Professional advice. Wisdom that no doubt came from twenty years of navigating federal prosecution without getting pulled into the undertow of D.C.'s power games.

But I'd never been good at staying out of the water.

I pulled a legal pad from my drawer and started drafting subpoena language, focusing on the work. Redmond's emails first—official Senate correspondence, personal accounts if we could establish probable cause. Then bank records—checking, savings, any investment accounts tied to her name or her husband's.

My pen moved across the page, legal citations flowing from memory. The Torres case had laid the groundwork. Now we followed the money upstream, traced it back to its source, built the wall of evidence brick by brick until it was too solid for any jury to ignore.

Outside my window, clouds gathered over the Capitol dome. The weather had turned overnight, November's false warmth giving way to the cold front I'd heard mentioned on the Metro this morning. Rain coming. Maybe snow, if the temperature dropped low enough.

I wrote until my hand cramped, until the subpoena language covered three pages of precise legalese. Then I pulled up the electronic filing system on my computer and started translating handwritten notes into formal documents.

The work consumed me. Hours vanished into case law and financial regulations, into tracing the web of shell companies Gulf Coast Strategies had used to hide their payments. Ramsey's firm had been clever. He'd layered enough legitimate business transactions between the bribes that untangling them required spreadsheets and flowcharts and several cups of coffee.

But patterns emerged if you looked long enough. Money flowed in predictable directions, leaving traces in bank statements and wire transfer records.

Find the pattern, follow the flow, build the case.

My phone buzzed at noon with a text from James.

Lunch? Need a break from this memo.

I glanced at the subpoena draft on my screen, half-finished.

Can't. Buried in case work. Tonight?

Dinner at my place. 7. I'll cook.

Perfect.

I set the phone aside and returned to the draft.

By three o'clock, I had subpoenas ready for Redmond's personal email, her Senate account, and five bank accounts tied to her and her husband's names. I saved the documents, printed hard copies for Banks's review, and leaned back in my chair.

My shoulders ached and my eyes burned from staring at the monitor. But the subpoenas were solid, the legal foundation sound. Banks would approve them, a judge would sign them, and we'd have our window into Redmond's finances.

One step closer to proving Kline's testimony. One step closer to a grand jury indictment. And then on to trial.

I stood and stretched, my vertebrae popping. Through the window, I could see that the rain had started. The light drizzle turned Pennsylvania Avenue slick and reflective. Pedestrians hurried past with umbrellas blooming like mushrooms, and I watched as a taxi splashed through a puddle.

D.C. in autumn. Cold and wet and gray. It felt so very different here.

I gathered the printed subpoenas and headed down the hall toward Banks's office. Her door stood half-open, light spilling into the corridor. I knocked on the frame.

"Come in," she called without looking up from whatever she was reading.

I entered and set the subpoenas on her desk. "Drafts for your review."

Banks picked up the first page, her eyes racing across the lines. Her pen moved, making small notations in the margins. She flipped to the second page, then the third.

"Good work," she said finally. "Clean language, proper citations. I'll have these filed by end of day tomorrow."

Relief washed through me, warmer than it should have been for such basic approval. But this was Helen Banks—legend of the Criminal Division, the woman who'd prosecuted governors and congressmen. Her approval carried weight here, and I found myself wanting it.

"Thank you," I said.

She set the subpoenas aside and met my eyes. "You did your homework last night."

"I did." There was no sense in denying it or trying to play coy. I'd worked hard on these documents.

"Keep doing that. Stay ahead of the case, ahead of the defendants, ahead of their lawyers. That's how you win in federal court." She picked up her pen again, returning to whatever document had occupied her before I'd arrived. "Close the door on your way out."

I left, pulling the door shut behind me.

The hallway stretched empty in both directions. Somewhere down the corridor, a phone rang unanswered. I walked back to my office, settled into my chair, and pulled up the next file.

United States v. Carla Redmond.

We were just getting started.

CHAPTER
FIVE

BY FOUR O'CLOCK, the case files had started blurring together. I'd reread the same paragraph three times without absorbing a single word. My coffee from this morning sat cold and abandoned on the desk, a ring of condensation staining the wood beneath it.

I needed air, movement and distance from these four walls. I grabbed my wallet and phone and took the elevator down to street level. Outside, the drizzle had stopped but left the sidewalks damp.

I was beginning to learn that the city measured itself in count-downs: orange hands flashing numbers on crosswalk signs, fifteen seconds to cross, then ten, then five. Everyone calculated their pace against the clock, against the next meeting, against traffic that never truly stopped. It already felt exhausting.

Two blocks down Pennsylvania Avenue, I found Compass Coffee tucked between a law firm and a dry cleaner. Light spilled out of the windows, warm against the gray afternoon. I pushed through the door. Heat hit first, then noise. Espresso machines hissed, conversations overlapped, indie music played at that perfect volume where you could still think but didn't have to.

The line stretched four people deep. I joined it, scanning the menu board above the counter even though I already knew what I wanted. A plain black coffee.

The woman ahead of me ordered an oat milk latte with two pumps of vanilla and a double shot. The barista nodded, already moving. Money was exchanged, the receipt printed. Next customer. The city was ruthless in its efficiency.

I ordered, paid, and moved to the pickup area near the windows. Outside, a Metro bus rumbled past, brakes squealing. Someone's phone rang behind me. The espresso machine screamed steam.

And eyes pressed against my back.

The sensation arrived suddenly. That awareness of being watched even without eye contact. I turned slowly, scanning the crowded shop.

A woman stood near the door. Mid-fifties, dark hair cut in a severe bob, charcoal suit that looked expensive even from across the room. She stared at me with an intensity that stripped away the coffee shop noise and narrowed the world to just the two of us and the space between.

I knew her. Or I should know her. I felt like I recognized her, but I just couldn't place her.

"Alex!" The barista called my name, voice cutting through my focus.

I turned to grab my coffee, and when I looked back, the woman was gone. The door swung shut, bell chiming. Through the windows, I caught a glimpse of the charcoal suit disappearing into the pedestrian flow, swallowed by foot traffic.

Pushing outside, I scanned both directions. Office workers streamed past, everyone in navy and black and gray. As if they were trying to match the weather.

There was no sign of her.

I stood there for thirty seconds, coffee steaming in my hand, searching faces in the crowd. But she was gone.

My mind began to wander, making connections that shouldn't have existed.

Texas. The chess pieces left at my apartment door. A bishop, then a queen. The gunman who'd cornered me in the airport security room, his voice flat: *You're just as smart as your mother was. But that's what got her killed.*

I'd thought leaving Houston meant putting distance between me and the worst of the threats. A new city, new badge, new rules. I told myself the network's tentacles stretched across Texas and the Fifth Circuit, but not this far north, not into the heart of the DOJ itself. I came here believing D.C. held the resources, the sealed files, the untouchable databases that could finally map the whole board and burn it down. Safe ground to fight from, not another square already claimed.

But maybe I'd been wrong about that, too.

They'd killed Judge Thatcher in Texas. They operated across state lines. And if they'd infiltrated the judiciary in Houston and Dallas, why not Washington?

I walked back toward the DOJ building, my coffee forgotten, lukewarm in my grip. The sidewalk stretched ahead, each face a potential threat. That man in the business suit checking his phone—was he watching me? The woman with the briefcase waiting at the crosswalk —had she been there when I'd left the building?

Stop. This was paranoia. The woman in the coffee shop could have been anyone—a lawyer, a government worker, someone who'd mistaken me for an old friend or colleague.

But her stare hadn't been an accident.

I rode the elevator back to the fifth floor, nodded at Marina as I passed her desk, and locked myself in my office. The coffee went on my desk next to this morning's abandoned cup. I dropped into my chair and stared at my computer screen, where Redmond's bank records still glowed.

Focus. Work. This was the story I kept repeating to myself: build a federal résumé, stack convictions, earn the trust that opened doors to sealed files and classified databases. The real reason I'd left Houston and taken James's offer sat in an encrypted drive hidden behind a false panel in my closet: Melissa Thatcher's evidence, the chessboard photos, every document that proved a nationwide judicial network shielded traffickers. I came to D.C. because only Main Justice had the tools to finish what my mother started in 2003. Katherine Hayes. The woman who disappeared the night she got too close to the same rot I was still chasing.

I just hadn't expected the network to greet me on day one. And I sure as hell hadn't planned on risking the career I needed as camouflage before I'd even unpacked my boxes.

My fingers moved to the keyboard before the rational part of my brain could intervene. I opened the DOJ shared drive and typed my mother's name into the search bar.

Nothing would come up. Why would it? She'd been a local prosecutor in Houston, not federal. Her cases wouldn't be in DOJ's system.

The search spun for three seconds.

One result appeared.

My pulse hammering in my ears, I clicked on the file.

2003 DOJ/FBI Nationwide Survey on Judicial Integrity and Public Corruption

The PDF loaded slowly, the progress bar crawling across the screen. Three hundred forty-two pages. Scanned documents, not digital text, which meant no search function, no way to jump directly to my mother's name. Just page after page of surveys and case studies and anonymized accounts.

I scrolled to the first page. Dense paragraphs filled the screen, formatted in that distinctive early-2000s typewriter font. The header read: *Joint DOJ-FBI Task Force: Post-9/11 Assessment of Judicial Vulnerabilities*.

The introduction outlined the document's purpose—a nationwide survey compiled after September 11th to assess how corruption, organized crime, and trafficking operations had infiltrated federal and state courts. Statistical data. Case studies. Interviews with prosecutors, judges, law enforcement.

I started reading, skimming paragraphs for anything relevant. Page five discussed bribery trends in Southern states. Page twelve analyzed influence-peddling schemes in municipal courts. Page twenty-seven included a case study from Louisiana where a judge had accepted payments from a drug cartel.

My eyes burned. The words bled together into meaningless shapes. But I kept scrolling, kept searching.

A knock on my door frame made me jump.

Rory Chambers stood there, jacket off, sleeves rolled to his elbows. "Got a minute?"

My hand moved the mouse by instinct, minimizing the PDF. The Redmond file sprang back to the screen, bank records filling the monitor.

"Of course." I gestured to the empty chair.

Chambers entered and settled into it. "Just wanted to check in. How's day two treating you?"

"Good. Great, actually." The words came automatically, as though I'd rehearsed them. "Banks has me drafting subpoenas for the Redmond case. Bank records, emails. Building the financial trail from Gulf Coast Strategies."

"She works fast." Chambers smiled, brief and approving. "What do you think of her?"

"She's incredible. Sharp, direct. Doesn't waste time."

"Give it a few weeks. The honeymoon phase wears off." His tone carried affection despite the warning. "Banks is brilliant, but she's also exacting. She'll push you harder than anyone you've worked with before."

"I can handle it."

"I know you can. That's why I paired you with her." Chambers's gaze drifted to my desk, landing on the Compass Coffee cup beside my monitor. "Did you try going there today?"

I glanced at the cup. "Yeah, just needed to clear my head after staring at financial documents all afternoon."

"Good choice. Their coffee's better than anything in this building." He leaned back, expression shifting into casual curiosity. "I heard through the grapevine that Eleanor Vance was there earlier. You didn't see her by chance, did you?"

My throat tightened. "No. I hate to admit it, but I wouldn't recognize her."

"Ah, well. Probably for the better, given the current situation." Chambers stood, rolling his shoulders back. "Keep up the good work. Banks speaks highly of your subpoena drafts."

He left, pulling my door half-closed behind him.

I stared at the coffee cup for five seconds, trying to make sense of our interaction before grabbing my phone. My fingers moved across the screen, typing *Eleanor Vance DOJ* into Google.

Images loaded.

The first result showed a professional headshot—mid-fifties, dark hair in a severe bob, sharp eyes and sharper cheekbones. The caption read: *Deputy Attorney General Eleanor Vance announces new public corruption initiative.*

My stomach dropped.

The woman from the coffee shop. The one who'd stared at me, who'd vanished the moment I'd turned away, was Deputy Attorney General Eleanor Vance.

The woman about to hold a press conference tomorrow about Franklin Pearce, about to drop dirt that had James working late and Chambers preparing for fallout.

She'd been watching me.

I set my phone down, hands not quite steady. Outside my window, the afternoon had darkened toward evening. Streetlights flickered on along Pennsylvania Avenue. Rain started again, harder now, droplets streaking the glass.

Did Eleanor Vance know who I was? Had she sought me out, tracked me to that coffee shop, studied me long enough to make sure I'd felt it?

I shook my head, trying to clear the paranoia.

I pulled up the minimized PDF, that massive document from 2003 with my mother's name buried somewhere in three hundred forty-two pages. The cursor blinked in the corner, waiting.

Was my fresh start already compromised? Had the network's shadow followed me from Houston and manifested in a Deputy Attorney General's stare and a document linking my mother to judicial corruption investigations twenty-two years ago?

I should close the file. Focus on Redmond. Build the case Banks expected, prove myself through work instead of chasing conspiracies.

But my hand moved to the scroll wheel anyway.

Page thirty-eight. Case study from Texas, 1999-2002. A trafficking operation used judicial connections to shield their activities from prosecution.

I kept reading.

Outside, the rain returned to hammer against the window. Inside, my office shrank with every passing second.

CHAPTER SIX

THE APARTMENT FELT SMALLER at night. Boxes still lined the walls, half my life packed in cardboard, waiting for energy I didn't have. I sat cross-legged on the couch, phone pressed to my ear, leftover Thai food congealing in its container on the coffee table.

"No, James, I'm telling you it was Vance," I said. "She was staring at me. Not casual people-watching."

"Maybe she was looking at something behind you." His voice carried that special tone he used when trying to talk me down from a ledge. "A painting on the wall, or someone else she recognized. Why would the Deputy Attorney General stare at you?"

I picked at the label on my water bottle, peeling it in strips. "I don't know. Why is Chambers having you look into her ahead of Friday?"

He didn't answer immediately. Traffic hummed outside my window. A siren wailed somewhere blocks away, dopplering into the distance. I was still getting used to the sounds of the city. It was so different than the quiet of my childhood home I'd gotten used to.

"I really can't talk about that," James said finally.

"Oh, come on. You're really not going to tell me?"

Another pause. Then a long and resigned sigh. "Okay, but you can't repeat this."

I straightened on the couch, ready to listen. "Fine."

"We have word that Vance is going to try to discredit Pearce. Before his confirmation hearing. And I'm trying to figure out if there's any validity to whatever she plans to say."

I stopped picking at the label. "Why would she do that?"

"I don't know. That's what I'm trying to find out." Frustration bled into his tone. "I owe it to Frankie to get ahead of this, make sure he's not blindsided."

"Isn't that a conflict of interest?"

"No. It doesn't affect my judgment. If it turns out there's truth to whatever Vance has, I'll disclose it. But until then—"

"How did this even land on your desk?" I stood, pacing the narrow strip between couch and window. I looked down at the wet pavement to see the streetlight patterns. "Shouldn't someone without a personal connection be handling it?"

"If a federal judicial nominee was involved in bad stuff, that involves PIN." James's voice hardened into bureaucratic justification. "We're getting ahead of potential fallout. D.C. optics."

"Right. Optics."

"Alex—"

"No, I get it." I pressed my forehead against the cool glass, my tone softening. "Good luck with all of it."

James cleared his throat. "What are you doing tonight?"

"Big report to read. Subpoenas to finalize for tomorrow." I decided not to mention the three-hundred-forty-two-page PDF currently sitting in my personal email.

"Get some rest," James said. "I'll see you Friday?"

"Friday."

We said our goodbyes. I ended the call and stood at the window for another minute, watching cars navigate the intersection below. Red light, green light, and a yellow light that a taxi sped up for.

Opening my laptop on the dining table, I pulled up my personal email. The file sat at the top of my inbox, sent from my DOJ account twenty minutes before leaving the office. It was probably stupid. But not as stupid as printing three hundred pages on the communal printer.

The PDF downloaded slowly while I cleared the Thai food container, dumped it in the trash, and washed my hands.

The download completed, and I clicked the file.

2003 DOJ/FBI Nationwide Survey on Judicial Integrity and Public Corruption

Page one loaded and I started reading where I'd left off, scanning dense paragraphs about trafficking operations in Southern states, judicial vulnerabilities, and patterns of corruption that had emerged in the years following September 11th. Or maybe just patterns that people noticed for the first time but had always been there.

My phone rang. I looked at it to see Erin's name on the screen. I answered on the second ring.

"Why didn't you tell me you were handling the Redmond case?" Her voice carried mock outrage, the teasing edge she used when she'd caught me in an oversight.

"I just got it assigned yesterday. What's it matter?"

"Alex." Erin laughed. "Lisa said the commute was getting to you, but wow. Did you seriously not put two and two together? I prosecuted Torres at the district level."

My hand stilled on the laptop keyboard. Torres. Robert Kline. Gulf Coast Strategies. The case that had given us Redmond in the first place.

"I didn't even think about it," I admitted.

"Clearly." Papers rustled on her end. "Okay, well, let me tell you what they're probably not telling you."

I grabbed a pen and legal pad, ready to take notes. "Go."

"They're gonna say Kline is full of shit. Desperate defendant making up stories to reduce his sentence. But I don't know, Alex. I think there might be truth to what he's saying."

"You think Redmond did it? Accepted bribes? Everyone here thinks it's a dead end."

"I'm not sure. But I'm also not sure she didn't do it." She paused. "Kline was consistent in his testimony. Details matched financial records we pulled from Gulf Coast Strategies. And when we mentioned Redmond's name during cross, he didn't flinch. Didn't hesitate. Just laid it out matter-of-fact."

I made notes, circling *consistent testimony* twice. "What about corroboration?"

"That's the problem," Erin said. "Kline claims all communication with Redmond went through Ramsey. Disposable phones, in-person meetings, nothing in writing. Smart if you're running a bribery operation. Impossible to prove after the fact."

"So we subpoena Ramsey's records," I said. "See if anything shakes loose."

"Already done at the district level. He lawyered up immediately. Claimed attorney-client privilege on half his communications, Fifth Amendment on the rest." Erin's frustration bled through the phone. "Guy's a ghost. Built his whole operation to leave minimal traces."

I tapped my pen against the pad. "What's your gut tell you?"

"My gut tells me Kline wasn't lying. Whether we can prove it?" She exhaled. "That's why they're handing it to you. See if federal resources can crack what we couldn't at the state level."

We talked for another ten minutes. Case strategy, witness credibility, the financial labyrinth Gulf Coast Strategies had constructed. Erin promised to send me her case notes, the interview transcripts that hadn't made it into official filings. Anything that might give me an edge.

"And Alex? Be careful. Redmond's connected. She's been in the Senate for twelve years, sits on Appropriations. Those kinds of people have reach."

I swallowed, nodding even though she couldn't see me. "I know."

"I mean it. Don't go rogue on this one. Work it by the book."

"When have I ever gone rogue?"

Erin laughed. "Do you want that list chronologically or alphabetically? I already have a PowerPoint started."

I laughed, and we said our goodbyes. Setting the phone down, I stared at my laptop screen, where the PDF waited.

Talking to Erin about a case she prosecuted without me was bittersweet. It made me miss home, but I pushed the thought aside.

I pulled the laptop closer and kept reading.

Page forty-seven discussed a Houston case from 2003. A trafficking operation that had used judicial connections to shield members from prosecution. The investigation had stalled when a key prosecutor went missing.

My breath caught.

Katherine Hayes, Assistant District Attorney, Harris County, initiated the investigation in January 2003. By March, she had identified three judges with suspected ties to a trafficking network. On April 12, 2003, Hayes disappeared. Her car was found abandoned near Buffalo Bayou. No body was recovered. The investigation was closed six months later due to lack of evidence and prosecutorial resources.

I read the paragraph three times. Four. Five.

My mother. Right here in black and white, in a federal document compiled by DOJ and FBI investigators. Her work acknowledged. Her disappearance recorded as fact.

And then this: *Hayes's preliminary findings suggested a trafficking network that extended beyond Houston, with connections to Dallas, Austin, and potentially federal judicial appointments. Her evidence was never recovered.*

I leaned back in my chair, my vision blurring.

The network had killed her for getting too close. For uncovering connections that threatened their operations. And someone at DOJ had known about it. Had documented it. Had included her name in this survey and then it got buried in three hundred pages of scanned documents nobody would ever read.

Outside my window, rain started again.

My mind went back to the coffee shop, where Eleanor Vance hadn't just spotted me, but recognized me. Had known I was Katherine Hayes's daughter. The prosecutor who'd taken down judges in Houston, who'd uncovered the same network her mother had died investigating.

And on Friday, Vance would hold a press conference about Franklin Pearce.

James's mentor. A judge from East Texas ascending to the Fifth Circuit.

Turning back to the PDF, I kept reading, searching for more mentions of my mother, for anything that might explain why her investigation had ended with her death instead of convictions.

CHAPTER
SEVEN

BANKS APPEARED in my doorway at 9:15 Wednesday morning, coffee in one hand and a manila folder in the other. She dropped the folder on my desk.

"You did a good job on the subpoenas," she said. "Which means you get more work."

I looked up from the case file I'd been reviewing. "What do you need?"

"Gulf Coast Strategies. Historical records." Banks settled into the chair across from me, taking a long sip from her mug. "They've been operating in Houston for fifteen years. I want to know their patterns. Who they've lobbied, which contracts they've won, any prior investigations that didn't result in charges."

"History of corruption."

"Exactly. PIN's record retention policies mean anything pre-2005 got shipped to the National Archives. You'll need to request access." She set her coffee down and opened the folder, pulling out a requisition form already half-filled. "Sign this. They'll pull the boxes for you."

I scanned the form. *Request for DOJ Criminal Division Records, 1998-2005, Subject: Gulf Coast Strategies LLC.*

"How long will this take?" I asked.

"Depends on how buried the records are. Could be a day. Could be a week." Banks stood, collecting her folder. "But Torres's prosecution left gaps. Kline's testimony only covers the last five years. I want to know if Ramsey was running similar schemes before that."

My chest tightened. "And if he was?"

"Then we establish a pattern. Show the jury this wasn't one corrupt deal with Redmond. This was business as usual for Gulf Coast Strategies." She paused at the door. "Archives are on Constitution Avenue. Take the afternoon. Bring back anything useful."

She left before I could respond.

I signed the requisition form, grabbed my coat, and headed for the Metro.

———

The National Archives building rose white and massive between 7th and 9th Streets, its Corinthian columns making the DOJ building look modest by comparison. I climbed the steps and pushed through heavy bronze doors. The marble lobby smelled like old paper and government authority.

A security guard directed me to the research room on the second floor. I handed over my requisition form to a clerk behind plexiglass who barely glanced at it before stamping approval.

"Boxes will be ready in twenty minutes," she said. "Wait in the reading room."

The reading room was long and narrow, lined with tables and those green-shaded lamps that belonged in old movies. A handful of researchers hunched over documents, some taking notes by hand, others typing on laptops. Late afternoon light filtered through high windows, casting an amber glow on the room.

I found a table near the back, secluded from the other researchers. The quiet pressed against my ears after the Metro's constant noise. Someone coughed three tables over. Pages turned. A pencil scratched against paper.

The clerk appeared with two archive boxes and set them on my table. "Ring the bell when you're done."

I opened the first box. Manila folders stacked neatly and chronologically. I pulled the top one. *Gulf Coast Strategies—Contract Awards, Harris County, 1998-2000.*

Pages of contracts. Infrastructure projects. Municipal bonds. Public works. Ramsey's firm had their fingers in everything, winning bids with a record of consistency. I made notes, tracking patterns. Certain commissioners appeared repeatedly as approving authorities. Certain banks had handled the bond transactions.

The second box contained correspondence. Letters between Ramsey and county officials. Nothing overtly criminal in the language, but the subtext hummed beneath professional pleasantries. *Appreciative of your consideration. Looking forward to continued partnership. Attached consulting fee as discussed.*

I was forty minutes into reading when footsteps approached from behind.

"Finding what you need?"

I turned, expecting the clerk.

I found Eleanor Vance instead, standing two feet away from me.

She wore a different suit than yesterday, navy instead of charcoal. Her familiar intense glare locked onto me.

My heart started to pound. "Deputy Attorney General."

"Ms. Hayes." She glanced at the boxes on my table, at the folders spread across its surface. "Gulf Coast Strategies. Interesting choice."

I didn't respond. Couldn't. My brain struggled to process why the Deputy Attorney General was here, in the National Archives, approaching me in a secluded corner of the reading room.

"I saw you're looking at the 2003 survey," Vance said, voice low enough that it wouldn't carry. "It's a tough read, but the Texas section might interest you. Page 132 has some history on Houston cases." She paused. "Your mother would've known those courts well."

My eyes widened. She knew. About my mother. About the document I'd downloaded to my personal email last night.

"Keep digging," Vance continued, already turning away. "But be careful who you trust at the DOJ. Some games have silent players. And some gavels don't make a sound when they come down."

"Wait—" I started to stand, the word coming out louder than intended.

Heads turned. A researcher three tables over glared at me. Someone behind me hissed for quiet.

By the time I looked back, Vance was gone. The reading room door swung shut behind her, the soft thud echoing in the silence.

I sat frozen, Vance's words circling my mind. *Page 132. Your mother would've known those courts. Be careful who you trust.*

I stared at the Gulf Coast Strategies files spread before me, but the words blurred into meaningless shapes. My hands weren't steady. I forced them flat against the table, pressing until my palms hurt.

Five minutes passed. Then ten. I gathered the files back into their boxes, returned them to the front desk, and left the building.

Outside, the temperature had dropped ten degrees this afternoon. My breath fogged as I walked toward the Metro station.

I pulled out my phone and called James.

He answered on the third ring. "Hey, how'd your day go?"

"Vance approached me." The words tumbled out fast. "At the National Archives."

"Alex, are you sure?"

Something hot flared in my chest. "Why are you doing that?"

"Doing what?"

"Always asking if I'm sure. You make me feel insane. Yes, I'm sure that Eleanor Vance approached me in the National Archives and spoke to me." I stopped walking, standing under a streetlight while pedestrians flowed around me. "She found me in the research room, James. Knew what I'd been looking at. Told me to keep digging but watch who I trust. Said something about silent gavels."

He was silent for a moment. "What were you looking at?"

"Gulf Coast Strategies records. For Banks. For the Redmond case." Not technically a lie. I had been looking at those files when Vance appeared. Just not the only thing I'd been investigating.

I could almost hear him thinking, probably weighing how to respond without setting me off further.

"Okay," he said finally. "I guess I'm just surprised. The Deputy AG doesn't usually corner junior prosecutors in the Archives."

I huffed. "Well, she did."

"Did she say anything else?"

I thought about page 132. About my mother. About the warning to keep digging. But telling James meant admitting I'd accessed that document, emailed it to my personal account, and chosen to investigate my mother's case instead of focusing on the work I'd been hired to do. James had encouraged me to come to DC, had said I'd have more resources here to look into what happened to her, but I knew that support didn't extend to me abandoning my actual cases to chase a twenty-two-year-old murder.

"No," I said. "Just the warning about trust."

"That's ..." James trailed off. "Strange."

"Yeah."

"Look, I need to go. I need to finish this Gulf Coast work for Banks before end of week, and it's not an easy lift."

"Okay. But you know I'm here if you need me, right?"

"Yeah. Okay."

Ending the call, I stood under the streetlight for another minute. Something about his reaction sat wrong with me, but I couldn't articulate what. I finally walked toward the station, descending into the tunnel. The platform was crowded with evening commuters. I found a spot near the yellow safety line and waited.

The train arrived. Doors opened. I pushed inside and found a handhold, wedging myself between a teenager with headphones and a woman reading something on her phone.

But as the train pulled away from the station, I found myself scanning faces. The man in the business suit near the doors. The woman with the briefcase standing two feet away. The college kid slumped against the window.

Any of them could be watching. Any of them could be network. Any of them could be one of Vance's *silent players*.

I rode to Cleveland Park, seeing threats in every face, feeling eyes that probably weren't there.

The walk from the station to my apartment seemed longer than usual. I took the route I'd walked twice before, but tonight every shadow felt populated. Every car passing too slowly appeared deliberate.

By the time I climbed the flights to my door, my shoulders ached from tension.

Inside, I locked the deadbolt and chain, drew the curtains, and turned on every light.

The laptop sat on the dining table where I'd left it this morning. I opened it and pulled up the PDF.

Right to page 132.

CHAPTER
EIGHT

THE HEADER SAT at the top of the page, part of a larger section titled *Texas State Judiciary: Case Studies in Organized Crime Influence.*

Case Study: Houston Trafficking Indictment, 2002 (Dismissed)

I read the first paragraph.

Then, read it again.

Then, a third time.

In 2002, the Harris County District Attorney's office prosecuted a major interstate human trafficking ring operating through Texas ports. Evidence included wiretapped communications, financial records, and victim testimony documenting the movement of victims across state lines. The case targeted a syndicate with connections to Houston's shipping industry and appeared strong by prosecutorial standards.

A state district judge dismissed the indictment on procedural grounds, citing insufficient evidence due to suppressed wiretaps. The dismissal occurred despite prosecutors' objections that the wiretaps had been properly obtained under state law. Twelve trafficking counts were dismissed. Twenty victims saw their cases dropped.

I leaned closer to the screen, reading faster.

The dismissal raised immediate suspicions of judicial bias. Financial records obtained by Source J-17 showed payments from Houston lobbying firm Gulf Coast Strategies to Capitol Ventures LLC, a shell company tied to *the judge's campaign finance committee. The payments totaled $50,000 over six months prior to the dismissal.*

Gulf Coast Strategies. The same firm funneling bribes to Senator Redmond. The same firm Victor Ramsey ran. An operation that had been corrupting Texas infrastructure deals for over a decade.

They'd been doing this in 2002. Bribing judges to dismiss trafficking cases.

I kept reading.

Source J-17, a local prosecutor, provided case files and financial data indicating external influence on the court. Further investigation was curtailed due to jurisdictional limits and source safety concerns. FBI interviews with Source J-17 are referenced in supplemental materials (see restricted file). A marginal note in the original survey indicates: "J-17: Houston DA, see restricted file."

Source J-17. A local prosecutor. Someone who'd gathered evidence against a corrupt judge. Someone whose safety had been a concern.

I scrolled up. Scrolled down. Searched the surrounding pages for any reference to J-17's identity.

Nothing.

Your mother would've known those courts well, Vance had said.

I read page 132 for a fourth time. A fifth. The words blurred together. *Gulf Coast Strategies. Capitol Ventures LLC. Source J-17. Restricted file.*

My mother had investigated trafficking. Had identified judges protecting the network. Had disappeared in April 2003.

This case was from 2002. One year before her death.

The timeline fit. The subject matter fit. Even the firm—Gulf Coast Strategies—connected directly to the corruption I was investigating now.

But Vance had pointed me here for a reason. She'd known the page number. Known what it contained and that it would matter to me.

What was I missing?

I pushed away from the table and grabbed my phone. Opened a search engine and typed: *Eleanor Vance Deputy Attorney General.*

News articles loaded. Official DOJ press releases. A Wikipedia page with her professional history. Standard biographical information—Yale Law, Southern District of New York, twenty years as a federal prosecutor before her appointment as Deputy AG.

I scrolled deeper. Added *recent* to the search.

Different results appeared. Op-eds questioning her judgment. Twitter threads speculating about her motivations. A Washington Post article from two days ago with the headline: *Deputy AG Vance's Unusual Press Conference Raises Questions About DOJ Leadership.*

I clicked on the article.

Deputy Attorney General Eleanor Vance's announcement of a Friday press conference regarding Fifth Circuit nominee Franklin Pearce has sparked confusion within the Justice Department. Sources close to the matter suggest Vance is acting without full departmental support, raising concerns about coordination between DOJ leadership and the White House. "This is highly irregular," said one former DOJ official who spoke on condition of anonymity. "The Deputy AG doesn't typically involve herself in judicial nominations unless there's a serious ethics concern. The timing and manner suggest something is off."

Vance, who has served as Deputy AG for eighteen months, has faced criticism in recent weeks for what some describe as erratic decision-making. She allegedly bypassed standard protocol on several recent cases, leading to tension with Attorney General McMahon. Observers note that Vance has increasingly acted independently, prompting speculation about internal power struggles within the department.

I opened Twitter and searched for Vance's name.

The feed exploded with commentary. Legal analysts dissecting her career. Political operatives questioning her motives. Conspiracy theorists spinning elaborate theories about deep state operations, judicial corruption, and lizard people in the government.

One tweet from a verified legal journalist read: *Sources tell me Vance has been compiling a "corruption file" on judges for months. No one at DOJ seems to know what's in it or why she's doing it. Friday's presser might be the tip of the iceberg.*

Another: *Eleanor Vance is either the bravest person at DOJ or she's having a breakdown. Time will tell which.*

A third, more pointed: *DAG Vance approached several junior prosecutors in recent weeks with vague warnings about "games" and "trust." Behavior consistent with paranoia or whistleblowing. Hard to say which.*

I set the phone down.

Vance had approached me, and apparently others, in a similar manner.

Was she trying to help? Or was she spiraling, seeing conspiracies everywhere, dragging me into whatever breakdown she was having?

The woman in the coffee shop had been focused. Her words in the Archives had been specific—page 132, Houston cases, my mother.

But the woman described in these articles and tweets was erratic.

I pulled my laptop closer and returned to page 132, reading it again, slower this time, searching for details I'd missed.

Source J-17, a local prosecutor, provided case files and financial data...

My mother had been a local prosecutor, investigated trafficking, identified corrupt judges. But so had dozens of other prosecutors in Harris County. The designation alone didn't prove anything.

... source safety concerns.

They'd stopped investigating because J-17 was in danger. Because continuing the probe would have put them at risk.

My mother had disappeared six months after this survey was compiled.

I stood and paced the narrow strip between the table and the couch. Vance knew about my mother. Had known enough to point me to this specific page, this specific case study.

But she was also possibly unraveling.

Which meant I couldn't trust her warnings. Couldn't assume her information was accurate or her motives sound.

But I also couldn't ignore that page 132 existed.

The pattern was there. The connection was real.

I just didn't know what it meant yet.

Lisa's name appeared on my phone with a new message.

How's DC treating you? Miss your face.

Buried in work. Miss you too. Dad doing okay?

Visited yesterday. He's building a dining table. Says hi.

I smiled despite the exhaustion pressing against my skull. Lisa checking on Dad, making sure he wasn't alone while I was hundreds of miles away chasing cases and ghosts.

Tell him I'll call this weekend.

Will do. Don't work too hard.

No promises.

I set the phone aside and stared at page 132 for another minute. Then, I opened a new document and started making notes.

Source J-17 - Houston DA - 2002 trafficking case dismissed by corrupt judge - Gulf Coast Strategies payments to judge's campaign - $50k through Capitol Ventures LLC - same shell company in Redmond case.

I added: *Vance pointed me here. Why? What does she know about Mom?*

And finally: *Vance possibly unreliable. Social media suggests erratic behavior. Can't trust warnings without verification.*

The notes stared back at me, incomplete and frustrating.

I closed the laptop and stood at the window. Below, the street was empty except for a lone pedestrian walking their dog.

I pulled the curtains closed and turned off the lights.

Sleep wouldn't come easy. But I'd learned to function on too little sleep, too much coffee, and the stubborn belief that the truth existed somewhere if I just kept digging.

CHAPTER NINE

THE FIFTH FLOOR buzzed with voices when I stepped off the elevator Thursday morning. People clustered in doorways, huddled near cubicles, all facing the same direction. Toward the break room, where a television mounted on the wall played news coverage.

I walked faster, scanning faces. Marina stood at the edge of the crowd, coffee clearly forgotten in her hand.

"What happened?" I asked.

She turned, eyes wide. "Didn't you hear? They found Eleanor Vance dead this morning."

The words didn't land right. I tried to process what she just said. Still, I asked, "What?"

"In her Georgetown townhome. Apparent suicide." Marina's voice dropped lower. "Neighbor heard a gunshot around six a.m. Called the police for a wellness check."

My vision narrowed as the hallway tilted.

Eleanor Vance. Dead. Suicide.

The woman who'd approached me yesterday in the Archives. Who'd told me to keep digging. Who'd known about page 132, about my mother, about games with silent players.

"Alex?" Marina touched my arm. "You okay?"

"Yeah. Just … shocked." The word came out flat and unconvincing.

I pushed through the crowd toward my office. People talked

around me, speculation flying. Someone mentioned the press conference that would never happen now. Someone else brought up the
rumors about her mental state, the erratic behavior, the tension with
the Attorney General.

I closed my office door and leaned against it, muffled chatter
continuing from behind.

Vance had been alive yesterday. Standing two feet from me,
speaking in a low, urgent voice about my mother's investigation.

She hadn't looked like a woman planning to end her life. She'd
looked focused, like someone with a mission.

Could I believe the official narrative? Apparent suicide. A gunshot
in Georgetown. Case closed.

Or was this what happened to people who dug too deep? Who
tried to expose corruption that reached too high?

A notification from James flashed across my screen.

James; *Just heard about Vance. You okay?*

I stared at the message for ten seconds before typing back.

Me; *In shock like everyone else.*

James; *Want to talk later?*

Me; *Maybe. Have a lot of work to do.*

I put the phone face-down and moved to the window. Below, Pennsylvania Avenue moved with its usual rhythm. Cars. Pedestrians.
Metro buses. The city didn't stop for dead Deputy Attorneys General.

A knock on my door broke me out of my trance.

"Come in," I called.

Banks entered, closing the door behind her. "I guess you heard the
news."

"Yeah." I turned from the window. "It's awful."

"It is."

Banks eased into the chair across from my desk. Her coffee mug
was absent today, as was her portfolio. Just her hands folded in her lap
and an expression I couldn't quite read.

"I spent too much time at the Archives yesterday," I said. "My
head's still spinning."

The lie came smoothly. I hadn't decided yet whether to tell anyone
else about Vance's approach, about the warning she'd given me.

Revealing that conversation would open doors I wasn't sure I was ready to walk through.

"Did you find anything useful?" Banks asked.

"Actually, yeah. Gulf Coast Strategies has a longer history than we thought." I pulled out my notes, the research I'd done before Vance had appeared. "I found a 2002 case—trafficking indictment in Harris County that got dismissed on procedural grounds. Financial records showed payments from Gulf Coast to a shell company connected to the judge's campaign. Same shell company structure they used with Redmond."

Banks's expression morphed with interest. "Capitol Ventures LLC?"

"Exactly. They've been using this pattern for over twenty years. Bribing judges, getting cases dismissed, protecting trafficking operations." I pushed the notes across my desk. "It establishes a clear history of corruption. Shows this wasn't a one-time thing with Redmond."

Banks picked up the notes and scanned them. "This is good work. Really good."

"We could leverage it to issue broader subpoenas. Dig into Gulf Coast's full financial history, map out every payment they've made to political campaigns over the past two decades."

"Hold on." Banks set the notes down. "This absolutely implicates Gulf Coast. Proves they've been playing dirty for years. But it doesn't necessarily implicate Redmond."

"It shows pattern and practice—"

"Of Gulf Coast's behavior. Not Redmond's." Banks leaned forward. "We already knew Gulf Coast was corrupt. Now we know they've been corrupt for longer than we thought, which is useful context. But a judge isn't going to let us go on a fishing expedition through twenty years of financial records just because we found one old case. We need evidence tying Redmond directly to Gulf Coast's payments. Without that, I'm not putting any of this before a grand jury."

My hands tightened on the armrests. "We could find that evidence if we had broader subpoena authority—"

"Or we waste months chasing leads that go nowhere while Redmond's lawyers file motion after motion claiming prosecutorial overreach." Banks's voice stayed patient. "I've seen it happen. Ambitious prosecutor thinks they've found the thread that unravels every-thing, pulls and pulls until the whole case falls apart. Don't be that prosecutor."

"I'm just trying to build a solid case," I protested.

"I know. And again, you're doing good work." Banks stood, collecting my notes. "But when you're a hammer, everything looks like a nail. Be careful about crafting the reality you want to make rather than looking at the true evidence in front of you."

I tried to keep the frustration out of my voice. "I am looking at the evidence."

"Then keep looking. Find me proof that ties Redmond to Gulf Coast's payments. Bank transfers, emails, phone records, meetings. Anything concrete." Banks moved toward the door. "Finalize your memo on the Gulf Coast history. It'll be useful background for the jury if we get that far. But don't chase patterns into dead ends."

She left, letting the door close behind her.

The silence in my office pressed down on me as I stared at the empty chair where she'd been sitting.

When you're a hammer, everything looks like a nail.

Was that what I was doing? Seeing connections that didn't exist? Letting my obsession with the network cloud my judgment about Redmond's case?

Gulf Coast Strategies had bribed judges in 2002. Had protected traf-ficking operations. Had used the same shell company structure they were using now with Redmond.

That wasn't coincidence. That was pattern.

But Banks was right about one thing—pattern didn't equal proof. Not the kind that would survive a grand jury. Not the kind that would hold up in court.

I needed evidence tying Redmond directly to Gulf Coast. Not just Kline's testimony. Not just historical corruption from two decades ago. Concrete proof that she'd taken payments and used her position to secure federal appropriations in return.

My phone buzzed. Another text from James.

> Chambers wants everyone in conference room at 2 for briefing on Vance situation. You'll be there?

> Yeah.

I pulled up a blank document and started drafting the memo Banks wanted. *Gulf Coast Strategies: Historical Pattern of Judicial Corruption, 1998-2025.* The facts flowed easily. Contracts, payments, dismissed cases. The 2002 trafficking indictment. The financial records showing payments to Capitol Ventures LLC.

But I left out Source J-17. Left out the survey data. Left out anything that would raise questions about how I'd found this information, about what I'd been reading in the survey.

The memo grew to twelve pages. Comprehensive and professional. Exactly what Banks had asked for.

I saved it and leaned back in my chair.

Outside my window, clouds gathered. I was learning that D.C. fall weather meant it was always gray and threatening to rain.

Eleanor Vance was dead. And I may have been the last person she'd spoken to.

Should I tell someone? Report the encounter to Chambers? To the FBI?

But what would I say? That the Deputy Attorney General had approached me in the archives and told me to keep digging into my mother's twenty-year-old cold case? That she'd pointed me toward a document I'd accessed without authorization and downloaded to my personal email?

That conversation would end my career before it even started.

So I'd keep quiet. Finish the memo. Build the case against Redmond with the evidence I could prove. Leave Vance's death out of it. Let it be what the official narrative claimed—a tragedy, a woman under too much pressure who'd made a terrible choice.

Even if I didn't believe it.

Even if her warning still echoed in my head.

CHAPTER
TEN

JAMES APPEARED in my doorway just after noon, tie loosened, and sleeves rolled to his elbows. "Lunch?"

I glanced at my computer screen where financial records from Gulf Coast Strategies glowed in neat columns. "I should probably work through it."

"You need to eat." He leaned against the door frame. "And I need to talk to you. Properly."

Something in his tone made me save the document and grab my coat.

We walked three blocks in silence, weaving through lunchtime pedestrian traffic. The temperature had dropped overnight. My breath fogged in the air. James led us to a restaurant on 9th Street with white tablecloths and a hostess who checked reservations on an iPad.

"This is pretty fancy," I said as we followed her to a corner table.

"Yeah, well." James pulled out my chair. "I guess I owe you an apology for yesterday."

We ordered. Water arrived in glasses with lemon wedges. I picked at the edge of my napkin while James studied the wine list as if it required serious consideration.

"What's happening with your investigation?" I asked. "Into Vance?"

James set the wine list down. "Chambers told me to press pause on it. Indefinitely."

"What? Why?" My voice came out sharp. A couple at the next table glanced over. I lowered my volume. "If Vance was right and Pearce shouldn't be confirmed, people should know. We should know the truth."

"I haven't found anything yet. And clearly she was unstable."

"We don't know that."

James leaned forward, dropping his voice. "Vance committed suicide."

"We don't really know that either," I muttered.

"Alex." His expression shifted into something between concern and frustration. "You don't seriously think …"

"Look, all I know is that she approached me yesterday. And she didn't look like a woman who was about to take her own life. Quite the opposite."

James's eyes widened. He glanced around the restaurant, checking if anyone was listening. "What are you trying to say?"

"I just think we should consider that she could have been silenced. For what she was planning to go public with tomorrow." I kept my voice steady. "Don't you think the timing is suspicious?"

"I think if you're looking for things to be suspicious, then they will be." James rubbed his face with both hands. "Maybe she had remorse. Or guilt. Or was overwhelmed. The timing right before a big press conference makes sense if you aren't looking for conspiracies."

I pushed back my chair, ready to leave.

"James! Good to see you, my friend!"

Turning, a man approached our table. Early sixties, sandy brown hair that had turned silver at the temples, wearing a tailored suit.

Franklin Pearce.

James stood and extended his hand. They shook, that firm grip men used to convey mutual respect and shared understanding.

"Frankie." James's voice carried genuine warmth. "How are you holding up?"

"As well as can be expected given the circumstances." Pearce's gaze shifted to me. "And who's this?"

"Alex Hayes. She just joined DOJ from Houston." James gestured between us. "Alex, this is Judge Franklin Pearce."

I extended my hand. His grip was just as firm.

"Pleasure to meet you," Pearce said. "Houston, you said? We could use more prosecutors willing to make the move to federal work."

While he spoke I studied his face. The lines around his eyes. The easy smile. The way he stood relaxed but attentive, giving James and me his full focus despite the restaurant full of other potential connections.

Could this man have orchestrated Vance's death? Could he be standing here twelve hours after her body was found, shaking hands and making small talk, if he'd ordered her silenced?

"Shame what happened with Eleanor," Pearce said, his expression shifting into appropriate solemnity. "Terrible tragedy."

"Yes, we were all shocked," James said.

"Well." Pearce straightened his cuffs. "I guess we need to put it all behind us at this point. Move forward. The work continues regardless of setbacks." He clapped James on the shoulder. "Let's grab coffee next week. After all this confirmation business settles down."

"Absolutely."

Pearce shook James's hand again, then turned to me. "Ms. Hayes, lovely to meet you. Best of luck at the DOJ."

"Thank you, Your Honor."

He moved off toward a table near the windows where another man in a suit waited. The waiter materialized at that moment with our orders. Salmon for James, chicken for me. The food looked expensive and artfully arranged.

I sat back down. Picked up my fork. The chicken was perfectly cooked, tender and seasoned with herbs. I ate mechanically, tasting nothing.

James cut into his salmon. "Frankie's a good man. One of the best legal minds I've encountered."

I didn't respond. Across the restaurant, Pearce laughed at something his companion said.

"Do you think he's involved," James said, setting his fork back down. It wasn't a question.

"I don't know what I think." I set my fork down too. "But Vance was about to hold a press conference about him. And now she's dead.

And he's here eating lunch, treating the whole thing like she'd just stepped away for a few days."

"What's he supposed to do? Wear black and sequester himself?" James's frustration bled through his features. "People die, Alex. Even people in positions of power. Even people with information. Sometimes they die because they're under too much stress and make terrible decisions. Not because there's some vast conspiracy."

"Sometimes they die because they know too much."

"And sometimes prosecutors see patterns that don't exist because they're looking for them." James pushed his plate away, food half-eaten. "I know what happened in Houston and I know what you went through with Leland and Thatcher and all of it. But this is different. This is D.C. The Deputy Attorney General committed suicide. It's tragic. It's awful. But it's not a murder."

"How do you know it isn't?"

"How do you know it is?"

We stared at each other across the white tablecloth and expensive food neither of us wanted anymore.

The waiter returned. "Can I get you anything else? Dessert? Coffee?"

James and I continued glaring at one another. He set his crumpled napkin on the table. "Just the check."

———

We walked back to the DOJ building in silence. The afternoon had grown colder. Wind cut through the gaps between buildings, making me pull my coat around me tighter.

At the security checkpoint, James stopped. "I'm worried about you."

I scoffed. "I'm fine."

"No, you're not. You're seeing conspiracies where there aren't any." He touched my arm, light and brief. "Alex, I know you came here partly to find answers about your mother. And I support that. But that doesn't mean the first person who dies is automatically connected to what happened in Houston. You survived a lot there, and I get why you're on edge. But you can't spend your career chasing ghosts or assuming every tragedy is part of some larger pattern." I turned to face him, scrunching my nose. "What if they're not ghosts?"

James didn't have an answer for that. We rode the elevator in silence, got off on the fifth floor, and walked to our respective offices without another word.

Franklin Pearce's face stayed clear in my memory. His easy laugh. His confident handshake. His casual dismissal of Vance's death as something to put behind us and move past.

The work continues regardless of setbacks.

That's what he'd called it. A setback. Not a tragedy. Not a loss. A setback to be overcome and forgotten.

I woke up my computer, opened a search engine and typed Franklin Pearce's name.

The results loaded. Professional biography. Cases he'd presided over. Law review articles he'd written. A Wikipedia page detailing his rise from Harvard Law to federal judgeship to Fifth Circuit nominee.

I scrolled deeper. Added East Texas to the search.

More results. His appointment to the Eastern District bench in 2015. Cases involving oil and gas disputes, environmental regulations, immigration enforcement. Nothing obviously connected to trafficking or corruption.

But the network was careful. They didn't leave obvious trails.

I opened a new search.

Franklin Pearce Gulf Coast Strategies.

Three results appeared. Two were tangential mentions in news articles about Texas politics. The third was a campaign finance report from 2014 showing a donation from Gulf Coast Strategies to a judicial retention campaign.

I clicked the link.

The report loaded. Tables of donors and amounts loaded onto the screen. I scrolled to the relevant section.

Gulf Coast Strategies LLC: $5,000 donation to Citizens for Judicial Integrity, supporting retention of Judge Franklin Pearce, Eastern District of Texas.

Five thousand dollars a decade ago. Nothing illegal about it. Judi-

cial retention campaigns accepted donations from law firms and businesses all the time.

But it was a connection. Tenuous, yes. Circumstantial, even, but
real.

Franklin Pearce had received money from the same firm bribing
judges and protecting trafficking operations.

I saved the report and made notes. It was probably nothing. Almost
certainly nothing.

But I couldn't ignore it.

My phone buzzed, and I looked at the screen to find a text from
Erin.

> Heard about Vance. You doing okay?

> > Yeah. Crazy day.

> Be careful up there. DC's a different animal.

> > I know.

> Seriously, Alex. People play different games in
> that city. Watch your back.

I stared at her message for a long moment before responding.

> > Always do.

Outside my window, clouds had rolled in, the afternoon darkening
toward evening even though it was barely two o'clock.

Eleanor Vance was dead. Franklin Pearce was alive and networking
over expensive salmon. And I was sitting in my office with a decade-
old campaign finance report and a growing certainty that James was
wrong.

CHAPTER ELEVEN

"BANKS WAS LOOKING FOR YOU," Marina said from my doorway.

"Thanks." I saved the document I'd been working on and headed down the hall toward the corner office that overlooked both Pennsylvania Avenue and 7th Street.

Banks's door stood open. I knocked on the frame.

"Come in." She gestured to a chair on the other side of her organized mahogany desk, her eyes still focused on what was in front of her.

I stepped inside and sat in the leather chair facing her desk. The office was twice the size of mine, with floor-to-ceiling bookshelves covering two walls. Two windows flooded the space with gray afternoon light. Legal treatises stood spine-out in alphabetical order. Case reporters filled the lower shelves, their burgundy and blue bindings worn from use. On the wall behind her desk hung framed diplomas and bar admissions, along with a photograph of herself shaking hands with someone who looked vaguely familiar.

"Marina said you were looking for me?"

Banks closed the file she'd been reading and set it aside. "Filed your subpoenas yesterday afternoon. Defense responded this morning with a motion to quash."

My stomach tightened. "Already?"

"Judge Richard Caldwell scheduled a hearing for tomorrow at ten a.m." Banks pulled a stapled document from one of her stacks and slid it across the desk. "You want to handle it?"

I picked up the motion, scanning the first page. Standard boiler-plate about overbroad subpoenas and undue burden. "You think I'm ready?"

"You handled full murder trials as first chair in Houston. I think you can manage a little motions practice." Banks leaned back in her chair. "What do you know about Judge Caldwell?"

I shook my head, pulling my hand away from the file. "Nothing. What should I know?"

"Eastern District of Virginia, sits in Alexandria but hears cases here occasionally when we need overflow capacity." Banks steepled her fingers under her chin. "He's conservative. Very conservative. Former corporate litigator who spent twenty years defending oil companies before Reagan appointed him to the bench. He's generally pro-busi-ness, skeptical of government overreach, and has little sympathy for prosecutors who can't dot every i and cross every t."

"So this might be an uphill battle."

Banks tilted her head. "The fact that he granted the hearing and scheduled it this quickly isn't the best sign." She pulled over another file, opening it to reveal highlighted sections of case law. "But those subpoenas comply with Rule 17. They're narrowly tailored, relevant to the investigation, and properly served. I don't see how he refuses them."

I nodded. "A make-us-jump-through-hoops exercise."

"Exhaust us at the initial phase. See if we're serious enough to fight for the evidence." Banks closed the file. "Defense does this all the time in white-collar cases. They know the subpoenas are valid, but they file motions anyway. Makes their clients feel like they're getting aggressive representation, and it costs us time and resources responding."

"Great."

Banks smiled briefly. "Think of these things as a game. Turn it into fun rather than an annoyance. You get to outmaneuver opposing coun-sel, show the judge you know the law better than they do, and walk out with what you came for."

I stood, taking the motion with me. "I'll draft a response tonight."

"Good. Email it to me by eight a.m. I'll review it before the hearing."

I left her office and headed back toward mine. Voices drifted from the reception area near Marina's desk. A cluster of people stood watching something on the monitor mounted to the wall.

I slowed, catching fragments of conversation as I approached.

" ... press conference starting now ..."

"MPD, I think ..."

Marina stood at the back of the group, arms crossed. On screen was a podium filled with microphones. The MPD shield hung on the wall behind it. A uniformed officer stepped up to the microphones, adjusting them slightly before speaking.

"At this time, the Metropolitan Police Department has concluded its preliminary investigation into the death of Deputy Attorney General Eleanor Vance. Based on evidence collected at the scene and statements from witnesses, we have found no signs of foul play. The Medical Examiner's office has ruled the death a suicide. Our condolences go out to Ms. Vance's family and colleagues during this difficult time. We will not be taking questions."

The officer stepped away from the podium. The feed cut back to a news anchor who began recapping Vance's career.

Around me, people continued to murmur. Someone said how sad it was. Someone else mentioned the pressure she must have been under. A third voice speculated about mental health resources at the DOJ.

"So sad that she would do that to herself," Marina said to no one in particular.

I kept walking, past the cluster of colleagues, past Marina's desk, into my office and closed the door.

No signs of foul play. Suicide. Case closed.

The official narrative, delivered by MPD at a press conference timed perfectly to quash speculation before it could spread. Exactly what you'd expect if everything was aboveboard.

Or exactly what you'd expect if someone needed the story buried fast.

I moved to my desk and pulled up the motion to quash, reading it more carefully this time. The defense argued that our subpoenas were overbroad, that requesting Senator Redmond's financial records going back five years constituted a fishing expedition, that we lacked probable cause to believe the records would contain evidence of criminal activity.

Standard arguments. Nothing creative or particularly compelling. But Judge Caldwell might buy them anyway if he was inclined to throw up roadblocks.

I opened a blank document and started drafting a response. I cited Rule 17's requirements for subpoenas in criminal cases. Referenced case law establishing that financial records were routinely discoverable in fraud investigations. Argued that Kline's testimony provided ample probable cause to believe Redmond had received payments from Gulf Coast Strategies.

My fingers moved across the keyboard, muscle memory from four years of writing motions and briefs in Houston. The legal arguments came easily. This was the work I knew how to do, the kind where facts and law intersected cleanly and the outcome depended on who made the better argument.

Not like chasing Vance's warnings. Not like trying to piece together my mother's investigation from twenty-year-old survey data.

This was simple and hopefully, the sort of work that wouldn't get me killed.

I wrote for hours, stopping only to reference case law and double-check citations. By seven o'clock, I had ten pages of argument explaining exactly why Judge Caldwell should deny the motion to quash and enforce our subpoenas.

I saved the document and emailed it to Banks. I stretched in my chair, reaching my hands high. Through my window, the street below had gone dark.

A text from James sat on my phone from an hour ago.

How'd the rest of your day go?

Fine. Drafted a motion response. Hearing tomorrow.

Want company tonight? I could bring dinner.

Rain check. Need to prep for tomorrow.

Okay. Good luck with the hearing.

I set the phone face down and returned to my computer, trying not to think about my feelings regarding James. I pulled up the search I'd done earlier on Franklin Pearce. The campaign finance report showing Gulf Coast Strategies' donation to his retention campaign.

Five thousand dollars donated a decade ago. It was probably meaningless.

But I saved the report anyway, adding it to a folder I'd created labeled *Background Research*. Nothing official. Nothing I'd share with Banks or put in any filing. Just information I wanted to keep track of, patterns I couldn't quite ignore.

My email dinged with a response from Banks: *Good work. See you at 8:30 tomorrow to review before we head to the courthouse.*

I closed my laptop and gathered my things. The fifth floor had emptied out while I'd been writing. Only a few offices still had lights on, other attorneys inside working late on their own cases.

The elevator descended in silence. I crossed the lobby and pushed through the revolving doors into cold night air, beginning the eight-minute walk to Metro Center. When I got there, the platform was nearly empty, just a handful of commuters heading home late.

The train arrived, and I found a seat and stared at my reflection in the dark window across from me. Behind my image, tunnel walls rushed past in streaks of concrete and graffiti.

Eleanor Vance was dead. Officially a suicide. No foul play. Nothing to see here.

CHAPTER TWELVE

THE MAILBOXES SAT in a brass panel near my building's entrance. Stopping to check mine before heading upstairs, I pulled out a stack of envelopes. Cellphone bill. Credit card offer. Something from my car insurance company. And at the bottom, a small package wrapped in plain brown paper.

I tucked the mail under my arm and climbed the three flights. Inside my apartment, I dropped everything on the kitchen counter and kicked off my heels. My feet ached against the cool tile floor. The motion response was solid, but I needed to review it again before tomorrow, make sure I hadn't missed anything.

Before I could turn my attention to the package, my phone rang. Dad's name lit up the screen.

"Hey," I said, wedging the phone against my shoulder while I sorted through the mail.

"Just wanted to check in," he said. I could tell from his tone that he was concerned. "See how you're doing after all the news today."

"I'm okay. Shocked like everyone else." I tossed the credit card offer in the recycling. "It's been all over the news here."

"I saw some of it. They're saying suicide?"

"That's the official word." I picked up the brown paper package, turning it over." MPD held a press conference this afternoon. No signs of foul play."

"You believe that?"

The package felt light in my hands. I pulled at the paper, tearing along one edge.

"I don't know what to believe. Everything's been chaos since I got here."

"Are you settling in okay otherwise?"

The paper came away easily. Inside was a small cardboard box, maybe two inches square. I opened the box.

A chess piece sat nestled in tissue paper. The white queen. The crown carved in delicate detail, the base smooth and rounded.

My hand froze.

"Alex? You still there?"

"Yeah." The word came out wrong. I forced my voice to relax. "Yeah, I'm still here. Sorry, the call just cut out a bit."

"Must be the cell service in your building. Lisa mentioned her calls drop sometimes when she's in her apartment."

I picked up the chess piece. The white porcelain felt cool against my palm. The piece wasn't new. The surface showed wear, some small scratches along the base. There was discoloration near the crown, like someone had handled it frequently. The piece looked like it could have hung on a chain, rubbed smooth from contact with skin or clothing.

"Dad, I need to go. I've got a hearing tomorrow morning, and I should prep."

"Of course. You'll do great. You always do."

"Thanks. Love you."

"Love you too, kiddo."

I ended the call and put my phone on the counter. I turned the chess piece over in my fingers. The packaging sat torn open beside it. I smoothed out the brown paper, looking for any indication of where it came from.

Nothing. No address label, no postage stamp, no return information. Someone had put this directly in my mailbox.

Grabbing the packaging, I headed back downstairs. The front desk attendant looked up from his phone as I approached. He was in his late twenties and wearing the building's uniform polo.

"Can I help you?"

"This was in my mailbox." I held up the brown paper. "But there's no address on it. Do you know who might have put it there?"

He frowned, taking the paper from me, examining it front and back. "Postman's the only one with access to the mailboxes. We don't let anyone put things directly inside residents' boxes."

"What time does the postman come?"

"Around seven-thirty each morning. You could try catching him tomorrow if you want to ask about it."

"Thanks."

I took the paper back and returned to my apartment. I placed the chess piece on the kitchen counter and stared at it. Then, I picked it up again, studying the wear patterns. This wasn't like the others. The bishop piece left at my Houston apartment had been new, sharp-edged, as if taken from a new set and sent to me to send a message. The queen piece that followed had been similar. Mass-produced. Identical to thousands of others.

This one was different. Used. Loved, even.

I went to my bedroom and pulled the lockbox from my closet. I entered the combination, and it clicked open. Inside were the other chess pieces, wrapped in tissue paper and tucked into a corner beside my mother's case files and the flash drive Rebecca Thatcher had given me.

I carried the box back to the kitchen and laid out all three pieces in a row. White bishop. White queen. White queen.

The first two matched. Same set, same craftsmanship, same pristine condition. The third stood apart. Different manufacturer. Different era, maybe. Worn smooth as if it had been used to play.

I thought about the DOJ report. Source J-17. My mother's investigation cut short by her disappearance. Eleanor Vance pointing me toward page 132, warning me about trust and silent players.

And now this.

Too much coincidence. Too many connections appearing in the span of a week.

Gathering the chess pieces, I returned them to the lockbox before putting the box back in my closet and locking it.

In the kitchen, my laptop sat waiting. I still needed to review the motion response. Judge Caldwell's hearing was in twelve hours. I should be focused on that, on the work Banks expected, on proving I belonged at the DOJ.

But I couldn't stop staring at my closet door. Couldn't stop thinking about who would send me a chess piece they'd worn smooth. Who would have access to my building's mailboxes without leaving any trace?

Who wanted me to know they were watching?

I poured coffee, opened my laptop, pulled up the motion response, and forced myself to read through it line by line, checking citations and arguments.

I read until midnight, making notes in the margins. Strengthened a few arguments. Added another case citation. By the time I closed the laptop, the motion was as good as it would get.

Tomorrow I'd stand in front of Judge Caldwell and argue about subpoenas. Present my case with confidence and competence. Show Banks I could handle federal practice. That I deserved to be here independent of my relationship with James.

But before that, I'd catch the postman at 7:30 a.m. and find out who'd put that package in my mailbox. Who was sending me messages through chess pieces.

I went to bed but didn't sleep. Instead, I lay in the darkness listening to the building settle and thinking about white queens, worn porcelain, and warnings from dead Deputy Attorneys General.

CHAPTER
THIRTEEN

THE POSTMAN HAD SHRUGGED when I'd caught him the next morning in the building lobby. "I delivered what came through the system. Anything without postage didn't come from me."

"So someone put it directly in my mailbox?"

"Not supposed to happen, but ..." He'd glanced at the front desk attendant, who'd suddenly become very interested in his computer screen. "Sometimes people slip things in if they know the building code."

I'd had to let it go. The hearing was in an hour, and I needed to get across town.

Now I stood on the steps of the E. Barrett Prettyman Federal Courthouse, staring up at marble columns and bronze doors. The building rose six stories, imposing in that particular way federal architecture demanded respect. Cars streamed past on Constitution Avenue. A group of lawyers climbed the steps ahead of me, briefcases swinging, already deep in conversation about some motion they needed to file by the end of the day.

This was real. My first federal hearing. Not in Houston, where I knew every courtroom, every clerk, every judge's quirks and preferences. Here, I was starting over.

I climbed the steps and pushed through the doors into a lobby that smelled like floor polish and old wood. Security funneled visitors through metal detectors. I showed my DOJ credentials to the guard, who waved me through the attorney lane.

The directory listed courtrooms by floor. Judge Richard Caldwell, Courtroom 4B, third floor.

I took the elevator up with three other attorneys who discussed discovery disputes in hushed tones. The doors opened, and I stepped into a hallway lined with dark wood paneling and marble floors that echoed every footstep. Courtroom doors stood closed, brass placards announcing the presiding judges.

4B sat at the end of the hall. I pushed through the doors into a gallery with twenty rows of wooden benches, half of them already occupied by attorneys waiting for other hearings. At the front, a mahogany barrier separated the gallery from the well of the court. Beyond that, two counsel tables faced the judge's bench.

The bench itself rose high, accessed by steps on either side. The federal seal hung on the wall behind it, flanked by American flags. To the right sat the jury box, empty today. To the left, the clerk's desk and court reporter's station.

I moved through the swinging gate and set my briefcase on the prosecution table. I pulled out my motion response, my notes, and a legal pad to write down potential arguments on the fly.

The door behind me opened. Banks entered, laughing at something the man beside her said. She wore her usual navy suit with her hair pulled back. The man was in his late forties, wearing an expensive charcoal suit, and his silver cufflinks caught the overhead lights.

"Alex." Banks gestured me over. "This is Jason Bellamy. He's representing Senator Redmond."

Bellamy extended his hand. "Ms. Hayes. I've heard good things."

His grip was firm and professional.

"Mr. Bellamy," I said.

"Please, call me Jason." He smiled with artificial charm. "No need for formality when we're going to be seeing a lot of each other over the next few months."

Banks moved to sit beside me, still chatting about some case they'd both worked years ago across the aisle. I sat and arranged my materials, trying to ignore the flutter in my chest. Just a motion hearing. Simple procedure. I'd done dozens of these in Houston.

But not in a D.C. federal court. Not with a judge known for skepticism toward prosecutors.

The clerk entered through a side door and took her seat. She was in her mid-fifties with colorful reading glasses on a chain, and she shuffled papers without looking up.

"All rise."

The command came sharply. Everyone in the gallery stood. I rose with them, straightening my jacket.

Judge Richard Caldwell entered from his chambers. He was in his seventies with white hair and black robes that made him look even taller than he probably was. He climbed the steps to the bench and settled into his chair.

"Be seated."

Caldwell pulled a file toward him and opened it.

"United States versus Carla Redmond. Motion to quash subpoenas." He looked up, scanning the courtroom. His gaze landed on me. "Alex Hayes, is it?"

"Yes, Your Honor," I said, standing.

"Welcome to federal practice, Ms. Hayes. I see this is your first appearance in my courtroom."

"It is, Your Honor."

"Well, let's see how you do." He turned to Bellamy, and I sat back down. "Mr. Bellamy, this is your motion. Tell me why the government isn't entitled to Senator Redmond's financial records."

Bellamy stood, buttoning his jacket. "Thank you, Your Honor. The subpoenas issued by the government are overbroad and constitute a fishing expedition. They request five years of Senator Redmond's personal and campaign financial records without any particularized showing that these records contain evidence of criminal activity."

"The government has a cooperating witness who testified that your client received bribes," Judge Caldwell said. "Doesn't that give them probable cause?"

"A cooperating witness with every incentive to fabricate testimony to reduce his own sentence, Your Honor. Robert Kline is facing twenty

years. He's desperate. His uncorroborated claims don't establish probable cause to invade Senator Redmond's privacy."

"Ms. Hayes?" The judge swiveled his chair toward me. "What's
your response?"

I stood as Bellamy sat back down. "Your Honor, Mr. Kline's testimony is detailed and specific. He identified the shell company Gulf
Coast Strategies used to funnel payments, Capitol Ventures LLC. He
described meetings between Victor Ramsey and Senator Redmond,
providing dates and amounts. That level of detail isn't fabrication."

"But you don't have corroboration," Judge Caldwell said.

"Which is exactly why we need the financial records. To corroborate
or refute Mr. Kline's testimony. We can't know what exists in those
records until we see them."

"That's circular reasoning, Ms. Hayes. You need the records to
prove probable cause, but you need probable cause to get the records."

This was it. The exact argument I'd prepared for.

"With respect, Your Honor, that's not accurate under Rule 17. The
government must show that the records are relevant to an ongoing
investigation and reasonably calculated to lead to admissible evidence.
Mr. Kline's testimony establishes relevance. The records will either
confirm or deny his claims."

Bellamy jumped in. "Your Honor, if that standard were sufficient,
the government could subpoena anyone's records based solely on an
uncorroborated allegation. That can't be the law."

Judge Caldwell leaned back in his chair. "What about narrowness,
Ms. Hayes? Five years seems excessive."

"Senator Redmond sits on the Appropriations Committee, Your
Honor. She's been in that position for eight years. Mr. Kline testified
that the bribery scheme has been ongoing since at least 2019. We need
to trace payments back to their origin to establish the full scope of the
conspiracy."

Caldwell nodded his head once. "And the campaign records? Why
do you need those?"

"Because Gulf Coast Strategies has a documented history of
funneling bribes through campaign donations," I said. "We found
evidence in a 2002 case where they used the same tactic."

Bellamy's head snapped toward me. "Your Honor, there's no mention of any 2002 case in the government's pleadings."

I pulled it back before Caldwell could respond. "It's background research, Your Honor. It shows Gulf Coast's pattern of using campaign contributions to disguise bribery."

"Inadmissible hearsay," Bellamy said, turning to face me. "And irrelevant to this motion."

Judge Caldwell held up a hand. "Let's stay focused. Mr. Bellamy, your motion argues the subpoenas are overbroad. But you haven't explained what narrower scope would be acceptable."

"Three years maximum, Your Honor. And only records directly related to the Houston municipal bond project. Not every transaction Senator Redmond has ever made."

"Ms. Hayes?"

I glanced at my notes.

"Your Honor," I said, "limiting our subpoena to transactions related to one specific project defeats the purpose. We're investigating a bribery scheme, not a single payment. If Senator Redmond received bribes, they won't be labeled 'bribe for Houston bonds.' They'll be disguised as consulting fees, campaign contributions, or payments to shell companies. We need the full financial picture to identify the pattern."

"You're asking for a lot of trust from this court," Judge Caldwell said, leaning back in his seat.

"I'm asking for the resources to do my job, Your Honor. Robert Kline came forward with specific allegations about a sitting United States Senator. We owe it to the public to investigate thoroughly."

The judge turned to Bellamy. "What about the bank records? Any objection to those specifically?"

Bellamy hesitated. "The personal accounts are particularly intrusive, Your Honor."

"But if bribes were paid, wouldn't they show up in personal accounts?"

"Or campaign accounts. Or nowhere, because the bribes don't exist."

Judge Caldwell picked up the briefs, flipping through pages. The courtroom went silent. Someone coughed in the gallery. The clerk's keyboard clicked softly as she typed notes.

I stayed standing, hands clasped in front of me. Banks sat motionless at our table. Bellamy shifted his weight, adjusting his cufflinks.

Thirty seconds passed. A minute.

Finally, Judge Caldwell set down the briefs. "I've read both submissions. Mr. Bellamy, your arguments about privacy concerns are noted. But Ms. Hayes is correct that Rule 17 doesn't require the government to prove its case before obtaining discovery. The cooperating witness testimony establishes sufficient relevance."

My chest tightened. Was he granting the motion?

"However," the judge continued, "I agree that five years is excessive. The subpoenas will be modified to cover three years from the date Mr. Kline testified the scheme began. That should give you enough scope to trace the alleged payments without invading every aspect of Senator Redmond's financial life."

Bellamy started to speak, but the judge raised a hand.

"The motion to quash is denied. Defense counsel will comply with the modified subpoenas within thirty days." He looked at me. "Ms. Hayes, I expect you to use these records responsibly. If I find out you've been fishing, we'll have problems. Understood?"

"Yes, Your Honor."

"Good. Anything else?"

"No, Your Honor," Bellamy and I said in unison.

"Court is in recess." Judge Caldwell stood.

"All rise," the clerk called.

Everyone stood as the judge descended from the bench and disappeared into his chambers. The moment the door closed, conversation erupted in the gallery.

I sat back down, hands trembling. We'd won. Not a complete victory, but enough for now. Three years of financial records would show the pattern, provide the evidence we needed.

"Nice work," Banks said, packing her briefcase. "You held your ground when Caldwell pushed back."

"Thank you."

Bellamy approached our table. "Well argued, Ms. Hayes. I look forward to our next round."

"Likewise."

He left through the gallery doors, phone already pressed to his ear.

Banks waited until he was gone. "Come on. Let's get out of here."

We walked through the courthouse halls, down the elevator, out into cold November air. On the steps, Banks paused.

"We should celebrate your first D.C. win."

"We really don't need to do that," I said.

"It's more self-serving." Banks started down the courthouse steps. "I want some good coffee."

I followed her toward the street, still processing what had just happened. My first federal hearing. My first courtroom argument as a D.C. DOJ prosecutor.

And I'd won.

Even if the victory felt smaller than it should have, overshadowed by chess pieces and dead Deputy Attorneys General and warnings I couldn't ignore.

CHAPTER FOURTEEN

THE COFFEE SHOP was two blocks from the courthouse. It was small and crowded and appeared to survive mostly on lawyer traffic. We ordered at the counter. Banks got an Americano. I went with regular coffee, black.

A television mounted in the corner played cable news on mute, closed captions scrolling across the bottom. I caught Pearce's face on screen, then footage of the Senate Judiciary Committee room.

The captions read: *Franklin Pearce confirmation hearing scheduled for Friday, November 7th. Senate sources say nomination expected to advance smoothly despite recent controversy surrounding Deputy AG Vance's planned press conference.*

"You think it's going to go through?" I asked Banks.

She glanced at the screen. "I don't see why it wouldn't at this point. Pearce has strong support on both sides. Whatever Vance had planned to say ..." She shrugged. "It died with her."

I wanted to push. Wanted to ask if she found the timing suspicious, if she wondered what Vance had discovered. But Banks's tone suggested the topic was closed. The nomination was moving forward. Case closed.

The barista called our names. We grabbed our cups and headed back outside.

The walk to the DOJ building took us past the National Archives. I kept my eyes forward, not looking at the building where Vance had approached me just days ago.

Banks sipped her coffee as we walked.

"What's our anticipated timeline for securing an indictment?" I asked.

"Depends on the financial records. Once we get those from Redmond. We also need to corroborate what Kline said. And figure out what the anonymous informant knows." She paused at a crosswalk, waiting for the signal. "The informant's tip was specific. Too specific to be a guess. They know details about Gulf Coast's operations."

"Do we really not know who the anonymous informant is?"

"FBI isn't saying anything. Either they don't know or they're not telling." The signal changed, and we crossed. "Sometimes we can figure it out based on what's in the case file. Cross-reference the information they provided with other evidence, see who would have access. But I haven't had time to really focus on that." She looked at me. "Maybe you want to give it a shot?"

"Sure, I'll take a closer look."

We walked another block in silence. The coffee warmed my hands through the paper cup. Cold wind cut through the gap between buildings, carrying the smell of exhaust and roasting nuts from a street vendor.

"The financial records will help," Banks said. "If we can trace payments from Gulf Coast to Redmond, show the pattern Kline described, that strengthens everything. But without corroboration …" She shook her head. "Defense will argue Kline's desperate. That he's fabricating testimony to reduce his sentence."

"What about the 2002 case?" I asked. "The one I found at the Archives?"

"It provides context. Shows Gulf Coast's history of corruption. But it doesn't directly implicate Redmond." Banks pulled out her phone as it buzzed. Scanned the screen. Her expression shifted. "Wiretaps are ready."

I nearly choked on my sip of coffee. "Already?"

"Mag judge signed off Wednesday. FBI's been recording Ramsey's calls since then." She looked up from her phone. "Want to take a listen?"

Victor Ramsey. CEO of Gulf Coast Strategies. The architect of the bribery scheme, according to Kline. Whatever he'd been saying on those calls could give us exactly what we needed.

"Sounds like a thrilling Friday afternoon," I said.

Banks smiled. "Welcome to federal prosecution. This is where the real work happens. Not in courtrooms. In offices, listening to hours of recorded conversations, looking for the one sentence that breaks the case open."

We reached the DOJ building, made our way through security, up the elevator, and down the fifth-floor hallway to Banks's office. She held the door open, and I walked in.

"Close that," she said, gesturing to the door. "These recordings aren't for general consumption yet."

CHAPTER FIFTEEN

BANKS'S OFFICE felt smaller with the door closed. She pulled up the wiretap files on her computer, the audio player interface filling the screen. A list of recordings appeared, each labeled with date, time, and a phone number.

"These took place last week, Tuesday through Thursday," she said, scrolling through the list. "Ramsey's office line and cell phone. FBI set up the tap after the magistrate judge signed the authorization Wednesday morning."

I leaned forward to see the screen better. "What's the legal threshold for a wiretap in a public corruption case?"

"Probable cause that the target's committing a crime, plus a showing that normal investigative techniques won't work or are too dangerous." Banks clicked on the first file. "The affidavit cited Kline's testimony and the anonymous tip. Argued that Ramsey's sophisticated enough to avoid leaving paper trails, so we needed real-time monitoring of his communications."

"Right. I've done one or two of these back in Texas when I was working in the Southern District."

Banks glanced at me. "Oh, that's right. I guess I keep forgetting you were federal for a bit."

"Just a year."

"Well, let's see what Ramsey's been saying." Banks hit play.

The speakers came to life. Then, a phone rang. Twice. Three times.

"Yes?" Ramsey's voice was clipped and impatient.

"It's me. We have a problem." A male voice responded, older maybe, but I couldn't place it. The connection wasn't great. The slight distortion suggested the use of a burner phone or bad reception.

"What kind of problem?"

"The queen on the board."

I went still.

"We may need to sacrifice her," the man continued. "Clear the path for the bishop."

There was a pause filled with the rustling of papers on Ramsey's end. "That's not a decision we make lightly."

"I understand. But the confirmation cannot have complications."

Ramsey stayed silent for a few more moments. Then, "Give me twenty-four hours. I'll make some calls."

The line went dead.

Banks stopped the recording. "That's a weird thing to say. Queen on the board? Bishop's path?"

My hands had gone cold. I pressed them flat against my thighs, trying to keep my face neutral.

"Maybe it's code," I managed. "For people involved in whatever they're planning."

"Could be." Banks pulled up the next file. "This one's from Wednesday afternoon. Different number but same voice on the other end."

She played it.

Ramsey again. "Talk to me."

"The queen's off the board now. It's done."

"When?"

"This morning. Clean. No complications."

"And the bishop?"

"Path's clear. Confirmation should proceed without issue."

Silence. Then Ramsey responded. "Good. Keep me updated if anything changes."

"Will do."

The call ended.

Banks stared at the audio player, forehead creased. "Queen's off the board. What does that mean?"

Wednesday morning. The day Vance's body was found.

My vision narrowed. The office walls pressed closer. Banks's voice sounded distant, like she was speaking through water.

"Alex?"

I forced myself to breathe. In through my nose. Out through my mouth. The walls stayed where they were.

"Sorry. Just thinking." I grabbed the edge of Banks's desk, grounding myself. "When exactly was this call?"

Banks checked the timestamp. "Wednesday at two forty-seven p.m."

Hours after Vance's death was announced. After the MPD held their press conference, ruling it suicide.

The queen's off the board now.

"There's more," Banks said. She played the remaining recordings. Ramsey talking to different people, always careful, always using the same chess metaphors. The bishop. The path. Clearing obstacles. Confirming timelines.

When the last recording ended, Banks leaned back in her chair. "Well, that was strange. Not what I expected."

I cleared my throat. "What were you expecting?"

"Direct discussion of bribes. Payments to Redmond. Something we could use in court." She gestured at the computer. "This is all metaphor and vague references. His lawyer will argue it's meaningless. Could be talking about actual chess for all we know or even a position on a board of directors."

"Do you believe that?"

"No. But I can't prove it's about our case." Banks closed the audio player. "I'll send these to the FBI, see if they can identify the voices Ramsey was talking to. Maybe that'll give us more context."

I sat quietly, my mind racing. They'd killed her. Or ordered it killed. However it worked in their network of corruption, someone had decided Eleanor Vance needed to be "off the board" so Franklin Pearce's confirmation could proceed.

And they'd talked about it on a wiretapped phone.

Either they didn't know about the wiretap—unlikely for someone as careful as Ramsey—or they didn't care. Maybe they thought the chess metaphors provided enough cover. Maybe they believed no prosecutor would connect the dots.

"Alex, you're being quiet." Banks's voice cut through my thoughts. "What's going on?"

I looked up. She was watching me with that assessing expression prosecutors developed, the one they used on witnesses and said *you're hiding something and I'm going to figure out what.*

Tell her. Don't tell her. The debate circled in my mind.

If I told her about the chess pieces, about Vance's warning, about my mother's investigation, she would probably think I was paranoid. That I was seeing patterns that didn't exist. Letting personal trauma color professional judgment. Just like everyone in my life eventually accused me of.

Or she'd believe me. And then what? We'd be investigating a conspiracy that reached into the highest levels of government, that had already killed my mother and Eleanor Vance, that was powerful enough to manipulate judicial nominations and eliminate threats.

But those wiretaps were real. Ramsey's words were recorded.

The queen's off the board now.

That wasn't paranoia. That was evidence.

"Alex." Banks leaned forward. "Talk to me. What's happening?"

I made a decision.

"You're going to think I'm crazy," I said. "But I know exactly what they're talking about."

Banks's expression shifted from concern to something sharper. "Start from the beginning."

I took a breath and started talking.

Banks didn't interrupt. She didn't react. She just listened.

I told her about the coffee shop first. Vance staring at me. Then the Archives, the warning about trust and silent players, the reference to page 132.

"What's on page 132?" Banks asked.

"A DOJ survey from 2003. Joint task force with the FBI assessing judicial vulnerabilities to corruption." I kept my voice steady even though internally I felt like I was crumbling. "It details a trafficking case from Houston in 2002. A judge dismissed it on procedural grounds despite strong evidence. Financial records showed payments from Gulf Coast Strategies to a shell company with ties to the judge's campaign."

"The same Gulf Coast Strategies we're investigating."

"Yes. Same shell company structure too. Capitol Ventures LLC."

Banks made notes on a legal pad. "Why did Vance point you to this?"

"Because my mother investigated that case. Or cases like it. She was a Houston prosecutor in 2003, working trafficking cases. She identified judges protecting the network. Then she disappeared." I paused. "They killed her. The same people who killed Vance. The same network we're investigating now."

"Alex—"

I held up a hand to stop her, knowing exactly what she was about to say. "I know how it sounds. But look at the timeline. Vance approaches me Tuesday. Warns me about the network, tells me to keep digging. Wednesday morning she's found dead. Wednesday afternoon Ramsey's on a wiretapped phone with someone saying 'the queen's off the board.'" I leaned forward. "That's not coincidence."

Banks set down her pen. "What else aren't you telling me?"

My chest tightened. This was the part that would make me sound unhinged. But I'd come this far.

"Someone's been sending me chess pieces. In Houston, before I left. A white bishop. A white queen. And last night, another white queen was in my apartment mailbox. No postage, no address. Someone put it there directly."

"Chess pieces." Banks looked almost incredulous.

"Yes. The network uses chess symbolism for their hierarchy. Bishops, queens, kings. I found references to it in my mother's case files. Judge Leland had a chessboard diagram in his house labeling different players."

Banks was quiet. I couldn't read her expression even though I was trying.

"You think Ramsey's chess metaphors on the wiretaps are connected to the pieces you received," she said finally.

"I think they're talking about real operations using chess code. The queen was Vance. The bishop is Pearce. They killed Vance to clear the path for his confirmation."

"That's—" Banks stopped. Rubbed her face with both hands. "That's a serious allegation."

"I know."

"You're saying Franklin Pearce, a respected federal judge about to be confirmed to the Fifth Circuit, is part of a criminal trafficking network. And that network orchestrated the Deputy Attorney General's death."

"Yes."

Banks stood, walked to her window, and stared out at the street below without speaking.

I waited. Let her process. Let her decide if I was paranoid or if the evidence supported what I was saying.

Finally, she turned back. "You realize how crazy that sounds."

I nodded. "I do. I told you it would."

"But?"

"But those wiretaps are real. Vance's warning was real. The chess pieces are real." I stood, facing her. "And my mother is dead because she asked questions about this same network twenty-two years ago. I'm not making connections that don't exist. I'm following evidence."

Banks crossed her arms. "Evidence that includes a two-decade-old survey, a dead woman's cryptic warning, and chess pieces left in your mailbox."

"And wiretaps of someone telling Ramsey 'the queen's off the board' hours after Vance died."

"Which could mean anything."

"But it probably means exactly what I think it means."

We stared at each other across her office. Banks moved back to her desk. She sat down and opened her legal pad to a fresh page.

"Tell me everything," she said, clicking her pen. "Every detail. Start with your mother's case and work forward. If we're going to do this, we're going to do it right."

Relief washed through me. She believed me. Or at least she was willing to listen.

So, I started talking.

CHAPTER
SIXTEEN

BANKS SAT BEHIND HER DESK, legal pad covered in notes. I'd been talking for twenty minutes, laying out everything that'd been circulating in my head for days.

"And you think this is connected to your mother's death," Banks said. She didn't phrase it as a question.

"Yes. I really do." My hands were clasped tightly in my lap. "She investigated the same network. Identified judges protecting trafficking operations. Then she disappeared."

"In 2003."

"April of 2003."

Banks made another note. "Twenty-two years ago."

"I know how long it's been."

"I'm not—" Banks shook her head and dropped her pen. "I'm just establishing a timeline. Your mother investigated judicial corruption tied to trafficking in 2003. She disappeared. Now you're investigating Senator Redmond for corruption tied to the same firm your mother was looking at."

I nodded. "Gulf Coast Strategies."

"Right." Banks leaned back in her chair. "And Eleanor Vance approached you about all this the day before she died."

Again, I nodded. "She pointed me to page 132 specifically. Told me my mother would have known those courts. Warned me to be careful who I trust at DOJ." I met her eyes. "Twenty-four hours later, she was dead."

She picked up her pen and tapped it against the legal pad. Once. Twice. Three times. Then set it down again, leaning in with her forearms against the table. "Let's say it's all true. What do you think is happening?"

I took a breath. This was the part that sounded the most insane. The part where most people decided I'd lost my grip on reality.

"I'm not one hundred percent sure," I started carefully. "But what it seems like is there's a very large conspiracy reaching into the highest levels of government. They're placing sympathetic judges and officials in positions of power. Creating a network that allows certain criminals —traffickers, mostly—to continue their operations with minimal to no consequences."

"And you think Franklin Pearce is one of those appointments."

"I don't know. I have no evidence to conclude that." I leaned forward. "But I do know that Vance was expected to speak against his confirmation. And she was silenced before she could. I also know that Thatcher and Leland were both considered 'bishops' in this network's hierarchy. And Ramsey just said something on those wiretaps about keeping the path clear for the bishop."

Banks sat motionless. Her expression gave nothing away. I couldn't tell if she was processing what I'd said or calculating how to gently suggest I take medical leave. Possibly in a padded, windowless room.

Maybe I'd made the wrong decision. Trusted the wrong person. This was how it ended—not with me uncovering the truth, but with everyone thinking I'd cracked under the pressure of moving to D.C., of leaving Houston, of never processing my mother's death properly.

Banks would tell Chambers. Chambers would put me on administrative leave. James would look at me with that furrowed brow and concern he'd been showing since before I even moved here. And the network would keep operating while everyone dismissed me as a paranoid conspiracy theorist.

Banks sighed, long and heavy. "I believe you."

I blinked. "I'm sorry?"

"I believe you." She met my eyes. "I'm not sure that what you think is happening *is* happening. But I believe that you believe it is."

"I'm not sure if that's better or worse."

Banks laughed. The sound broke the tension that had been pressing against my chest. "What I'm trying to say is that it's worth considering. Worth looking into. I'm not going to dismiss it just because it sounds crazy."

"Really?" The word came out smaller than intended.

"Yes. Really." Banks pulled the legal pad back toward her. "Because we've got evidence of Ramsey on the phone talking about queens and bishops. You're getting chess pieces delivered to your apartment. And Eleanor Vance, the Deputy Attorney General of the United States, sought you out specifically to warn you about something before she died." She tapped the pad. "There's no such thing as coincidence. Not this many times."

Relief washed through me, so sudden and overwhelming that my eyes burned with tears. I pressed my palms against my thighs, trying to ground myself.

"Okay," I managed. "So where do we go from here?"

"Give me everything you have on all of this." Banks opened a drawer and pulled out a flash drive. "The DOJ survey. Your mother's case files. Anything about Leland and Thatcher. The chess pieces, if you still have them. Notes on Vance's warning. Everything."

I almost sputtered. "I can get most of it tonight."

"Good. Because we're going through all of it this weekend." Banks checked her watch. "It's five-thirty now. Go home. Gather what you have. Come back tomorrow morning at eight. Bring coffee. And I hope you didn't have anything planned for the weekend."

"I'm an attorney. What's a weekend?" I stood, legs not quite steady. "Thank you. For believing me. Or at least for not thinking I'm completely insane."

" I think you might be a little insane." Banks smiled. "But the best prosecutors usually are. They see patterns other people miss. Connect dots that shouldn't connect. Sometimes that makes them paranoid.

Sometimes it makes them right." She closed her legal pad. "We're going to figure out which one you are."

Grabbing my bag, I headed for the door.

"Alex."

I turned back.

Banks's expression had shifted to concern. " If you're right about any of this, if there really is a network operating at this level, they've already killed your mother and Eleanor Vance. Don't give them a reason to add you to the list."

"I won't."

"I mean it. No going rogue. No investigating on your own. We do this together, by the book, with documentation of everything. Understood?"

"Understood."

I left her office and walked back to mine. The fifth floor had mostly emptied out for the weekend. A few offices still had their lights on, other attorneys working late. I grabbed my coat and messenger bag and shut down my computer.

James sent me a text.

> Still good for dinner? Thinking Thai food might be easier.

I'd completely forgotten about dinner.

> Yeah. My place? I've got some work stuff spread out, but we can order in.

> Perfect. See you at 7.

I locked my office and headed for the Metro. The commute home passed in a blur of stops and transfers, my mind already cataloging what I needed to pull together for Banks. The lockbox in my closet held most of it. But I'd need to organize it, make it presentable. Show Banks I wasn't just chasing phantoms but following actual evidence.

At my apartment building, I checked the mailbox out of habit. Bank statement. Another credit card offer. Nothing in an unmarked plain brown paper mailer. I breathed a sigh of relief.

Upstairs, I unlocked my door and dropped my bag on the kitchen counter. I pulled the lockbox from my closet and opened it on the dining table.

I laid the three chess pieces in a row, studying the wear on the second white queen.

Who had used this enough to wear the porcelain? And why send it to me now?

I pulled out my mother's case files next. Photocopies of her notes, witness statements, financial records she'd gathered before disappearing. I'd received them from my father after his release, had spent hours reading through her handwriting, trying to understand what she'd been chasing.

The same thing I was chasing now. The same network. Just different players.

James: *Leaving the office now. Want me to grab the food on the way?*
Me: *Yeah. Usual order.*

Spreading the case files across the table, I organized them by date and subject. Then I created piles for different judges my mother had been investigating, cross-referenced names with the DOJ survey.

Martin Crawford. Elizabeth Stern. Robert Foley. All three had been on my mother's radar. All three had escaped prosecution.

Pulling up my laptop, I started a timeline document. Listed every relevant event from 2002 to now. The trafficking case dismissed in 2002. My mother's disappearance in 2003. Leland's arrest. Thatcher's murder. Vance's death.

Patterns emerged. Judges dismissed cases. Prosecutors disappeared or died. The network adapted, replaced compromised pieces, continued operating.

And now they were placing Franklin Pearce on the Fifth Circuit. The bishop, whose path needed to be clear.

Three sharp knocks interrupted my work.

I crossed to the door and checked the peephole. James stood in the hallway, takeout bags in both hands.

I unlocked the deadbolt and let him in.

"Hey." He leaned in for a kiss before moving to the kitchen. "Got your usual. Extra spring rolls because I know you've had a long—"

He stopped. Stared at the dining table covered in files and documents and chess pieces.

"Whoa. What happened here?"

I closed the door and locked it. "If you really want to know, Banks thinks I might be onto something. With the conspiracy."

CHAPTER SEVENTEEN

JAMES SET the takeout bags on the kitchen counter and stared at the dining table. Documents covered every inch of surface. Case files stacked in piles. Laptop open to a timeline I'd been building. And in the center, three white chess pieces lined up like evidence.

James turned from the table to look at me. "Alex, are you sure about this?"

The question felt wrong, and anger flared in my chest. After Banks had believed me, agreed to look at the evidence, validated that these patterns existed, James's doubt felt particularly loud.

"I asked for your support on this." I knew I was raising my voice. Also knew this would likely turn into a fight, but I felt helpless to stop it. "Now someone finally believes me, and you're questioning that too? Why are you so against this?"

"I'm not against it." James moved away from the table and started unpacking the food containers he'd brought. Spring rolls. Pad Thai. Tom Yum soup. "I just don't know that you're going about this the right way."

I swallowed hard. "And what, exactly, would be the right way?"

"Not accusing a federal judge of being part of a criminal conspiracy based on chess metaphors and a dead woman's warning?" He pulled plates from my cabinet. "Not dragging Banks into whatever this is."

"Whatever this is?" I crossed my arms and tried to breathe through my nose. "This is my investigation. My mother's murder. The network that killed Eleanor Vance."

"Alex, you don't know that Vance was murdered."

"The timing—"

"Could be coincidence. Could be exactly what the police said. Suicide." James set the plates on the counter harder than necessary. "You're connecting dots that might not connect, Alex. And you're pulling a respected prosecutor into it with you."

"Banks is choosing to help. I didn't force her. She's got decades of experience on me."

"Because you convinced her with chess pieces and twenty-year-old documents." James ran his hand through his hair. "Do you hear yourself? This is exactly what I was worried about."

"You're the one who suggested I come here," I said. "You told me DC would give me access to resources to look into what happened to my mother."

"Yeah, but I didn't think you'd let it affect your work. I didn't think you'd bring it into the office with you." His voice rose slightly. "You came to DC and immediately started seeing the network everywhere. It's exhausting!"

"Because they are everywhere," gesturing at the table. "Gulf Coast Strategies has been bribing judges since at least 2002. Ramsey's on wiretaps talking about queens and bishops. Vance warned me the day before she died. How is any of that me being paranoid?"

"I didn't say paranoid—"

"But you implied it. Just like you implied it at lunch yesterday when I told you about Vance approaching me." My chest tightened. "James, I need you to support me on this. Not question every conclusion I reach. Not act like I'm losing my grip on reality. Sometimes you make me feel actually insane."

James's jaw tightened. "Supporting you doesn't mean I have to buy into your conspiracy theories."

"They're not theories. I have evidence."

"Evidence of what? That Gulf Coast is corrupt? We already knew that. That Ramsey talks in code? Criminals do that. None of it proves there's some vast network placing judges or that Franklin Pearce is involved." Moving toward the table, he pointed at the files. "All I see is you obsessing over your mother's death and trying to connect it to everything happening now."

"My mother was killed by these people." I could feel my rage building, all mixed up with the hurt of someone who I thought loved me tearing me down, yet again.

"No." James's voice went flat. "You only think that's what happened. You don't actually know it. And you might drag a good man's name through the mud chasing this theory."

I narrowed my eyes at him. "Why are you protecting him? You can't even entertain the idea that he might not be this bastion of virtue you think he is." I all but pointed a finger at him to make my point.

He scoffed, returning to face the food. "That's ridiculous."

"I don't think so. Every time I mention Pearce you defend him. He's your mentor; he's brilliant; he's incapable of corruption." I stepped closer. "What if you're wrong about him?"

"I know this man." James's voice rose. "I've known him for fifteen years. Studied under him. Worked with him. I can vouch for his character."

"People vouched for Leland too. And for Thatcher. They had reputations. They seemed respectable. And they were protecting traffickers. One of them murdered his own daughter!"

"Pearce isn't Thatcher!"

"How do you know?"

"Because I know *him*. And I'm not going to stand here and watch you destroy his reputation because you're chasing ghosts."

"Then maybe you should leave."

The words came out before I could stop them. I knew they were harsh, and as soon as they left my lips, I wondered if they meant something deeper.

James froze. "What?"

I looked at him, really looked at him for a moment, and then I solidified my resolve. "If you're not going to support me in this, if you're just going to question everything and defend Pearce no matter what evidence I find—" My throat tightened, but I forced the words out. "Then maybe you should leave."

He stared at me. "That's what you want?"

"What I so want is for you to believe me. For you to not to make me feel like I should be committed. But if you can't—"

"Fine." James grabbed his coat from the chair he'd draped it over and pulled it on. " But I don't want this. I'm leaving because you asked me to."

Walking to the door, he unlocked it, pausing with his hand on the knob.

"Alex—"

I shook my head. I could see it in his eyes. James wasn't going to budge, and neither was I. Maybe our personalities were incompatible. Maybe we could be together after I'd gotten the proof I needed. The whole thing made me sad and made my heart ache with several feelings I couldn't even describe. But none of them could overcome the lack of support he exhibited towards me on a constant and consistent basis.

"Goodbye, James."

He left. The door closed behind him. It clicked softly, but it somehow felt louder than if he'd let it slam.

In the sudden silence. the apartment felt emptier than it had five minutes ago. The takeout containers sat on the counter, food going cold. Spring rolls I wouldn't eat. Soup I wouldn't drink.

My eyes burned. I pressed my palms against them, fighting back tears that wanted to come. No. I didn't have time for this. Banks expected everything organized by tomorrow morning. This was my one chance to get someone to believe me. To see what I was seeing. To harness the support she was offering to me. I had work to do.

Grabbing the takeout containers, I dumped them in the trash. All of it. The food, the containers, the paper bags James had carried up three flights of stairs. Gone.

Then I turned back to the dining table. To the files and documents and chess pieces waiting. This was more important than a fight with James. More important than whether he believed me or supported me or understood what I was trying to do.

My mother had died investigating this network. Eleanor Vance had died trying to expose it. I wasn't going to stop just because I had a fight with my boyfriend.

I slid my laptop closer and kept working on the timeline. Added notes about Ramsey's wiretapped conversations. Cross-referenced the dates with Vance's death.

Tuesday: Ramsey's contact says the queen is problematic and needs to be sacrificed.

Wednesday morning: Vance found dead.

Wednesday afternoon: Ramsey's contact says the queen is off the board.

The pattern was there. It wasn't a conspiracy. The evidence was right there, plain as day.

But James couldn't see it. Or wouldn't. Because Pearce was his mentor, and the idea that his mentor could be corrupt was impossible for him to accept.

I tried to stop myself from thinking about James right now. Whatever was happening between us I could try to fix later, if there was anything left to fix.

Grabbing my mother's case files, I started reading through them again. Her handwriting filled the margins. Notes about judges she suspected. Financial records she'd gathered. Witness statements from people who'd disappeared or recanted.

She'd been building the same case I was building now. Following the same trails. And they'd killed her for it.

You only think that's what happened, James had said. *You don't actually know.*

But I did know. Maybe not with courtroom-quality proof. Maybe not with evidence that would survive a defense attorney's cross-examination. But I knew in the way prosecutors learned to trust their instincts after years of working cases.

My mother hadn't disappeared randomly. Hadn't walked away from her family and her career. She'd been murdered because she'd gotten too close to the truth.

And now I was getting close to that same truth.

A text from Lisa buzzed on my phone.

> How's your weekend going? Miss our
> Saturday dinner dates.

I stared at the message. Dinners with Lisa in Houston sounded so far away. Like a completely separate life, left fourteen hundred miles behind.

> Me too.

> Everything okay?

> Yeah. Just busy.

> Call me if you need to talk?

I set the phone aside without responding. I did need to talk but I couldn't verbalize my feelings at the moment. So, I pulled the DOJ survey back up on my laptop and navigated to page 132, distracting myself by reading through the case study again, this time making detailed notes.

Everything pointed to my mother being Source J-17, the one who'd provided case files and financial data showing Gulf Coast's payments to a judge. But the survey had been anonymized. The restricted files it referenced weren't accessible through normal channels.

I added a note to my timeline: *Confirm J-17 identity. Request restricted files from FBI?*

Banks would know how to get them. Or whether we could get them at all. Tomorrow we'd go through everything together. Build the case properly. With documentation and evidence and all the procedural safeguards that would survive scrutiny.

By midnight, I'd organized everything into folders. Mother's investigation. Leland and Thatcher cases. DOJ survey. Vance's warning. Chess pieces. Wiretaps. Financial records.

Each folder had a summary document outlining the key evidence and how it connected to the larger pattern. I hoped it would show Banks that I wasn't just paranoid but that I was following a legitimate trail.

I saved everything to the flash drive and shut down my laptop.

The apartment was silent except for the hum of the refrigerator and distant traffic. I stood at the window, looking down at the empty street. A car passed. Then another.

James thought I was wrong. Thought I was chasing ghosts and seeing patterns that didn't exist.

But Banks believed me. Or at least believed me enough to spend her weekend helping me investigate.

It was something, and for right now, something had to be enough.

CHAPTER EIGHTEEN

I REACHED the DOJ building at 6:30 Saturday morning. The lobby was empty except for one security guard manning the checkpoint and looking half-asleep. My credentials got me through without conversation.

The fifth floor was dark and silent. I unlocked my office and turned on the lights, the fluorescent glaring against the windows. I spread my files across the desk and booted up my computer, taking the moment to make coffee in the break room. It tasted burnt even when it was fresh.

By 7:15, I had everything organized. After I printed and highlighted the timeline, I sorted the case files by date, then labeled the flash drive with scanned documents. I wrapped the chess pieces in tissue paper and placed them in a small evidence bag I had found in my desk drawer.

Banks arrived at eight on the dot, but this wasn't the Banks I had seen all week. The navy suit was gone. In its place, she wore jeans and a Georgetown sweatshirt with her hair down around her shoulders. She carried two paper bags and a coffee carrier.

"Wow." Setting the bags on my desk she handed me a cup. "You look like shit."

"Yeah, well. Not everyone in my life is supportive of me following this lead."

Banks pulled out breakfast sandwiches from one of the bags. They were egg and cheese on English muffins. "Ah yes. I did know about you and Holloway having a relationship. I'm assuming you mean him?"

"Yeah." I unwrapped the sandwich. I wasn't hungry, but I hadn't eaten since yesterday. "We fought last night about all this. About Franklin Pearce."

This was my own personal business, but I felt helpless to keep it inside me.

Banks took a bite, chewed, and swallowed. "He's protective of his mentor. I can't fault him for loyalty."

"But I can when that loyalty means he won't even consider the evidence."

Banks sat in the chair across from my desk and crossed her legs. "You know, my ex-husband and I met in law school. Both of us were ambitious and wanted big careers. Got married right after graduation." She sipped her coffee. "For the first five years, his career moved faster. He made partner before me and got bigger cases with better clients. I was happy for him and celebrated every win.

"But then I started winning bigger cases than his. Got appointed to the U.S. Attorney's Office while he was still grinding out civil litigation. Suddenly my career was taking off ahead of his." Banks's expression went flat. "He couldn't handle it. Started questioning my judgment and undermining my decisions. Made little comments about how maybe I should slow down and focus on family instead."

Taking a bite of my sandwich I swallowed, understanding her parallel to my current predicament. "What did you do?"

"Divorced him." She said it matter-of-factly. " I wasn't the type of person who could live with myself if I didn't chase what I knew was right. He should have known that about me. Should have supported it instead of trying to make me smaller so he could feel bigger."

"I don't *want* James to feel like my career is taking off ahead of his." I set down the sandwich. "I mean, he got me this job, and I'm grateful for that. But I have to pursue what I feel is right without him trying to silence me."

"Then my advice is to keep doing what you think is right." Banks leaned forward. "If he can't get behind that, that's on him. You're not the type of person who's going to be able to live with yourself if you back down. James should know that about you by now."

Her words made sense. They may have been the only thing that made sense in the last year. "Thanks."

"Alright, enough talk about men. Show me what you've got." Banks stood and moved to my side of the desk, surveying the organized files.

I walked her through everything. I started with my mother's investigation in 2003, showing her the judges my mother had identified and explaining her disappearance in April. Then I moved forward to Leland's arrest, Thatcher's murder, and the flash drive with Melissa Thatcher's evidence.

"Wait a second." Banks picked up one of the financial documents from Thatcher's files. "This shell company is Bayfront Holdings LLC. I've seen that name before."

She pulled out her phone and opened an email, scrolling through attachments until she found what she wanted. "Here it is. In the Gulf Coast Strategies preliminary financials, Bayfront Holdings received payments from Gulf Coast in 2018 and 2019."

My pulse quickened. "So Thatcher's shell company was receiving payments from Gulf Coast?"

"It looks like it." Banks compared the documents side by side. "The account numbers are the same, and the routing information matches. Gulf Coast was paying Thatcher through Bayfront Holdings."

"Then Gulf Coast directly paid a judge who's been confirmed to have protected trafficking operations."

"They didn't just pay him. The amounts here …" Banks pulled up a calculator on her phone. "This is over two hundred thousand dollars across eighteen months."

Grabbing my timeline, I added the information. I drew a line connecting Gulf Coast to Thatcher and another line from Thatcher to Leland. The web was taking shape.

"What about Capitol Ventures?" I asked. "That's the shell company from the 2002 case that also appears in Redmond's investigation."

Banks flipped through more documents. "Here it is. Capitol Ventures received payments from Gulf Coast starting in 2001 and continued through at least 2023 based on what we have." She looked up at me. "They've been using the same shell company structure for over twenty years."

"And now they're using it with Redmond."

"Allegedly, we still need proof that Redmond received payments." Banks held up a hand. "But the pattern is clear. Gulf Coast creates shell companies and funnels money through them to judges, politicians, and whoever they need to protect their operations."

I pulled out the DOJ survey. "This is what Vance pointed me to. Page 132."

Banks took the document and read it. Her expression shifted as she scanned the information about the 2002 trafficking case, the dismissed charges, Gulf Coast's payments to Capitol Ventures, and Source J-17.

"A local prosecutor provided the evidence," she said. "But they curtailed the investigation due to source safety concerns?"

I nodded. "I think J-17 was my mother. The timeline fits her investigation of trafficking and corrupt judges in 2002 and 2003. She had access to court records and financial data. She disappeared six months after this survey was compiled."

"But you don't know for sure, that she was J-17."

"I don't know for certain because the survey is anonymized. I need to find the actual case and see who the prosecutors were."

Banks set down the survey and pulled a chair up beside my computer. "Let's find it then. We can do a Westlaw search for Harris County trafficking cases from 2002."

I logged into Westlaw. I entered the search parameters for trafficking cases in Harris County, Texas from 2002 that were dismissed.

Eight results appeared.

We clicked through them one by one. We found drug trafficking cases and immigration violations, but none of them matched the survey's description of a major interstate operation involving victims transported through Texas ports.

The seventh result made me pause.

The case was titled *Texas v. Garrett Simmons, et al.*, Cause No. 02-CR-8847, in the 177th District Court of Harris County, Texas.

I clicked on the case summary.

A twelve-count indictment charging defendants with human trafficking, conspiracy, and racketeering. The case involved victims transported through the Port of Houston for forced labor and prostitution. The indictment was dismissed in November 2002 on motion of the trial court citing insufficient evidence.

"That's it," Banks said. "This is a major trafficking operation with twelve counts that was dismissed in 2002."

I scrolled down to the party information where I could see the defendants, defense attorneys, and trial judge.

Under State's Attorneys, I saw Katherine Hayes listed as Assistant District Attorney for Harris County, along with Arthur Kennedy as Assistant District Attorney for Harris County.

My mother's name appeared right there in the official court records.

My hands started shaking, and I pressed them flat against the desk to steady myself.

Banks leaned closer to the screen. "The case was filed in May 2002 with trial scheduled for September and dismissed in November." She pulled up the docket sheet. "Your mother was lead prosecutor and Kennedy was second chair."

I swallowed the knot in my throat. "The survey says Source J-17 provided case files and financial data showing Gulf Coast's payments to the judge."

"Judge Allen Morrison presided over this case." Banks made a note. "We should look into him and see if he's still alive and on the bench."

"The survey said Source J-17's safety was a concern and that they curtailed the investigation to protect the source." I looked at Banks. "My mother disappeared six months later. They didn't protect her. They just stopped investigating and left her exposed."

"Alex, we don't know that's what happened."

"What else could it be? If she was J-17, then she provided evidence showing a judge was taking bribes from Gulf Coast to dismiss trafficking cases. The DOJ task force noted safety concerns but didn't follow up. Then she disappeared."

Banks was quiet as she stared at the screen where my mother's name sat in blue hypertext.

"We need to confirm Morrison was the judge taking payments," she said finally. "We also need to find out if the restricted files mentioned in the survey still exist. If your mother provided evidence to the FBI, there should be interview records and documentation."

"Can we access those files?"

"We might be able to. The FBI maintains files on public corruption investigations even if they don't result in charges. But it'll take authorization because we can't just request twenty-year-old restricted files without good cause."

"We have good cause. We're investigating Gulf Coast Strategies for bribing Senator Redmond using the same shell company and tactics they used in 2002."

"That might work as justification." Banks took out her phone and jotted down a note. "I'll put in a request Monday morning. I'll cite the Redmond investigation and argue that the historical pattern is relevant to proving the current scheme."

I saved the case to my files and printed the docket sheet. I stared at my mother's name in Times New Roman font.

Katherine Hayes had been the lead prosecutor, built this case and gathered evidence against a trafficking ring. She had identified the corrupt judge protecting them and provided information to federal investigators.

Then she had disappeared.

She hadn't disappeared randomly or because she had walked away. They had killed her to stop the investigation.

"Alex."

I looked up and saw that Banks was watching me with concern.

"Let's stay objective," she said. "I know this is personal, and I know finding your mother's name on that case makes this real in a way it wasn't before. But we can't let emotion drive the investigation."

"I'm not letting that happen," I said even as I questioned it myself.

"You are, and I can see it." Banks's voice was gentle. "I understand why this matters to you. But we are following evidence and building a case. We're not avenging your mother."

I pursed my lips. "Those things aren't mutually exclusive."

"They are if the second one clouds your judgment on the first." She closed the Westlaw tab. "We investigate this properly through channels and with documentation. Our job is to prove Gulf Coast has been bribing judges for decades and that they're continuing now with Redmond. We show there's a pattern of corruption. But we don't make it about your mother unless the evidence takes us there naturally."

I wanted to argue with her. Wanted badly to say this was already about my mother and that everything connected back to her investigation and her death. But Banks was right about the approach. Going into this with vengeance as a motivator would compromise the case and make us look biased. It would give defense attorneys ammunition to discredit everything we found.

"I understand," I said. "We'll investigate it properly."

"That's what I wanted to hear." Banks stood and stretched. "It's nine-thirty now, and we've been at this for an hour and a half. Let's take a break and walk around the block. We can clear our heads and come back to dive into the actual case details."

Grabbing our coats we headed downstairs. The morning had warmed up slightly with November sun breaking through clouds. For two blocks we walked without talking as we just moved and breathed and let the coffee kick in properly.

"You did good work pulling this together," Banks said as we turned back toward the building. "The connections you've found between Gulf Coast and Thatcher, the 2002 case and your mother, the timeline with Vance's death—all of it is worth investigating."

"But we need more than that?" I said it as a question, but I already knew her answer.

"Yes, we do. Right now we have patterns and coincidences. We need evidence that proves causation and shows that Gulf Coast isn't just corrupt but actively orchestrating a network. We need to prove that judges aren't just individually bad but part of a coordinated system." She held the door open as we entered the building. "That's what we're looking for this weekend. We need the proof that turns your theory into fact."

CHAPTER NINETEEN

BACK IN MY OFFICE, we settled in at my desk, and Banks pulled up the docket sheet for *Texas v. Simmons* again. "Let's start with the actual case. We should read the pleadings, see what your mother alleged and why Judge Morrison dismissed it."

The docket sheet showed a timeline that stretched from May 2002 through November 2003. Eighteen months from filing to dismissal.

"Your mother filed the indictment in May 2002," Banks said, scrolling through entries. "Trial was scheduled for September 2002, but it got continued. Multiple times."

I leaned closer to the screen. "Why the continuations?"

"Defense motions. Discovery disputes. Standard delay tactics." Banks clicked on one of the entries. "But look at this. Your mother was still listed as lead prosecutor through March 2003. Then, her name disappears from the docket."

April 2003. The month she had disappeared.

"Who took over?" I asked.

Banks scrolled further. "Arthur Kennedy. He was second chair originally, then became lead after your mother's death. Case went to trial in August 2003 and was dismissed two months later."

She opened the actual case documents. The indictment appeared first. I recognized my mother's style from the files I had gotten from my father. It was direct and thorough, leaving no room for ambiguity.

The charges were involuntary servitude, smuggling of persons, and organized crime under Texas Penal Code sections 20.04 for smuggling and 71.02 for organized crime. There was federal overlap under the Trafficking Victims Protection Act of 2000, specifically 18 U.S.C. section 1589 for forced labor.

"This is a big case," Banks said as she read through the indictment. "Not just smuggling. Organized trafficking with victims forced into labor."

I read over her shoulder. The allegations detailed a Houston-based trafficking ring that smuggled migrants from Mexico and forced them into labor at Bayou Shipping warehouses. My mother had built the case methodically. She had gathered wiretapped communications between Simmons and his co-conspirators. She had secured victim testimonies from workers who had escaped the warehouses. She had obtained financial records showing payoffs to local officials who looked the other way.

"This should have been an easy conviction," I said. "She had everything."

Banks scrolled to the motion practice section. "Keep reading."

Page after page of defense motions appeared. Motions to suppress the wiretaps. Motions to exclude the financial records. Motions to dismiss based on insufficient evidence. Every tactic defense attorneys used to chip away at a strong case.

Most of the motions were denied while my mother was still lead prosecutor. She had fought back with well-reasoned responses and solid legal arguments. The wiretaps were properly obtained. The financial records were relevant and authenticated. The evidence was more than sufficient.

Then, her name disappeared from the docket in April 2003.

David Kennedy took over, and the tone of the filings changed. His responses were shorter, less detailed. He seemed to be going through the motions rather than fighting to protect the case my mother had built.

The trial finally happened in August 2003. I clicked on the trial transcript. Witnesses testified about being smuggled across the border and promised jobs. They described being locked in warehouses and forced to work eighteen-hour shifts for no pay. They identified Simmons and his associates as the ones running the operation.

The evidence seemed overwhelming. But something had gone wrong.

Banks found it first. "Here. The dismissal order. November 2003."

She opened the document, and we both read.

Judge Allen Morrison had presided over the trial. In his order, he ruled to suppress key evidence, including the wiretaps and financial records. His reasoning was procedural grounds, specifically that the warrant authorizing the wiretaps had been improperly obtained.

"That's bullshit," I said. "My mother's motions responses showed the warrant was valid. She cited the authorizing statute and the magistrate's approval."

"Morrison disagreed." Banks scrolled through his reasoning. "He says the affidavit supporting the warrant lacked sufficient grounds, particularity about the communications to be intercepted."

"But that's not how wiretap warrants work. You can't specify exact conversations before you record them. You specify the subjects and the probable cause for believing criminal communications will occur."

"We both know that. But Morrison ruled otherwise." Banks leaned back in her chair. "With the wiretaps suppressed and the financial records excluded as fruit of the poisonous tree, the case collapsed. The prosecution couldn't prove the conspiracy without those records."

I kept reading. After Morrison's evidentiary ruling, the case fell apart. Kennedy tried to proceed with just the victim testimony, but the defense tore them apart on cross-examination. Without corroboration from the wiretaps or financial records, the jury would have seen it as a he-said-she-said situation.

Kennedy withdrew the charges. Simmons and his co-conspirators walked free.

Well, not entirely free. Simmons eventually pled guilty to a reduced charge. Minor immigration violations. He served eighteen months in county jail instead of the twenty years he should have gotten for trafficking.

"Morrison killed this case," I said. "My mother had everything she needed for convictions, and Morrison destroyed it with a bogus evidentiary ruling."

"The question is whether he did it because he was paid to or because Kennedy was an ineffective prosecutor without your mother as first chair." Banks pulled up her notes from our research. "The DOJ survey said Source J-17 provided financial records showing payments from Gulf Coast Strategies to a judge. If those payments went to Morrison, then this wasn't just a bad ruling. It was corruption."

"We need to find those financial records."

"They'd be in the restricted FBI files. The ones we're requesting access to." Banks made another note. "But even without them, the pattern is clear. Gulf Coast pays judges to dismiss trafficking cases. They did it in 2002 with the case on page 132 of the survey. They did it in 2003 with your mother's case. They're probably still doing it now."

I scrolled back to the top of the dismissal order and stared at Judge Allen Morrison's name at the bottom.

"Morrison," I said slowly. "Why does that name sound familiar?"

Banks looked up from her notes. Her expression shifted to recognition. "Morrison was the one who heard the Torres case."

My stomach dropped. "What?"

"The case Erin prosecuted. United States v. Daniel Torres. The one where Robert Kline testified about Senator Redmond." Banks pulled up her phone and scrolled through emails. "I remember seeing his name in the case materials. Judge Allen Morrison presided over the trial."

"So Morrison dismissed my mother's trafficking case in 2003," I said, "then twenty years later he's hearing another trafficking-related corruption case?"

"He's not on the state bench anymore. He was appointed to the federal bench." Banks set down her phone. "Southern District of Texas. And if he was corrupt in 2003, he's probably still corrupt now. Just operating at a higher level."

I thought about what that meant. Morrison had dismissed my mother's case using bogus legal reasoning. Had allowed traffickers to walk free. Had taken bribes from Gulf Coast Strategies to protect their operations.

And now, two decades later, he was still hearing cases. Had been elevated into a position to protect the network. Still corrupting the justice system from the bench.

"Erin would know about his rulings in the Torres case," I said. "She'd know if he made questionable calls during trial."

Banks nodded. "Call her. Put her on speaker. Let's find out what Morrison did in that courtroom."

I took out my phone and dialed Erin's number. It rang three times before she picked up.

"Hey, what's up? You surviving D.C.?"

"Hey, so I have you on speaker with Helen Banks. She's the lead prosecutor on the Redmond case I'm working."

"Oh, hi Helen. Erin Mitchell. I worked the Torres case at the district level."

"Good to talk to you, Erin." Banks leaned toward my phone. "We have some questions about Judge Morrison and his rulings during Torres."

"Morrison." Erin's tone shifted. "What do you want to know?"

"Were there any pretrial motions that he denied that he really should have allowed through?" Banks asked. "Or evidentiary rulings that seemed questionable?"

"Yeah, actually. Several."

CHAPTER TWENTY

"JUDGE MORRISON SUPPRESSED SOME PERIPHERAL EVIDENCE." Papers rustled on Erin's end of the call. "He threw out a minor wiretap segment on technical grounds. The warrant had a typo in the time range or something equally minor. But he allowed the core testimony from Robert Kline, which was what we really needed."

"So the case was still winnable?" I asked.

"Absolutely. And we did win it. Kline's testimony was solid, and the financial records backed him up. But there were some things Morrison did that felt off." Erin paused. "He limited cross-examination when defense tried to dig into Gulf Coast Strategies' broader ties. Shut it down pretty quickly, said it was beyond the scope of the charges."

Banks and I exchanged looks. Morrison protecting Gulf Coast, the way he had with my mother's case.

"Did you dig into Gulf Coast's operations at all?" I asked. "Beyond those related to Torres?"

"I didn't have the time or resources to, and we were still able to prove Torres was taking bribes from them. Then it was case closed." Erin sounded apologetic. "Should I have?"

"No, you did your job. You got the conviction." I pulled my laptop closer and opened a search browser. "I'm just trying to understand how deep Gulf Coast's connections go."

I typed Gulf Coast Strategies into the search bar and hit enter. Pages of results loaded. Press releases about infrastructure contracts. News articles about their CEO Victor Ramsey. A company website with generic corporate language about building better communities.

I scrolled past the first few pages of results, looking for something more substantial. Financial disclosures, regulatory filings, anything that would show their corporate structure.

On page four, I found it. A link to an SEC filing. I clicked it.

Banks leaned over to see my screen. "You find something?"

"I'm looking at an SEC filing that mentions Gulf Coast." I scanned the document header. "But this filing isn't for Gulf Coast. It's for Bayou Shipping."

"Wait, is Gulf Coast a public company?" Erin asked through the phone. "I don't remember seeing any public filings during our investigation."

"No, they're not public." I scrolled down through the document. "But Bayou Shipping is. This looks like their initial public disclosure from when they went public."

Banks pointed at the screen. "This is their S-1 registration statement. Companies have to file these with the SEC when they first offer stock to the public. It includes financial information, business operations, and ownership structures."

I kept scrolling until I reached the section on corporate ownership. The page listed major shareholders and their percentage stakes in the company. Institutional investors held the majority. A few individual executives owned significant blocks.

And there, buried in the middle of the list, was Gulf Coast Strategies LLC with a four percent ownership interest in Bayou Shipping Corporation.

"Holy shit," I said.

"What?" Erin's voice came through the speaker. "What did you find?"

"Gulf Coast owns part of Bayou." I stared at the screen. "Four percent according to this filing."

Banks leaned closer. "When was this filing dated?"

I checked the header. "March 2019. That's when Bayou went public."

"So Gulf Coast had an ownership stake in Bayou for at least the past six years." Banks pulled out her legal pad and made notes. "Possibly longer if they held the shares before the company went public."

Bayou Shipping was the company my mother investigated. Garrett Simmons and Bayou Shipping Corporation had been charged with trafficking. My mother had built a case showing they smuggled migrants and forced them into labor and worse at Bayou warehouses.

Judge Morrison had dismissed that case by suppressing evidence. If Gulf Coast had paid him to do that, they weren't just protecting Simmons. They were protecting their own financial interest in Bayou.

"Do we know who owns Gulf Coast?" I asked. "Was that in any of the discovery you did, Erin?"

"I'd need to look," she said. "It would be back in the office archives at this point. Off the top of my head, I don't know if we even pulled that information. Like I said, we focused on proving Torres took bribes from Gulf Coast. We didn't dig into Gulf Coast's ownership or corporate structure."

"Can you check on Monday when you head in?"

"Yeah, I can do that. I'll pull the files and see what we have on Gulf Coast's corporate setup." Erin paused. "What do you guys think you're onto?"

I looked at Banks. She gave a small nod.

"I'm not entirely sure," I said. "But things seem a little too connected at this point for it to be coincidence. Gulf Coast bribing judges in 2002, paying off Torres in 2020, possibly connected to Redmond now. And they had a financial stake in a company that was trafficking people."

"Jesus." Erin let out a long breath. "Okay, I'll dig through the archives Monday morning. If we have anything on Gulf Coast's ownership, I'll send it over."

"Thanks, Erin. I really appreciate it."

"No problem. Be careful up there, Alex. If this is as big as it sounds, you're playing with some serious people."

"I know. Talk to you Monday."

I ended the call and dropped my phone on my desk. Banks was still writing notes.

"So Gulf Coast has been protecting Bayou for at least twenty-three years," she said without looking up. "They paid Morrison to dismiss your mother's case in 2003. They had an ownership interest in the company when it went public in 2019. And now they're bribing Senator Redmond to secure federal contracts."

"It's not just about infrastructure deals. They're protecting a trafficking operation." I pulled up the SEC filing again and printed the ownership disclosure page. "Bayou was smuggling migrants and forcing them into labor. Gulf Coast had a financial interest in keeping that operation running."

"Which means every judge they bribed, every case they got dismissed, every politician they paid off was protecting more than just their consulting business." Banks set down her pen. "They were protecting an actual trafficking network."

This wasn't just corruption. This was corruption in service of something far worse. People were being smuggled, exploited, and forced into labor. And Gulf Coast was profiting from it while using bribed judges and politicians to make sure nobody stopped them.

"We need to find out who owns Gulf Coast," I said. "If we can trace the ownership up the chain, we might find the people actually running this operation."

"Agreed. Hopefully, Erin finds something in the Torres files." Banks checked her watch. "It's almost two o'clock. We worked well past lunch."

"I'm not really hungry. This stuff always steals my appetite."

"I can see why." Banks reached across my desk and picked up the white queen chess piece. She turned it over in her fingers, studying the worn porcelain. "So you have no idea how this made its way into your mailbox?"

"None. The mailman claims he doesn't recognize the packaging. Didn't even have an address on it."

Banks set the piece back down carefully. "Whoever delivered it knows where you live."

"Wow, that's so comforting," I said.

Banks smiled slightly. "What's life without a little risk?"

"I preferred my life with slightly less risk of being murdered by a trafficking network."

"Fair point." Banks stood and stretched. "But you're in it now. We both are. Might as well see it through."

I looked at her. She seemed completely unbothered by the danger we were walking into. No fear. No hesitation. Just a prosecutor doing her job.

"What's your story?" I asked. "How did you get here? To this job, this level of work?"

Banks was quiet for a moment. She looked at the chess pieces on my desk, at the files spread across the surface, then back at me.

"That's better left for another day." She grabbed her coat from the back of the chair. " Let's get some lunch. We can come back and keep working after we eat something."

I wanted to push. Wanted to know what had driven Banks to become the sort of prosecutor who would spend her weekend investigating conspiracy theories with a junior attorney she barely knew. But her tone made it clear the conversation was over.

I grabbed my own coat and followed her out of the office. We locked the door behind us and headed for the elevator. The fifth floor was empty on a Saturday afternoon.

"There's a good sandwich place two blocks from here," Banks said as we stepped into the elevator. "They make a decent turkey club."

The elevator doors opened, and we walked through the lobby into cold November air. Traffic streamed past on Pennsylvania Avenue. People hurried along the sidewalks with their heads down against the wind.

We walked two blocks to the sandwich shop Banks had mentioned. Ordered at the counter and found a table near the window. The food arrived quickly. I forced myself to eat even though I felt slightly nauseous.

"Monday we request the FBI files," Banks said between bites. "See if we can get access to the restricted materials from the 2003 survey. If your mother gave them evidence about Morrison taking payments, it should be in there."

"And if they won't give us access?"

"Then we build the case without it. We have enough to show pattern and practice. Gulf Coast bribed judges for two decades. Ownership interest in a trafficking operation. Current bribery scheme with Redmond." Banks wiped her hands on a napkin. "It won't be easy to prove without the FBI files, but it's possible."

"What about Pearce?" I asked quietly. "The bishop Ramsey mentioned on the wiretaps?"

Banks was quiet for a long moment. She stared out the window at the people passing by on the sidewalk.

"We follow the evidence," she said finally. "If it leads to Pearce, then it leads to Pearce. But we can't go after a federal judicial nominee without ironclad proof. The political blowback would be massive."

"Vance was about to do it."

"And Vance is dead." Banks met my eyes. "Which should tell you how dangerous that path is. We move carefully. We document everything. We don't make accusations we can't prove."

I nodded. She was right. But part of me wanted to charge ahead anyway. Wanted to expose Pearce before his confirmation hearing. Wanted to stop the network from placing another corrupt judge on the federal bench.

But that wasn't how you won cases. That was how you got people killed. This was the lesson I was starting to learn.

We finished eating and walked back to the DOJ building. We spent the rest of the afternoon reading through more case files. Looking for other instances where Gulf Coast might have interfered with trafficking investigations. Building the timeline of corruption that stretched back over two decades.

By six o'clock, my eyes burned from staring at documents. Banks called it a day, and we packed up our materials. I locked everything in my office and headed home.

The Metro was crowded with weekend travelers heading into the city for dinner and entertainment. I wedged myself into a corner and stared at my phone. No messages from James. Nothing since our fight.

Part of me wanted to text him. Wanted to explain what Banks and I had found. Wanted him to understand why this mattered.

But he had made his position clear. He thought I was chasing conspiracy theories. Thought I was risking Pearce's reputation based on nothing.

He was wrong. But I couldn't prove that to him. Not yet.

CHAPTER TWENTY-ONE

MONDAY MORNING ARRIVED with gray skies and the threat of rain. What I was learning was the normal for fall in D.C. I reached the office at 7:30, coffee in hand and my messenger bag stuffed full with the files Banks and I had worked through over the weekend. We had spent most of Saturday and Sunday going through documents, building timelines, and becoming more confident that we could secure a grand jury indictment against Redmond.

The fifth floor was quiet as I walked down the hallway. I unlocked my office and settled in, turning on my computer and pulling up my email while the system booted. There was still nothing from James. Pushing the thought aside I focused on organizing the case files spread across my desk.

I had just taken my first sip of coffee when my phone rang at 8:15. Erin's name lit up my screen.

"Hey," I answered. "Did you find anything?"

" Took me until midnight, but I pulled everything we had on Gulf Coast from the Torres case." Papers rustled on her end. "I'll send you a big data dump over the next few hours. Sorry I don't really have the time to sort through it all and give you a summary."

"Don't worry about it," I said. "It's not your case anymore. I'll go through it."

"There's a lot here, Alex. Corporate filings, financial records, discovery materials we subpoenaed but never really dug into because we didn't need it for the Torres prosecution." She paused. "Tell me what you find, okay?"

"Yes, I will. Thanks, Erin. I really appreciate you doing this."

After saying goodbye I shifted my attention back to my screen. The inbox was already loading the first attachment from Erin. A PDF file labeled *Gulf Coast Corporate Structure 2019*. I downloaded it but didn't open it yet, wanting to wait until I had Banks with me to review the materials together.

A knock on my door frame made me look up.

James stood there with files tucked under his arms, looking tired. His tie was loosened even though the workday had barely started. Dark circles shadowed his eyes as if he hadn't slept well over the weekend.

"Can I sit down?" he asked.

I didn't know how I felt about him showing up at my office unannounced like this. Part of me wanted to lay into him immediately. Why hadn't he called me back the entire weekend? Why did he have to question everything I believed in every time I brought it up? Why couldn't he support me in what I was trying to do? But I didn't say any of those things.

Instead, I just nodded and said, "Yeah, I guess," gesturing to the chair across from my desk.

James sat and hesitated for a moment before sliding the files across to me. "This is what Chambers had me working on. The Vance investigation. Everything he asked me to review and compile."

I stared at the files but didn't reach out to look through them.

"I want you to know that I do believe in you," James said. His voice was missing that usual confidence. "I do support you. If this is what it takes to make you believe that, then this is what it takes."

His words made my heart soften.

I swallowed my feelings and pulled the first folder toward me, flipping it open. Information on Eleanor Vance stared back at me. Her schedule in the days before her death. Case files from the past six months. Email communications with other DOJ officials. Everything

Chambers had tasked James with reviewing to determine what Vance had been planning to reveal about Pearce.

"Thank you so much," I said, looking up at him. "Truly."

"Don't mention it." His voice dropped even lower. "Seriously, don't mention it. I'm not sure Chambers would be happy about me sharing this with you. He thinks I'm still compiling analysis. Doesn't know that I've already finished and decided to show you the raw materials."

I opened my mouth to respond, but another knock interrupted us. My eyes widened as Chambers appeared in the doorway. He glanced between James and me. A smile that seemed too knowing played at his lips.

"Chambers wouldn't be happy about what?" Chambers asked, clearly having heard at least part of James's last sentence.

James didn't miss a beat, the raw vulnerable version of him was gone in an instant as he turned to look at Chambers. "Oh, you know. Office romance stuff. Whether we should grab lunch together or if that's too obvious."

Chambers laughed and shook his head. "Yeah, well, we sort of all knew you two were an item. Thankfully, that happened before Alex got here, so I guess you're grandfathered in. Just try to keep it professional during work hours."

Either Chambers believed James's cheap lie, or he was excellent at playing along.

My face heated, but I forced a smile. James gave me a pointed look, and I quickly slid the Vance files to the side, stacking them with my other materials where they wouldn't be immediately obvious.

James stood and asked, "How's it going with Banks and the Redmond case, by the way?"

"Great, actually." I tried to sound casual even though my heart was racing. "I think we may be able to secure that indictment against Redmond after all. Banks and I spent the weekend going through everything."

Chambers' eyebrows raised to his hairline. "Really? And Banks agrees with that assessment?"

"Yeah, but we should probably get an update from Helen directly." I stood as well. "She's the lead on this, after all."

As if summoned by the conversation, Banks appeared behind Chambers in the hallway. Carrying her own coffee and a legal pad covered in notes.

"Oh, Alex. Good, you're here." Banks looked past Chambers at me. "Rory, I was just coming to tell you that we're probably going to go ahead and try for the indictment."

"Do you think you're on the side of caution?" Chambers asked, his expression shifting to concern. "A failed indictment against a sitting senator would be a disaster."

"We think it's better to be proactive rather than reactive," Banks said smoothly. "Let's talk about it in detail and I can walk you through what we found."

She looked at me and I caught something in her expression. A warning, maybe? Did she want to talk to Chambers alone, without me there to potentially reveal too much about what we had actually been investigating? Did she not trust me to read the room about what to reveal?

"But clearly if we don't secure it, it could be a media frenzy," Banks continued. "Why don't you come to my office and we'll let Alex work on important things in the meantime?"

I was about to argue that I should be part of that conversation, but Banks shot me a look that said she knew exactly what she was doing. I shrunk back on myself and stayed quiet.

"I also have a lot more to read," I said, gesturing at the extra files on my desk. She didn't have to know they were actually for the Vance case. "Erin just sent over discovery materials from the Torres case. I should go through those."

Banks nodded. " Then we'll catch up later this morning after I brief Rory."

She and Chambers started walking down the hall; their voices faded as they got further away from my office. James lingered in my doorway for a moment.

"I really am sorry about Friday," he said quietly.

I looked at him, and I could tell that he really meant it. "I know."

"So ... we can talk tonight? Properly? I'll make dinner."

I wrapped my arms around myself, nodding, finding it hard to look into his eyes. "Yeah. Tonight."

He gave me a small smile and left. I listened to his footsteps moving down the hall before turning back to my desk. The Vance files sat where I had pushed them aside when Chambers appeared. I pulled them back toward me and started reading through them carefully.

The documents painted an interesting picture of Eleanor Vance. The memos and reports James had compiled suggested she had become increasingly paranoid about corruption in the DOJ and the judicial branch as she advanced in her career. There were notes from colleagues describing her behavior as erratic. Emails where she questioned routine decisions and saw hidden agendas in standard bureaucratic processes. Memos where she raised concerns that seemed overblown to the people receiving them.

But was it paranoia if she had been right?

I kept reading and taking notes. The files eventually switched focus from Vance's behavior to Franklin Pearce himself. Background checks from his initial judicial appointment. Financial disclosures from various points in his career. Documentation related to his current nomination to the Fifth Circuit. All the standard materials that would be compiled for any judicial nominee going through the confirmation process.

I found the form that included Pearce's most recent financial disclosures, filed ahead of his confirmation hearing. In it was a myriad of property holdings, investment accounts, stock portfolios, and advisory positions with various companies and organizations.

Reading through the list of board positions he'd held over the past decade, most were exactly what you would expect for a federal judge. Legal aid organizations. Bar association committees. Law school advisory boards.

And then I saw it.

Right there in black and white on an official financial disclosure form filed with the Senate Judiciary Committee.

Franklin Pearce had served on the board of directors of Bayou Shipping Corporation from 2015 to 2018.

.   .   .

Not as a passive investor. Not as someone who owned a few shares, but as a board member. Someone involved in corporate governance and strategic decisions. Someone who, presumably, would have known what Bayou's operations entailed.

Staring at the disclosure form, my hands trembled, and I set down my coffee cup before I dropped it. This was the connection, the proof that Franklin Pearce wasn't just some innocent judge being promoted through normal channels. He was part of the network. He had direct financial ties to the very companies Gulf Coast protected through judicial corruption.

I grabbed my phone and texted Banks.

> Need to see you immediately. Found something in the files.

Her response came within seconds.

> Give me ten minutes. Still with Chambers.

I looked back at my monitor and kept reading. Kept following the trail Erin had sent me. The pieces were falling into place. The pattern was becoming clear.

And I understood why Eleanor Vance had been killed.

BANKS RETURNED from her office fifteen minutes later. She closed my door behind her and dropped into the chair across from my desk.

"Well, what was that about?" she asked. "Your text sounded urgent."

"I found something in the files James gave me." I turned my monitor so she could see it better. "And in the discovery materials Erin sent over."

Banks leaned forward. "What am I looking at?"

"Pearce's financial disclosure form. The one he filed ahead of his confirmation hearing." I pointed to the relevant section. "Look at his board positions from 2015 to 2018."

Banks read in silence for a moment. Then her expression changed. "Bayou Shipping Corporation. He was on their board."

"For three years." I pulled up a document on my monitor. "And here's what Erin found in the Torres case archives. Gulf Coast Strategies' ownership structure from 2019."

I showed her the corporate filing. Pointed out Gulf Coast's ownership stake in Bayou. Then showed her the list of limited partners and silent investors who held pieces of Gulf Coast itself.

Banks studied the screen carefully. She didn't say anything for a long moment.

"So, Pearce was on the board of a company that Gulf Coast had an ownership interest in," she said finally. "A company that was actively engaged in human trafficking, according to your mother's case."

"And that's not all." I pulled up the email from Erin with additional attachments. "Look at this."

I opened another corporate filing. This one showed a different shell company structure. Payments flowing from Gulf Coast through various intermediaries to individuals whose names were redacted in the original discovery but visible in the unredacted version Erin had pulled from the archives.

"These are payments Gulf Coast made to what they called 'legal consultants' and 'advisory board members,'" I said. "But the amounts are way too high for legitimate consulting work. We're talking hundreds of thousands of dollars to individuals who don't appear to have provided any actual services."

Banks scrolled through the payment records. "This looks like a payoff structure. They're disguising bribes as consulting fees."

"Exactly what they did with the judges. Same pattern." I pulled up another document. "And look who received one of these payments in 2016."

I watched Banks's reaction as she looked at the name on the screen. Her entire body went still.

"That's circumstantial," she said after a moment. "Receiving a consulting payment doesn't prove criminal activity. Pearce could have legitimately advised them on legal matters."

"While serving on the board of their subsidiary company?" I shook my head. "That's not a consulting relationship. That's a conflict of interest at minimum. And more likely a payoff disguised as legitimate business."

Banks sat back in her chair. She didn't say anything right away. I could see her mind working through the implications. How we would prove this in court.

"Let me ask you something." She turned to face me. "Are we looking into this because we genuinely believe Pearce is part of the network? Or are you trying to protect something else? Some other theory that doesn't quite fit?"

The question took me slightly aback. "What do you mean?"

She let out a breath through her nostrils. "I mean that we're two prosecutors looking at a federal judge nominee and finding connections that could be explained multiple ways. Yes, he was on Bayou's board. Yes, he received payments from Gulf Coast. But board memberships and consulting arrangements aren't inherently criminal. We need to be honest with ourselves about whether we're following evidence or pointing fingers because someone disagrees with our theory."

A familiar defensive heat rose in my chest. "You think I'm making this up?"

"I think you've been through a lot." Banks's voice was gentle but firm. "I think anyone in your position would have a tendency to see patterns. I'm not saying that the patterns aren't real. I'm just saying we need to be absolutely certain before we go after someone like Franklin Pearce."

"I'm not just seeing patterns. I have documentary evidence." I gestured at the screen. "Pearce was on the board of a trafficking company. He received payments from the same firm that's been bribing judges for twenty years. The wiretaps caught Ramsey talking about keeping the bishop's path clear. Vance was about to expose him, and then she died."

"All of which could be circumstantial depending on how a defense attorney spins it." Banks pulled her legal pad toward her and started making notes. "But you're right that there are connections. Real ones. The question is whether they're strong enough to overcome the political firestorm that would come from accusing a judicial nominee of being part of a criminal conspiracy."

"What about the survey?" I pulled up the PDF on my computer. "Page 132 shows the 2002 case where Gulf Coast paid a judge to dismiss trafficking charges. That same pattern continued with my mother's case in 2003 where Judge Morrison dismissed charges against Bayou. Now we have Pearce connected to both Gulf Coast and Bayou, receiving payments during the same time period."

Banks leaned forward to read the survey. "The 2002 case doesn't name the judge who was bribed. It just says a state judge dismissed a trafficking case after receiving payments from Gulf Coast through Capitol Ventures."

"But we can figure out who that judge was. We can pull the case files and see who presided." I was already typing into Westlaw, searching for trafficking cases from Harris County in 2002 that involved Gulf Coast-related defendants.

"Even if we identify the judge, that doesn't directly implicate Pearce." Banks watched me search. "It shows a pattern of Gulf Coast corrupting the judiciary. But proving Pearce knew about that pattern and participated in it is a different matter."

"Unless we can show he benefited from it." Clicking on search results, I scanned case summaries. "If Pearce was receiving money from Gulf Coast while they were actively bribing judges to protect Bayou's operations, that's not coincidence. That's participation."

Banks was quiet while I continued searching. After a moment she said, "We need to think carefully about how to approach this. If we go to Chambers right now and say we think Pearce is corrupt, he's going to ask for ironclad proof. And if we can't provide it, he's going to shut down our investigation and possibly refer us for exceeding our authority."

I paused my incessant scrolling and leaned back in my chair. "So what do you suggest?"

"Let's keep building the case against Redmond. That's our official assignment. But we also quietly investigate the Gulf Coast network and see where it leads." Banks tapped her pen against the legal pad. "We subpoena merger documents and financial records to see who was getting payouts when Bayou went public. We wait for the FBI files from the 2003 survey to see if they identify the judges who were bribed. And we follow the money and see if it connects to Pearce in a way that's undeniable."

"And in the meantime, his confirmation hearing is in a week." I felt my frustration building. "If we wait too long, he'll be on the Fifth Circuit, and we'll have missed our chance."

"If we move too fast, we'll get shut down and lose any chance we had." Banks met my eyes. "I know you want to stop this. I know you feel like we're running out of time. But we have to be smart about it.

We can't just throw accusations at a federal judge without evidence that will stand up to scrutiny."

I wanted to argue. Wanted to say we had enough evidence already. In the past, I might have. But working with Helen had given me some perspective, and I could see her point. What we had was suggestive. The connections were all suspicious, but not conclusive. Any competent defense attorney would shred our theory in minutes if we couldn't prove direct criminal activity.

"Okay," I said. "I can get behind that, but I also don't want to linger."

"Agreed." Banks stood. "I'll draft a follow up FBI request this afternoon and get it submitted. You work on identifying the cases from page 132. Let's figure out which judges were taking bribes in 2002 and 2003. If we can connect them to the current network, that strengthens everything."

She moved toward the door but stopped to face me. "Alex, I need to ask you something."

"What?"

"If we're going to go after someone at Pearce's level, we need protection. Lifetime tenure for federal judges means they're almost impossible to remove once confirmed. But if we're building a case that could block his confirmation or even lead to criminal charges, we need to think about how that affects us." Her eyes glistened, reflecting the cloudy day from the windows. "This kind of investigation could end our careers if it goes wrong. Chambers will need to know what we're looking into. We need his backing before we go too much further."

"Do you think he'll support us?"

She hesitated a moment. "I think he'll ask hard questions. But if we have solid evidence, he'll back us." Banks opened the door. "Keep digging into those cases. Find judges who took bribes from Gulf Coast. Give me names and dates and amounts."

When she left, I went back to my computer and pulled up the Westlaw search results. Started reading through Harris County trafficking cases from 2002, looking for the one described in the survey. Looking for the judge who had taken Gulf Coast's money and let traffickers walk free.

The work consumed me. Hours passed without me noticing. My coffee went cold. The sky outside my window grew darker as afternoon turned to evening.

By six o'clock I had compiled a list of seven judges who had dismissed or reduced charges in trafficking cases between 2002 and 2018. Not all of them had obvious connections to Gulf Coast yet. But I knew the pattern.

I saved everything to a flash drive and backed it up to the secure server. Made copies of the most important documents. Organized it all into folders that Banks could review.

Then I gathered my things and headed home. The Metro was crowded with evening commuters. I found an empty seat all the way to the back of one of the trains and pulled out my phone.

A text from James waited.

> Dinner at 7? My place?

> Yeah. Need to talk to you about what we found.

> Looking forward to it. And to apologizing properly for Friday.

Before I could set my phone down, it pinged with a text from Erin.

> Did you get everything I sent? Let me know if you need clarification on any of it.

> Got it all. This is exactly what we needed. Thank you.

Then I texted Lisa.

> Having difficulty sitting on my hands with this case. Every reason to trust Banks but feeling impatient. I don't know why I sent it, exactly. Maybe I was looking for comfort? For reassurance?

Her response came fast.

Trust the process. You've got good instincts,
but don't let them make you reckless.

Lisa was right. Banks was being smart about this. Building a case that would survive scrutiny instead of rushing forward with accusations we couldn't prove.

But knowing that didn't make the waiting any easier.

CHAPTER
TWENTY-THREE

AROUND 6:45, the train rolled into the station, and I headed up the escalator towards James's apartment. It was in a renovated brownstone near Dupont Circle. Climbing the exterior stairs to the third floor, I knocked on the dark green door with brass numbers marking unit 3B.

He answered immediately, pulling the door open with a dish towel slung over his shoulder. The smell of garlic and tomato sauce drifted out from behind him.

"Hey." Stepping aside to let me in. "Perfect timing. Pasta's almost ready."

I walked into the apartment and took in the space. The entry opened directly into a living room with exposed brick on one wall and tall windows overlooking the tree-lined street below. A leather couch faced a bookshelf crammed with legal treatises and hardcover novels. The coffee table held a neat stack of case files and a half-empty glass of red wine.

The kitchen was separated from the living space by a granite counter with three bar stools tucked underneath. Pots simmered on the stove, and a cutting board held the remnants of chopped vegetables.

"Make yourself comfortable." James gestured toward the couch. "Wine?"

"Please."

He poured a glass and brought it to me, then returned to the kitchen to check on dinner. I settled onto the couch and set my bag beside me, case files weighing against my hip.

"So I did what you asked," James said from the kitchen, stirring something in a pot without looking at me. "I went through the Vance materials again. Really dug into what Chambers had me compile."

"And?"

"And I found some things that made me reconsider my position." He turned down the heat on the stove and came to sit beside me on the couch, picking up his own wine glass. "Vance was obsessed with old DOJ surveys on judicial corruption. There were notes in her files referencing a 2003 report. She kept calling it the key to unlocking the whole game."

My heart began to race. "The 2003 survey. The one she pointed me to at the archives."

"She had files on it going back months. Notes about something called a J-17 source. Someone who provided information about judges taking bribes in Houston." James pulled out his phone and opened his photos. "I took pictures of some of her notes. Look at this."

He showed me a photograph of a handwritten memo discussing silent players in nominations and a reference to Houston '02 followed by the initials K.H. and the phrase "paid the price."

"K.H.," I said quietly. "Katherine Hayes?"

"I thought that might be what it meant." James swiped to the next photo. "She also had notes about family ties in old cases. Companies like Bayou Shipping, where judges' relatives held stakes. She thought there was a pattern of judges protecting businesses that employed or enriched their family members."

"Did she have specifics?" I asked. "Names and dates?"

"Some. But Chambers pulled most of the files after her death. Said they were speculative and not relevant to Pearce's nomination." James set his phone down, his gaze resting on me. "Which in retrospect seems like he was trying to bury what she found rather than investigate it properly."

"Banks and I found something similar." I pulled my own files from my bag and spread them on the coffee table. "Pearce's financial disclosures show a small ownership stake in Bayou Shipping Corporation from the 2006 timeframe. We traced it back using EDGAR filings to a 2006 merger where Gulf Coast Strategies acquired several smaller shipping companies, including one that Pearce had invested in years earlier."

James leaned forward to study the documents. I watched his expression shift from curious to concerned as he read through the merger details and ownership structures.

"So Pearce ended up with shares in Bayou because of a corporate merger," he said. "That's not necessarily suspicious on its own."

"Except Gulf Coast is the same firm that Redmond took bribes from. The same firm that paid judges to dismiss trafficking cases in 2002 and 2003. The same firm that had an ownership interest in Bayou when they were actively trafficking people." I pulled out another document. "And look at the timing. The merger happened in 2006. Pearce joined Bayou's board in 2015, nine years later. He made a conscious choice to get *more* involved with a company he knew had Gulf Coast ties."

James went quiet. He picked up his wine glass and took a slow sip, then set it down carefully on a coaster on the coffee table.

"There's something else," he said finally. "A touchstone about Pearce's family connections that Vance had noted but never fully investigated. His wife's maiden name is Whitaker. Her brother, Thomas Whitaker, was a board member at Bayou Shipping back in the early 2000s."

I went very still. "Before my mother's case?"

"During." James's eyes pierced through me, causing chills to erupt on my arms. "Thomas Whitaker served on Bayou's board from 2000 to 2002. Then, he sold his shares right before some scandal broke. I don't remember the details, but Franklin mentioned it once. Said his brother-in-law had been smart to get out when he did but that it was all hushed up quickly. Nothing illegal on paper, but Thomas knew something was coming."

"The scandal was probably my mother's investigation." I pulled up the case file on my laptop and showed James the timeline. "She filed charges against Bayou in May 2002. If Thomas Whitaker sold his shares around that time, he was getting out before the prosecution became public."

"Which means he knew about the trafficking operation." James dragged his hands down his face. "And if Thomas knew, then Franklin probably knew too. They're close. Family dinners every Sunday according to Franklin. One of those families that talks business over wine."

Pearce's brother-in-law had been on Bayou's board during their trafficking operations. Had sold his shares right before the prosecution. Had gotten out clean while my mother built a case that Judge Morrison would eventually dismiss.

"Vance thought it was a conflict pattern for judges. Family members profiting from companies that appeared in their courtrooms or court-rooms of judges they associated with. She didn't have proof, but she suspected Pearce's nomination was about protecting the network rather than his qualifications."

"Did she identify who was running the network?" I asked. "Who was at the top of the hierarchy?"

"Not explicitly. But she kept coming back to Gulf Coast Strategies as the common thread. Every corrupt judge, every dismissed case, every protected company—Gulf Coast was involved somehow." James stood and walked to the window, staring out at the street below for a moment before turning back to me. "I owe you an apology. A real one. I dismissed what you were saying because I didn't want to believe Franklin could be part of something like this. He's been my mentor for fifteen years and I respected him. But the evidence you've found combined with what Vance documented …" He sighed and ran a hand through his hair. "It's too much to ignore."

"I know this is hard for you." I joined him at the window. I'd felt so distant from him through all of this. Until just now, I hadn't even real-ized how alone it was making me feel. "I know you don't want to believe someone you trusted could be corrupt."

"It's more than that." His voice was quiet. "If Franklin is part of this network, then I've been helping him advance his career. I've been vouching for his character to people who asked. I've been complicit in putting someone corrupt on the federal bench."

Wrapping an arm around his waist, his body settled against mine. "You didn't know."

"But I should have known. I should have asked harder questions when he mentioned his brother-in-law's shares in Bayou. I should have dug deeper when Vance started making noise about his nomination." He turned to face me. "I chose loyalty over due diligence, and people were harmed because of it."

Walking over to the couch, I reached into my bag, pulling out the white queen chess piece. The one that had signs of wear. I held it out to James.

"Someone sent me this last week," I told him. "No address, no postage. Just left it in my mailbox."

James took the piece and turned it over in his hands. "It's heavy. Feels like real porcelain, not plastic."

"It's been worn smooth. Like someone carried it for years." I watched him examine it. "The network uses chess pieces to communicate. Bishops for judges, queens for high-level targets. Why do you think they're sending these to me?"

"To intimidate you? Maybe even to threaten." James set the piece down on the windowsill. "Have you told anyone else about this?"

"Banks knows." I hesitated, then decided to be fully honest. "I didn't tell you on Friday because I thought you'd dismiss it as more conspiracy theory. Thought you'd tell me to stop investigating and trust that Pearce was clean."

"I probably would have." James moved back to the couch and sank into the cushions. "I'm sorry for that. Sorry for not listening when you first tried to tell me about the network. Sorry for defending Franklin without looking at the evidence you were presenting."

"Thank you for saying that." I sat beside him and let him wrap his arm around me. "And thank you for going back through Vance's materials. For taking the time to reconsider instead of just doubling down on your initial position." I sighed. "I know how easy it would have been to do that because I did that with my father for years."

"What Banks said is right, though. I do jump to conclusions sometimes. I make assumptions based on what I want to be true rather than what the evidence shows." He picked up his wine glass and swirled the liquid inside. "It's a flaw I've been trying to work on. But clearly I have further to go."

The timer in the kitchen went off. James stood and went to check on dinner. I followed him and watched as he drained pasta and plated it with the sauce that had been simmering. Rich tomato and garlic floated into my nostrils and made my mouth water and stomach growl. We carried our plates back to the couch and ate while going through more of the documents I had brought.

"So what's the plan?" James asked between bites. "Banks isn't going to let you go after Pearce without ironclad proof. And Chambers will shut down the investigation if he thinks you're overreaching."

"Yes," nodding my agreement. "Our official assignment is the Redmond case, so that's what we're going to focus on. Meanwhile, we keep our eyes open for the Gulf Coast network and see where it leads." I showed him the list of judges I had compiled. "Seven judges who either dismissed cases or reduced charges in trafficking cases between 2002 and 2018. All with potential Gulf Coast connections. If we can prove they were taking bribes as part of a coordinated network, that strengthens our case that Pearce is part of the same system."

"What about the FBI files from the 2003 survey? Can you get access to those?"

"Banks is making the request. She plans to reference the Redmond investigation and make the case that the historical pattern is essential to establishing the current bribery scheme." I set down my fork. "But even if we get the files, we still need more to connect Pearce directly. Right now we have circumstantial evidence. Board memberships and family ties, and suspicious timing. A defense attorney would shred that in minutes."

"Unless you find the money trail." James pulled out his phone again and opened his notes app. "Vance had a theory that Gulf Coast used consulting payments to disguise bribes. She thought if you traced the payments through their shell companies, you'd find a pattern of money going to judges and politicians who protected their interests. She just never had time to prove it before she died."

"We're working on that. Erin sent over discovery from the Torres case that includes some of Gulf Coast's financial records. Banks and I are going through them looking for the payment patterns Vance suspected."

The buzzer from the oven broke us out of our reverie. "Garlic bread," James said, giving me a soft kiss before getting off the couch. For the rest of the night, we ate together and didn't talk about Pearce or nominations or conspiracies. It was nice to put all of that aside for a moment and just have a normal dinner with my boyfriend.

We finished dinner and settled back in on the couch. James put on jazz music low in the background. Sitting close together, his arm around my shoulders, we talked about nothing in particular for another hour.

By ten o'clock I was exhausted. The weekend of research plus today's discoveries had drained me completely. I leaned my head against James's shoulder and closed my eyes.

"Stay tonight," he said quietly. "It's late, and you're tired."

"I should probably go home. I have work tomorrow, and all my stuff is at my place."

"You can borrow something to sleep in. I'll make you breakfast before we head to the office and we can grab a cab to your place so you can change and still be on time." His hand moved to my hair, fingers running through it gently. "I want to make up for Friday. For not believing you. For making you feel like you couldn't trust me with this."

I lifted my head to look at him. His expression was open and vulnerable. His usual bravado was gone, and instead there was some-thing softer. Something closer to what made me fall in love with him in the first place.

"Okay," I said. "I'll stay."

He smiled and kissed me. Gentle at first, then deeper as I responded. We stayed on the couch for a while, kissing and talking quietly, before eventually moving to his bedroom. He gave me one of his t-shirts to sleep in, and we lay in the darkness talking about every-thing except the case.

About his childhood in Boston. About my years in Houston. About the small details of our lives that we hadn't shared yet.

Eventually, we fell asleep tangled together in his bed. I slept better than I had in days. No nightmares about chess pieces or dead prosecutors. Just the warmth of James beside me and the quiet rhythm of his breathing.

CHAPTER
TWENTY-FOUR

JAMES'S ALARM went off at 5:30, pulling me from sleep in his unfamiliar bedroom. He groaned and reached across me to silence it.

"Sorry," he mumbled against my shoulder. "Early meeting with Chambers. I completely forgot."

I rolled over to face him. "What time is the meeting?"

"Seven. I need to be in the office by six-thirty to prep." He kissed my forehead and climbed out of bed. "You can stay and sleep longer if you want. Just lock up when you leave."

"No, I should get home and change before I go in." I sat up and looked around for my clothes.

Twenty minutes later I was dressed and standing on the sidewalk outside his building while a yellow taxi idled at the curb. James kissed me goodbye and promised to text later, then headed back inside to finish getting ready for his meeting.

The cab dropped me at my apartment just after six. I showered quickly and changed into fresh clothes, then made coffee and sat at my kitchen table with my laptop. Banks had forwarded wiretap recordings at six-thirty with a message that read simply, *Listen to these before you come in.*

I pulled up the audio files while the coffee cooled against my palm. More calls from Victor Ramsey's phone. The recordings were from

Sunday and Monday, conversations that had been flagged by the FBI analyst as potentially relevant to our investigation.

I clicked the first file and listened as Ramsey's voice filled my apartment.

"It's done," an unfamiliar male voice said. "The queen's dead drop was confirmed."

"And the package?" Ramsey asked.

"Delivered as instructed. No issues."

The line went dead. I sat staring at my laptop screen as my coffee stopped steaming.

Was the package referencing the white queen chess piece? The one that had appeared in my mailbox with no address and no postage?

I had to be careful not to jump to conclusions based on what I wanted the evidence to show. Proof was needed, not speculation. It was a shift in how I was approaching this. Old Alex would have been bursting at the seams to tell someone that this was definitely the conclusion. But, working with Banks was giving me perspective on how to approach things more through logic and less with my gut.

I listened to the rest of the wiretaps. More coded language about bishops and pawns and clearing paths. Nothing explicit enough to use in court but enough to make the pattern clear. The network was coordinating something big. And they might even know I was investigating.

Quickly finishing my coffee, I got ready for work. I sat quietly in a back seat on my commute, my mind circling back to those wiretaps. The queen's dead drop. The delivered package and what it all meant.

Banks was waiting in my office when I arrived at 8:15. She had her legal pad and a cup of coffee that smelled significantly better than what I had made at home.

"Did you think about the expanded subpoena?" she asked before I had even set down my bag.

I hung my coat on the back of my chair and sat down. "Not yet, but what did you manage to arrange?"

"A call with Robert Kline and his attorney. They agreed to answer follow-up questions about the wiretaps and the chess piece references we've been tracking." Banks checked her watch. "Video call in fifteen minutes. So far, he's cooperated fully. His attorney indicated that they want to keep this short because, in their eyes they've already done their part. Kline wants to move on with his life and put this all behind him. But I think we can get more out of him if we ask the right questions. I'm going to let you lead the call."

"What? Why?"

"Because I think you have the best sense for what he might know and what we can get out of him." Banks sat down in the chair across from my desk. "I've heard that you've been very successful on cross-examination in the past. You have a way of circling wins that no one thought could be done. I'm going to trust you to go into this. Just try not to go too far off the rails."

I nodded slowly. Leading the interview with a cooperating witness was a significant responsibility. If I pushed too hard, Kline could shut down, or his attorney could end the call. If I didn't push hard enough, we would miss our opportunity to get information that could break the case open.

"I'll meet you in conference room U in ten minutes," Banks said. She stood and moved toward the door. "Think about what you want to ask him."

Pulling out a legal pad, I started making notes about what I wanted to know. The chess pieces. The references to queens and bishops and pawns. Whether Kline had ever heard the name Whitaker or Pearce. Whether he knew about the network's structure beyond what he had already testified to.

Ten minutes later I walked down the hall to conference room U. Banks was already there, setting up the video call equipment. She gestured for me to take the seat facing the camera.

"You're on," she said quietly. "I'll be right here if you need me to step in."

The video call connected. The screen split into two boxes. On the left was Robert Kline, sitting in what looked like a home office. He was in his late forties with thinning brown hair and tired eyes. He wore a polo shirt and looked like he had lost weight recently. The stress of cooperating against his former associates had clearly taken a toll.

On the right side of the screen sat his attorney. Mid-fifties, with an expensive suit. He was the poster boy for an attorney who specialized in white-collar criminal defense. He had a legal pad and a pen in front of him, clearly ready to take notes.

"Good morning," I said. "I'm Alex Hayes, Assistant United States Attorney with the Criminal Division. Thank you both for making time for this call."

"Let's keep this brief," the attorney said. "Mr. Kline has already cooperated extensively. He's provided testimony, documents, and information that led to multiple convictions. He's fulfilled his obligations under the plea agreement."

"I understand. We just have a few follow-up questions based on recent wiretap evidence." I pulled up my notes. "Mr. Kline, in your previous testimony you described receiving instructions from Victor Ramsey regarding payments to Senator Redmond. I want to ask you about some specific language that appeared in communications between you and Mr. Ramsey."

Kline shifted in his seat. He glanced at his attorney before responding. "What kind of language?"

"References to chess pieces. Queens, bishops, pawns. Do you recall Mr. Ramsey or anyone else in the organization using those terms?"

He was quiet for a moment. The attorney leaned over and whispered something I couldn't hear. Kline nodded and turned back to the camera.

"At first I was reluctant to talk about that," he said slowly. "I thought it might make me sound crazy or like I was making things up. But yeah, there were some mentions in emails I was copied on. I knew about a queen in D.C. I always thought that was weird, that maybe it was just a nickname for someone. You know, like calling someone a queen as a compliment or that sort of thing."

"What about other chess piece references?" I asked. "Did you ever hear anyone described as a bishop or a pawn?"

"I mean, the pure hell is that people talk about pawns all the time, right?" Kline's voice sounded defensive. "Like someone being a pawn in someone else's scheme. That's common parlance. It doesn't necessarily mean anything criminal."

"But in the context of the organization you were part of, did those terms have specific meanings?" I leaned forward. "Were they code words for specific people or positions?"

His attorney interrupted. "Mr. Kline has already answered your question. He understood them as common expressions, not coded language."

"I'm just trying to establish whether there was a systematic use of chess terminology within the organization." I kept my tone professional and neutral. "Mr. Kline, did you ever hear the name Whitaker mentioned in connection with any of these chess piece references?"

Kline's expression changed. Recognition moved across his face before he could hide it.

"That was one of the names," he said. "You would have to look through a copy of the financials to be sure. But I remember seeing Whitaker on some of the documents. Family name, I think. Someone connected to one of the board members or investors."

I made a note on my legal pad. Tried to keep my expression neutral even though my pulse was pounding.

"Do you remember which company or entity the Whitaker name was associated with?" I asked.

"Not off the top of my head. Like I said, you'd need to look through the financials." Kline glanced at his attorney again. "Is that all? I've told you what I remember."

It wasn't all. I had more questions. I wanted to push harder. I wanted to ask about judges and nominations and whether he had ever heard Franklin Pearce's name said by anyone at the company. But his attorney was already shifting in his seat, preparing to end the call. If I pushed too far, they would shut it down completely.

I turned to Banks. She gave me a small nod that said, "Good work, but time to wrap it up."

"I think I'm good," I said. "Helen, do you have any follow-up questions?"

"No, I think that covers it." Banks leaned forward, so she was visible on camera. "Thank you both for your time and for continuing to cooperate with this investigation."

The attorney nodded curtly. "We'll expect that Mr. Kline's cooperation today will be noted in his file and considered when the court reviews his sentencing."

"Of course," Banks said. "We'll make sure the judge is aware."

The call ended. The screen went black. Banks and I sat in silence for a moment, both of us processing what we had just heard.

"So what do you think?" I asked finally.

"I think we need to subpoena some emails." Banks closed her laptop and stood. "Kline clearly knows more than he's saying. He recognized the name Whitaker immediately. "

"And the chess pieces?"

"He tried to downplay them, but his reaction suggested they meant something within the organization. The way he referenced 'a queen in D.C.' like it was a specific person rather than just a nickname." Banks gathered her things. "We need to find those emails he mentioned. The ones where chess piece terminology appeared. If we can show a pattern of coded language referring to specific targets, that strengthens everything."

We walked back to my office together. Banks left to start drafting subpoena requests for the email communications Kline had referenced. At my desk I pulled up the wiretap recordings again. I listened to Ramsey discussing the queen's dead drop and the delivered package.

They had to be talking about Vance, her death, and the chess piece that had been left in my mailbox as a warning.

But knowing it and proving it were two different things.

The phone buzzed.

James: *How did the Kline call go?*

Me: *Good. Got some useful information. Tell you about it tonight?*

James: *Dinner at my place again? I'll cook.*

Me: *Sounds perfect.*

I set the phone down and turned back to my computer. Pulled up the financial documents Erin had sent yesterday. Started searching for any mention of the name Whitaker. Cross-referencing payments and corporate structures and ownership charts.

I barely noticed the time passing as I dug deeper into the records, following the money trail from Gulf Coast through various shell companies and intermediaries. Looking for the connections that would tie everything together.

By one o'clock I had found what I was looking for. A series of payments from Gulf Coast to a consulting firm called Whitaker Advisory Services. The payments started in 2001 and continued through 2018. Hundreds of thousands of dollars over nearly two decades. All of it disguised as legitimate business expenses, but the amounts were far too large for actual consulting work.

Saving the documents, I emailed them to Banks with a message. *Found the Whitaker payments. This is what Kline was talking about.*

Her response came within minutes. *Come to my office. We need to talk about next steps.*

CHAPTER TWENTY-FIVE

I WALKED into Banks's office with my laptop and the files I had been reviewing. She was at her desk with her own computer screen filled with documents, reading glasses low on her nose as she scrolled through page after page of corporate filings.

"Close the door," she said without looking up.

I shut the door behind me and slid into the chair across from her desk. "I found the Whitaker payments. Gulf Coast paid a consulting firm called Whitaker Advisory Services from 2001 through 2018. The amounts are substantial. Way more than you would pay for legitimate consulting work."

"I saw your email." Banks finally looked up from her screen. "I've been going through the rest of Erin's discovery materials. She managed to find Gulf Coast's corporate disclosure documents from multiple years. The problem is that most of their ownership charts and internal documents are heavily redacted."

I twisted my lips. "How heavily?"

"Enough that we can't see who actually owns what. The names are blacked out. The ownership percentages are visible but not the people holding them." Banks turned her monitor so I could see. Page after page of financial documents with thick black lines obscuring the most important information. "Erin said she didn't press for unredacted versions during the Torres case because she didn't need them to win.

Her case was against Torres, not Gulf Coast. She had what she needed to prove he took bribes."

"But we need to know who owns Gulf Coast. We need to see the full ownership structure to prove the network exists." I leaned forward to study the redacted documents. "Can we get unredacted versions now?"

"We can try. But usually people don't redact things like this unless there's a legal reason for it. Trade secrets. Privacy protections. Ongoing investigations." Banks closed the file and removed her glasses. "The fact that these are redacted suggests someone fought to keep that information private."

I sat back in my chair and stared at the ceiling.

"There have been so many dead ends," I said. "Every time we get close to something concrete, we hit a wall. Judge Morrison's financial records are sealed. The FBI files from 2003 are restricted. Now Gulf Coast's ownership documents are redacted. It feels like the entire system is designed to prevent us from finding the truth."

"That's because it is designed that way." Banks's voice was matter-of-fact. "Powerful people don't stay powerful by being careless. They build layers of protection. Legal barriers that take time and resources to overcome. By the time you fight through one barrier, they've built three more."

"So what do we do?"

"We keep pushing. Find the cracks in their defenses." Banks pulled up another document on her screen. "Speaking of which, I have good news and bad news about the email subpoena."

"What's the bad news?"

"We barely got the subpoena filed before the defense attorney submitted a motion to quash it. He's arguing that the emails are privileged attorney-client communications and that we're on a fishing expedition." Banks handed me a printed copy of the motion. "Judge scheduled a hearing for Thursday."

"And Pearce's confirmation hearing is scheduled to start on Friday."

I scanned the motion. The arguments were predictable but well-crafted. Any delay in getting those emails meant we wouldn't have them in time to potentially stop Pearce's confirmation.

"I know the timing is tight." Banks pulled the motion back and set it aside. "But sometimes timing just doesn't work out the way we want it to. We do our best with what we have."

"No way. There has to be another way we can go about this." I stood and started pacing in front of her desk. My mind raced through possibilities. Ways to get information faster. Ways to circumvent the normal process that was designed to move slowly and put up road-blocks. "What if we hit the company that stores their data with a subpoena? Most corporations use third-party data storage companies these days."

Banks tilted her head, considering. "The defense would still file a motion to quash. We wouldn't have much time before they shut it down."

"But we would have some time. Maybe enough to get what we need." I stopped pacing and faced her. "And if we deliver the subpoena in person to the storage company, there's a chance they'll give us the information before the defense has an opportunity to stop it. Storage companies are third parties. They're not represented by Gulf Coast's attorneys. We can talk to them without breaching any ethical bound-aries as long as we simultaneously deliver a copy of the request to the defense."

"That's true." Banks pulled up a search engine on her computer. "Do you know which storage company Bayou uses? Or Gulf Coast?"

I grabbed my laptop and opened it on her desk. I started searching through the corporate documents Erin had sent. Looking for any mention of data management or information technology services. A company as large as Bayou would outsource their data storage. Most of the national data storage companies had their offices clustered in areas with good infrastructure and favorable business climates.

"Here." I found a reference in a 2019 annual report. "Bayou contracts with DataSecure Solutions for enterprise data management and cloud storage services. It says they transitioned to DataSecure in 2018 as part of a company-wide technology upgrade."

Banks typed the company name into her search. Their website loaded. Their corporate headquarters were in Reston, Virginia. Just outside D.C. in the technology corridor that had grown up around the government's need for secure data infrastructure.

"Perfect." I felt my enthusiasm returning. This could work. This could actually work. "They're headquartered in Reston. Just like I thought. Most data storage companies these days have their offices there. Virginia made itself super attractive for server sites with tax incentives and infrastructure investments."

Banks was already pulling up directions. "Reston is about thirty miles from here. We could drive, but traffic on I-66 is unpredictable."

"We can catch the Amtrak from Union Station. The Silver Line goes through Reston. We could be there in an hour." I checked the train schedule on my phone.

"You want to go today? Right now?" Banks looked at me over her reading glasses.

"If we wait until after our hearing, we won't have the information in time for Pearce's confirmation." Closing my laptop, I started gathering my things. "If we go today, serve the subpoena in person, there's a chance DataSecure gives us access before Gulf Coast even knows we're looking. Once the defense finds out, they'll file motions and tie everything up in court. But if we move fast, we might get a window."

Banks was quiet for a moment. I could see her weighing the risks. Going to Reston without telling Chambers. Serving a subpoena in person to put pressure on a third-party company. It was aggressive. Maybe too aggressive. But it might be our only shot at getting the information before Pearce was confirmed.

"This is a gamble," she said finally. "If it doesn't work, if DataSecure refuses to cooperate or if the defense shuts us down before we get anything useful, we'll have wasted a day we could have spent on other parts of the investigation."

"But if it does work, we might get everything we need. Corporate emails. Financial records. The unredacted ownership documents." I met her eyes and tried to show her how much I believed in this. "I know it's a risk. But we're running out of time. We need to take some chances if we want to stop this."

Banks stood and tossed her coat over her arm. "You know what, you're right. Sometimes you have to move fast and deal with the consequences later. I guess this is one of those times."

I could barely contain my surprise. "So we're doing this?"

"We're doing this. But I'm drafting the subpoena on the train. I want to make sure it's airtight before we serve it." She pulled out her phone and checked the time. "If we leave in the next five minutes, we can make the next train."

I was already moving toward the door.

"Alex." Banks's voice stopped me. I turned back. "This is good work. You're thinking creatively and finding solutions when the normal channels aren't working. That's what makes a good prosecutor great."

"Thanks." The praise felt good after days of dead ends and frustration. "I just want to stop them before they put another corrupt judge on the bench."

"Me too." Banks pulled on her coat and picked up her briefcase. "Let's go catch a train."

Hurrying out of her office we headed for the elevator. The fifth floor was busy with midmorning activity. Nobody looked twice at two prosecutors leaving together carrying briefcases and laptops.

In the elevator, Banks grabbed her phone and started typing. "I'm emailing Chambers that we're following up on a lead in the Redmond case. He doesn't need details right now. If this works, we'll brief him later. If it doesn't work, there's no point in getting him involved."

The elevator descended. We walked through the lobby and out into cold November air. The walk to Union Station took fifteen minutes at a brisk pace.

Inside, the station was crowded with travelers. We bought tickets at a kiosk and headed for the platform. We found seats in a quiet car and settled in. Banks pulled out her laptop and started drafting the subpoena while I watched over her shoulder, suggesting language and checking citations.

"We need to be specific about what we're requesting," Banks said as she typed. "All electronic communications and data storage records related to Bayou Shipping Corporation and Gulf Coast Strategies LLC for the period of January 2000 through present might be considered overbroad."

"Add language about corporate ownership documents and financial disclosures," I suggested. "Anything that shows who owns what and how money flows between entities."

Banks added the language and kept writing. The legal framework for the subpoena took shape on her screen. Proper citations to federal rules of criminal procedure. References to our ongoing investigation into Senator Redmond and the relevance of historical corporate records. Arguments for why DataSecure should comply immediately rather than waiting for judicial review.

The train pulled out of the station right on schedule. We rolled through the city and into the Virginia suburbs. Banks typed steadily, pausing to refine her wording or check a citation. Pulling up information about DataSecure on my phone, I read through their website and corporate structure, trying to anticipate what arguments they might make for not complying with our subpoena.

By the time we reached Wiehle-Reston East station, Banks had finished the draft. She turned the laptop toward me. "Read through this. Make sure I didn't miss anything."

I read carefully. The subpoena was comprehensive and well-reasoned. It established our authority to request the records, explaining the connection between DataSecure's data storage services and our investigation. Provided legal justification for immediate compliance.

"This is perfect," I said. "If they have any questions, this gives them everything they need to feel comfortable cooperating."

"Let's hope their legal department sees it that way." Banks saved the document and pulled up an email. "I'm scheduling this to send to defense in ten minutes. That way they can't claim they weren't given proper notice." She closed her laptop after a few more keystrokes.

We gathered our things and stood as the train slowed. The doors opened and we stepped onto the platform. Cold wind hit us immediately.

"The DataSecure building is about a mile from here," I said, checking the map on my phone. "We can walk it in fifteen minutes or grab a cab."

"Let's take a cab. I don't want to show up looking windblown." Banks flagged down a taxi that was dropping off passengers at the station. "Hard to project authority when you're shivering."

We climbed into the cab and gave the driver the address, first to a FedEx to print the subpoena and then to our actual destination. He nodded and pulled away from the station, navigating through the corporate parks and office buildings that filled this part of Reston. Everything looked new and clean. Glass and steel buildings housing technology companies and government contractors.

"Are you nervous?" Banks asked quietly.

"A little," I admitted. "I know this was my idea, but this is a lot more aggressive than I'm used to. Walking into a company unannounced and demanding they turn over data."

"It's within our authority as federal prosecutors. We have every right to serve this subpoena and request cooperation." Banks's voice was steady, and it made me feel more confident. "Just remember that we're not asking for a favor. We're executing our duties as officers of the court. They're required to comply with lawful subpoenas."

"I know. I just hope they see it that way."

When we pulled in front of the FedEx, I hopped out to grab the subpoena. Another few minutes of driving and the cab arrived at a modern glass building. The DataSecure logo hung above the entrance in brushed steel letters. We paid the driver and stepped out into the cold.

"Ready?" Banks asked.

I adjusted my coat and squared my shoulders. "Ready."

We walked through the glass doors into a bright lobby. A receptionist sat behind a curved desk made of white marble. She looked up as we approached. Her professional smile looked forced and perpetually in place.

"Good afternoon," Banks said. "We're with the Department of Justice. We're here to serve a subpoena."

The receptionist's smile wavered. "Of course. Let me call our legal department for you."

We waited while she made the call. My heart beat faster than normal. This was it. The moment where we would find out if our gamble would pay off.

CHAPTER TWENTY-SIX

BANKS and I moved to a seating area near the windows. Everything in the lobby looked expensive and designed to project an image of technological sophistication. It was as if the company was trying to justify their premium rates because their clients needed to believe their data was being stored by the best.

Reaching for my phone, I pretended to check emails, trying to calm my racing pulse. We were about to walk into a conversation where we would demand cooperation from a company that had no obligation to help us beyond what the law required. If their legal department decided to fight us, we would have nothing. But if they agreed to cooperate, we might get everything we needed.

"Remember what we talked about on the train," Banks said quietly. "We're not asking for favors. We're executing our authority as federal prosecutors. Stay confident."

Nodding, I wondered if Banks could sense my self-doubt. "I will."

Five minutes passed. Then ten. A man in his mid-forties finally emerged from the elevator bank at the back of the lobby. He wore khaki pants and a button-down shirt with the DataSecure logo embroidered on the pocket. His receding hairline and wire-rimmed glasses screamed, "man who spent his entire career in legal compliance departments." His name tag identified him as Toby Gordon, Legal Operations Manager.

"Good afternoon." He extended his hand to Banks first, then to me. "I'm Toby Gordon. I handle legal compliance here at DataSecure. I understand you're here from the Department of Justice?"

"That's correct." Banks pulled the printed subpoena from her briefcase and handed it to him. "I'm Helen Banks, and this is Alex Hayes. We're federal prosecutors investigating public corruption charges. We need access to data stored by your company on behalf of Bayou Shipping Corporation and Gulf Coast Strategies LLC."

Gordon took the subpoena and scanned it quickly. His expression remained neutral, but I caught the slight tightening around his eyes. This was clearly not a normal occurrence for him. Companies like DataSecure dealt with subpoenas regularly, but usually through formal channels with weeks of advance notice.

"I'll admit it's a little odd to have the DOJ come in person to deliver a subpoena," he said. His eyes moved back and forth between the document and us. "One we just received, for that matter. This isn't typically how these requests are handled in my experience."

"Unfortunately, it's a time-sensitive request," I said, hoping that I was keeping my voice steady. "We were hoping you could help us with that."

Gordon folded the subpoena and looked between us. His expression told me he was already formulating his response.

"Well, by law we are allowed fourteen days to respond to subpoena requests," he said. His tone was pleasant but firm. "And under our contract with clients, we need to give notice to the company whose data is being requested. That notification period is typically forty-eight hours. It allows them time to review the subpoena and file any protective motions they feel are necessary to safeguard their proprietary information."

"With all due respect, Mr. Gordon," I said, "subpoenas are self-operable and have the force of the court when issued by the DOJ in regard to an ongoing investigation. You're legally allowed to comply by releasing the records while sending prompt notice that such action was taken. The notification to your client is a professional courtesy, not a legal requirement that supersedes the force of the subpoena itself."

Gordon was quiet for a moment. He looked down at the subpoena in his hands, then back up at us. I could see him weighing his options. He could stick to the company's standard procedures and risk the ire of federal prosecutors. Or he could comply immediately and potentially face complaints from a client who might be unhappy about the quick turnaround.

Something shifted in his expression. He let out a short laugh that sounded more frustrated than amused.

"You know what? This company has screwed us lately." He gestured with the subpoena toward nothing in particular. "They've been late on their payments to us for the past three months. Every single month we send notices, they promise the money is coming, but nothing ever actually arrives. We've been more than patient with them."

He looked at both of us and seemed to come to a decision.

"So I'm going to do you this solid," he continued. "Go ahead and wait here in the lobby. I'll pull what we have from our servers. It should take around thirty minutes to compile everything and load it onto a drive you can take with you."

Relief flooded through me, but I kept my expression neutral and professional. "Thank you so much, Mr. Gordon. We really appreciate your cooperation with this investigation."

"No problem. Professional courtesy between people just trying to do their jobs." He turned and headed back toward the elevators.

As soon as Gordon was out of earshot, Banks turned to me with a small smile. "That went better than I expected. His frustration with their payment issues definitely helped our case. I guess it's a good reminder to always pay your bills."

Chuckling, I settled back into my chair and pulled out my laptop. "Now we just have to wait and hope the files actually contain what we need."

Banks did the same, opening her own laptop and starting to work on something. But, as much as I tried, I found it impossible to focus on the documents on my screen. My mind kept racing ahead to what might be in the files we were about to receive. Would they contain the unredacted ownership documents? Would they show the connections between Pearce and the network? Would they finally give us the proof we needed to stop his confirmation?

After about ten minutes of pretending to work, I gave up, closed my laptop and reached into my coat pocket. My fingers found the white queen chess piece. The one that had been left in my mailbox with no address or postage.

I pulled it out and turned it over in my hands. I kept turning it over and over. Running my thumb across the smooth surface. Looking for anything that might tell me who had owned it or why they had sent it to me. But there was nothing. Just worn porcelain and the weight of years of handling.

My finger found a rough spot at the top of the piece. Right where the crown met the neck. There was dirt or grime accumulated there in a ring. It was the only part of the piece that hadn't been worn completely smooth. I ran my finger along the area, feeling the rougher texture.

Banks glanced over at what I was doing but didn't comment, turning back to her laptop while I continued my examination of the chess piece. It had become almost meditative. Something to focus on besides the anxiety building in my chest about what we might or might not find in the DataSecure files.

The minutes crawled by. Banks kept typing on her laptop. The lobby remained quiet except for the occasional visitor checking in at the reception desk.

After what felt like hours but was probably closer to thirty-five minutes, the elevator doors opened again. Toby Gordon emerged carrying a small envelope. He walked across the lobby toward us.

As he approached, his eyes landed on the chess piece in my hand. His expression shifted. Recognition flickered across his face, followed by something that looked like nostalgia or fond memory.

"Oh cool," he said as he reached us. He stopped in front of my chair, his attention fixed on the piece in my hand. "I've not seen one of those recently. May I?"

I looked down at the chess piece, then back up at him. Why would a legal operations manager at a data storage company be interested in a chess piece?

I held it out for him.

Gordon took the piece carefully. He turned it over in his hands, examining it from different angles.

"You haven't seen a chess piece?" I asked, confused by his reaction. Everyone had seen chess pieces before. They were hardly rare objects.

"Haha, nah." Gordon held the piece up to the light streaming through the lobby windows. "Whitaker and Sons made these until they went bust back in the early thousands. Was a shame, really. They were good guys with a clever idea for how to craft these pieces. But you know how it goes. Overseas manufacturers stole the design and could produce them cheaper. Whitaker couldn't compete with the pricing and eventually had to shut down."

My stomach dropped. Whitaker and Sons? Another connection to the Whitaker name that kept appearing throughout our investigation. Thomas Whitaker, Franklin Pearce's brother-in-law. Now, a chess piece manufacturing company with the same family name? The connections were piling up too quickly to be coincidence.

Gordon continued examining the piece, seemingly oblivious to my reaction. His fingers found the same rough spot mine had been worrying, the ring of dirt and grime around what I had thought was just decoration at the seam where the crown met the neck.

"These pieces were beautifully made," he said, almost to himself. "Real craftsmanship. They had this clever design feature built in."

He gripped the crown portion of the piece with one hand and the body with the other. Then, with a gentle twisting motion, he pulled.

I heard a soft click.

The crown section separated from the body of the queen. As it came apart, I could see metal gleaming inside. USB connectors integrated into the base of the piece.

"The whole chess piece is the drive," Gordon said. "Pop off the top, and the USB connector is built right into it."

He held it up so we could see. The bottom portion of the chess piece had a USB plug extending from where it had been hidden beneath the crown. From the outside, it looked like a normal antique chess piece. But it was actually a functional USB drive disguised as decorative porcelain.

I stared at it in complete shock. My mouth opened, but no words came out. My brain struggled to process what I was seeing. Someone had sent me a USB drive, and I had been carrying it around for days without knowing.

Banks stood up so quickly her laptop nearly slid off her lap. "That's a USB drive?"

"Yeah, pretty clever design." Gordon twisted the crown back onto the body, hiding the USB connector again. "The weight feels right because it's got the drive components inside. You'd never know unless you knew to twist the top off. Whitaker and Sons made a bunch of these as novelty items before they went under. Collectibles, basically. Chess enthusiasts loved 'em."

He handed the piece back to me and I took it with shaking hands. Someone had wanted me to find the data stored inside the drive.

Gordon was still standing there, holding the envelope he had brought down from upstairs. "Are you alright? You look like you just saw a ghost."

I swallowed hard and tried to find my voice. "I'm fine. Just surprised. I didn't know it was a USB drive."

"I can imagine that was quite a shock." He held out the envelope to Banks. "Here's everything you requested from our servers. Corporate emails, financial records, data storage logs for both Bayou Shipping and Gulf Coast Strategies. All organized by date and client. Should be everything you need for your investigation."

Banks took the envelope but kept her eyes on me.

"Thank you for your cooperation, Mr. Gordon. This is extremely helpful to our investigation. "

"Happy to assist." Gordon gestured toward the envelope. "There's some chain of custody paperwork you'll need to sign. Just standard procedure to document that I handed over the files and you received them. Protects both of us if there are any questions later."

Banks finally tore her eyes away from me and focused on Gordon. She signed the necessary forms while I sat frozen in my chair, still staring at the chess piece USB drive in my hand. Still trying to process what this meant.

Gordon finished up the paperwork and made copies for his records. He handed Banks the copies for our files.

"If you need anything else, feel free to reach out," he said.

Banks shook his hand before he nodded to both of us and headed back toward the elevators. As soon as he was gone, Banks looked at me.

"Alex." Her voice was gentle but firm. "We need to see what's on that drive. But not here. Not until we're somewhere secure where we can properly document what we find and preserve the chain of custody."

I nodded but couldn't quite form words yet. My eyes were still fixed on the chess piece in my palm.

"Can you stand?" Banks asked.

"Yeah." I forced myself to my feet. My legs felt unsteady, but they held. I carefully placed the chess piece USB drive in my coat pocket. "Yeah, I'm okay. Let's go."

CHAPTER
TWENTY-SEVEN

THE TRAIN RIDE BACK to Washington felt like an eternity. Every stop seemed to take twice as long as it should. Every delay between stations stretched endlessly. I sat with my hand in my pocket, fingers wrapped around the USB stick that had been hidden inside the chess piece.

I wanted to pull out my laptop right there on the train. Wanted to plug in the drive and see what was on it. What evidence had been hidden all this time?

But Banks put her hand on my arm as I reached for my bag.

"Don't," she said quietly. "Not here. Not on a computer connected to the internet."

"Why not?"

"Because we don't know what's on that drive. It could have spyware or malware or anything else that could compromise our investigation if we connect it to a networked computer." Banks kept her voice low, even though our train car was mostly empty. "We need a clean machine. Something that can't go online. Something isolated that we can use to look at the contents without risk."

I pulled my hand away from my bag. She was right. Of course she was right. But the waiting was excruciating.

"I have an old laptop at my place," Banks said. "A MacBook Air that I've been meaning to donate for years. We can use that. It hasn't been connected to the internet in at least three years. Should be clean enough for our purposes."

"Can we go straight there?"

"Yes. We'll take a cab from Union Station straight to my place in Georgetown."

The train finally pulled into Union Station. Gatherin our things, we pushed through the evening crowds to the taxi stand outside. Banks gave the driver her address in Georgetown, and we settled into the back seat.

The cab wound through Washington traffic. I watched the city pass by outside my window but didn't really see any of it. My mind was racing.

"I recognize this neighborhood," I said as we turned onto a tree-lined street with elegant townhouses on both sides.

"Yeah, well, live in D.C. long enough and you'll eventually decide that you want to live in Georgetown," Banks said with a slight smile. "It's expensive, but it's worth it. Quiet streets, good restaurants, close enough to work but far enough away that you can actually relax when you get home."

The cab pulled up in front of a narrow brick townhouse with black shutters and a small front garden. Banks paid the driver, and we climbed out. She unlocked the front door and ushered me inside.

I barely had time to take in the entryway before a large golden retriever came bounding toward us. The dog's tail wagged so hard his entire back end swayed. He jumped up, putting his paws on my chest before I could react.

"Sorry, he's a bit of a jumper," Banks said. She grabbed the dog's collar and tried to pull him down. "Barkley, down. Down boy."

I laughed. "That's okay. I like dogs."

Nudging Barkley off of me, I scratched his neck as he landed back onto the floor. I wouldn't have pegged Banks as a dog person.

"That's a good sign. He's usually my meter for whether or not people are shit. If he doesn't like someone, I don't trust them either."

I chuckled and bent down to pet Barkley properly. He licked my hand like it was covered in salt.

"Glad I passed the test," I said.

"So am I." Banks headed for the stairs. "Wait here. I'll grab the laptop."

She disappeared upstairs while I stood in the entryway with Barkley pressing against my legs. The townhouse was tastefully decorated. Comfortable furniture in neutral tones. Bookshelves lined with legal texts and novels. Framed photos on the walls showed Banks at various points in her career.

Banks came back down the stairs carrying an old silver MacBook Air, and we moved into her living room. Banks cleared off the coffee table and set the laptop down. She plugged in the charger and we waited for the device to power on.

"This is going to take a few minutes," Banks said. "Can I get you something to drink? Water? Coffee?"

"Water would be great."

She disappeared into the kitchen. I sat on the couch with Barkley's head resting on my knee.

The townhouse had the comfortable, lived-in feel of someone who actually used their space rather than just staging it for guests. Bookshelves lined one wall, packed with legal texts mixed with fiction paperbacks. Framed photos showed Banks at various career milestones —swearing-in ceremonies, awards dinners, candid shots with colleagues. A worn throw blanket was draped over the arm of the couch. The coffee table had water rings and a stack of magazines that looked actually read rather than decorative. My hand was back in my pocket, fingers wrapping around the USB stick. So close now. Just a few more minutes and I would finally see what was on it. Banks returned with two glasses of water. She handed me one and sat down beside me on the couch. We waited in silence for the laptop to charge.

Finally, the screen lit up. Banks opened the laptop and pressed the power button. The old Apple startup sound played. The screen showed the login screen for her old user account.

"I haven't used this in years," Banks said as she typed in her password. "I completely forgot what was even on here."

The desktop loaded. Banks went into the system preferences and disconnected the wireless networking. Made sure the laptop had no way to connect to the internet. Then she took a deep breath.

"Ready?" she asked.

I pulled the USB stick from my pocket and handed it to her. "Ready."

Banks inserted the drive into the USB port. We both held our breath, waiting for something to happen. Seconds ticked by. We remained unblinking, staring at the screen.

A minute had passed.

Nothing happened.

Banks clicked on the Finder icon and waited for the window to open. When it did, the USB drive appeared in the sidebar. The device's name made my breath catch.

Dead Drop.

"That's what they were saying in the wiretaps," I said. "Ramsey said something about the queen's dead drop. Do you think this could be it? Do you think they were talking about this drive?"

Banks stared at the screen. "I don't know. But it would be one hell of a coincidence if it weren't related."

"So, someone sent the piece to me. Either they didn't know about the drive, or they wanted me to find it."

"Or it's a trap," Banks said.

She double-clicked on the drive icon. The window expanded to show the contents.

There was a single folder inside. The label read, "To Alex."

My heart was pounding. Someone had made this for me. Had labeled it with my name.

"At least now we know for certain that this wasn't delivered to you by accident," Banks said quietly.

She double-clicked on the folder. A password prompt appeared.

"Of course there's a password," I said. "Nothing about this case has been easy."

"If someone wanted you to access this, they would have chosen a password you could figure out," Banks said. "Something personal to you."

"But I don't know who created this. How am I supposed to guess a password when I don't even know who chose it?"

Banks sat back. "Let's think about this logically. Someone went to a lot of trouble to get this drive to you. They disguised it in a chess piece. They made sure it was labeled with your name. They wanted you to find it and open it. So the password has to be something you can guess."

"Try my birthday," I suggested. "December 2, 1995."

Banks typed in my birth date in various formats. Month day year. Year month day. Just the month and day. Nothing worked.

We tried other obvious options. My middle name. My hometown. The name of my law school. Every password prompt came back with the same error message. Incorrect password.

After the tenth failed attempt, I sat back in frustration. "This isn't working."

"Why don't we give it a rest for tonight?" Banks said gently. "We can come back to it with fresh eyes."

"We don't have time," I said. "Pearce's confirmation hearing is in thirty-six hours."

Banks was quiet for a moment. "Let me do some thinking on whether I know anyone who might be able to help us crack this. We have contacts who work with computer forensics. Maybe someone can get past the password protection."

She stood and walked over to her bag, pulling out the envelope that Toby Gordon had given us at DataSecure.

"Besides," Banks said, holding up the envelope, "you've got discovery to go through. Let that occupy your brain, and maybe something will click about the password."

She handed me the envelope. It was heavier than I expected. Probably hundreds of pages of documents inside.

"Even if we can't stop Pearce's confirmation tomorrow, we can still build the case against him," Banks continued. "If we get him charged with something afterward, there are mechanisms to remove him. It's been done before."

I couldn't keep the frustration out of my voice. "So we just let him get confirmed?"

"We don't have a choice at this point. We don't have enough evidence yet to go public with accusations. But we keep working." Banks tapped the envelope in my hands. "And in the meantime, we focus on what we can prove. The Redmond case. The connections to Gulf Coast. That's still our primary assignment."

I looked down at the envelope. She was right. We still had work to do.

She stood and gestured toward the door. "Why don't you head back to your office? Go through the DataSecure materials. See what connections you can find. Build the case we can actually prosecute right now."

I stood as well, tucking the envelope under my arm. "What about the USB drive?"

"I'll keep working on it here. Try some things. See if I can figure out what password someone would have used for you." Banks walked me to the door. "If I get anywhere, I'll call you immediately. But you should focus on what we can control. The discovery. The evidence we already have."

Barkley followed us to the door, his tail still wagging. I bent down to give him one more pet before leaving.

"Thank you," I said to Banks. "For everything today."

"We're going to figure this out," Banks said. "It might take time. But we'll get there. Someone wanted you to have this information. We just need to figure out how to access it."

I nodded and stepped out into the cold evening. The cab ride back to the DOJ building gave me time to think. About the password. About who had created that folder. About what was so important that someone had disguised it as a chess piece and sent it to me.

I checked my phone to find a text from James sent an hour ago.

> Still on for dinner tonight?

I had completely forgotten we had made plans. I typed back.

> Raincheck? Got a ton of discovery to go through tonight.

> Are you sure you're okay? You've been quiet today.

> Yeah all good. Just buried in work. Talk tomorrow?

Okay. Let me know if you need anything.

I put the phone away without responding. I wanted to tell him about the chess piece USB drive. About what we had found at DataSecure. But something held me back. Maybe it was the password-protected folder labeled "To Alex." Maybe it was the uncertainty about who had sent it and why. Or maybe I just wasn't ready to have another conversation about evidence and conspiracy theories when I didn't even know what was on the drive yet.

Back at my office, I spread the DataSecure materials across my desk. Hundreds of pages of corporate emails and financial records. The work of building a federal case.

I STOOD outside Banks's office door the next morning with a stack of papers clutched under my arm. My coffee had gone cold hours ago, but I was too wired to care, pacing back and forth in front of her door.

I had been awake for twenty-four hours straight. My hands shook slightly as I clutched the stack of papers. My eyes were bloodshot from staring at documents all night. I had consumed so much coffee that my heart was fluttering and adrenaline pulsating. But I didn't care.

Because I had found it.

Everything we needed to bring down Redmond. Everything we needed to implicate Pearce. It was all there in the DataSecure discovery, buried in corporate emails and financial records.

When Banks finally appeared at the end of the hallway, she took one look at me and her expression shifted to concern.

"Have you been here all night?" she asked as she approached.

"Yeah." I held up the stack of papers. "But I found it. Everything we need."

Banks unlocked her office door and ushered me inside. She closed the door behind us and gestured for me to sit down.

"You look like you've had about ten cups of coffee," she said.

"Closer to fifteen, but who's counting?" I moved to her desk and started spreading out the papers haphazardly. "Banks, this is it. This is everything. Direct evidence of Redmond taking bribes. References to

Vance right before she died. Explicit mentions of Pearce and his connection to the network."

Banks set down her bag and came around to look at what I was laying out. "Show me."

I yanked the first document off the table. "This is an email chain from May 2023. It was in the Bayou Shipping corporate files that Gordon gave us."

Banks leaned forward to read. The email header showed it was sent from Victor Ramsey at Gulf Coast Strategies to multiple recipients. The subject line read: Houston Flood Control Project - Funding Strategy.

"Email Chain 1: Bribery Setup and Queen Reference," I said, pointing to the notation I had written at the top. "Dated May 20, 2023."

Banks started reading aloud. "From Victor Ramsey. To Carla Redmond at her private secure email archive. Robert Kline at Bayou Builders. And the subject is Houston Flood Control Project - Funding Strategy."

She kept reading, her voice getting quieter.

"Senator Redmond, following our call, Gulf Coast Strategies will deliver $150,000 to your re-election PAC by Q3, structured through Capitol Ventures LLC to stay FEC-compliant. In exchange, we need your assurance on the $60M federal earmark for the Houston flood control bonds. Bayou Builders is positioned to take the lead on contracts. This keeps our operations smooth."

Banks looked up at me. "This is explicit. He's offering her money in exchange for steering a federal earmark to Bayou."

"Keep reading," I said.

Banks's eyes moved back to the email. "A certain queen in D.C. has been asking questions about our past projects, but we're managing it. The bishop's path is still clear. His family's support, especially TW, has been repaid through contributions over the years. His move to the circuit will lock in our interests. Confirm your committee vote?"

She stopped reading. Her finger was still on the page, but her eyes had gone wide.

"The bishop here," I said, "is Franklin Pearce. And TW is Thomas Whitaker, his brother-in-law. They're talking about Pearce's nomination to the Fifth Circuit. About how his family has been paid off through contributions. About how getting him on the circuit court will lock in their interests."

"And the queen," Banks said slowly. "They're talking about someone asking questions about past projects. Someone in D.C."

I nodded. "Eleanor Vance."

Banks kept reading. There was a reply from Carla Redmond dated May 21, 2023.

"Victor, $150K noted. Send it by July. Earmark is in the appropriations draft. I'll push it through. Re: the queen, keep her quiet. FP's got my vote. His brother-in-law's old Bayou work was helpful, and he's proven reliable. Let's keep this tight. CR"

Banks sat back in her chair. She looked at me with an expression I couldn't quite read. Shock? Maybe a little bit of fear.

"It doesn't exactly prove that they are responsible for Vance's death, but it's pretty strong circumstantial evidence."

"Here are the implications." I pulled out another sheet of paper where I had written my analysis. "This email directly confirms Redmond's bribe. $150,000 for earmarks that would benefit Bayou Builders. That's enough for a grand jury indictment under 18 U.S.C. § 201 and § 1343. Bribery of a public official and wire fraud."

"What about the rest of it?" Banks asked.

"Like you said, the queen reference provides circumstantial evidence regarding Vance's death. Ramsey says they're managing her, and then ahead of her moving to speak publicly, she's found dead. That's not coincidence. That's evidence of conspiracy to commit murder." I pointed to another highlighted section. "And here's where it ties to Pearce. Ramsey explicitly states that Whitaker has been repaid through contributions over the years and that Pearce's move to the circuit will lock in their interests."

Banks was reading through the email again, more carefully this time. "The reference to Bayou work from 2002. That's the trafficking case. The one your mother was prosecuting before it got dismissed."

"Exactly. Redmond is acknowledging that Pearce is part of the network. That they're orchestrating his nomination."

"But it's coded language," Banks said. "A defense attorney would argue this is all vague references. That we're reading intent into language that could mean anything."

"Except we have context now." I spread out more documents on top of what was already on the table. "We have the financial records showing Gulf Coast payments to Capitol Ventures LLC. We have corporate filings showing Thomas Whitaker served on Bayou's board during the 2002 trafficking case. We have Pearce's disclosure forms showing he controlled the family trust that held Bayou shares." I grasped and shook the printed email exchange. "And now we have this, explicitly connecting all of them to a bribery scheme and discussing how to manage someone who was asking too many questions. All we need is reasonable doubt." I looked at all the documents covering the desk, as if one of them would start blinking with a sign that read *Reasonable Doubt Here*. "Not even. Because if we're able to secure an indictment, I bet you people will start talking."

Banks stood and walked to her window. She stared out at the morning traffic on Pennsylvania Avenue. Her reflection in the glass looked tired. For a moment, I thought that I was losing her.

"This changes everything," she said without turning around. "We can indict Redmond today if we want. We have her in writing agreeing to accept money in exchange for steering federal funds. That's textbook bribery."

"What about Pearce?" I asked.

"Pearce is harder." Banks turned back to face me, and I could already see from her expression that I wasn't going to like what she was about to say. "This email implicates him as part of the network. It shows Redmond vouching for him based on past work connected to Bayou. But it doesn't show him directly taking bribes or committing crimes. A good defense attorney would argue he had no knowledge of his brother-in-law's activities. That his nomination to the circuit court was legitimate and any suggestion otherwise is speculation."

Frustration burned in my chest. "So we can get Redmond but not Pearce?"

"Not yet. But we do have probable cause to dig deeper into Pearce's finances, subpoena his communications." Banks came back to her desk and reached for the email printout. I handed it to her. "The reference to the queen also gives us grounds to reopen the investigation into Vance's death. If Ramsey was managing Vance ahead of her death, that's evidence of a conspiracy."

"What do we do first?" I asked. "We should go to Chambers, right? Let him know?"

Banks's voice was quiet but serious. "I'm not sure about Chambers."

"What do you mean?"

"Look, Chambers did assign us to the Redmond investigation." She looked away from me and shook her head. "But this goes way beyond Redmond. This implicates a federal judicial nominee. This suggests corruption at the highest levels of the DOJ and the judiciary. And Chambers is part of that system."

"You think Chambers is involved?"

Banks pressed her lips into a thin line. "I don't know. But I'm not convinced his hands are completely clean either. He shut down Vance's concerns about Pearce. He reassigned her investigation. He told you to be careful about making accusations without proof." She shook her head. "What if he's not just being cautious? What if he's protecting something?"

My stomach sank. Chambers had seemed like an ally, but that was Vance's warning, wasn't it? Be careful who you trust.

"So what do we do?" I asked. "If we can't trust Chambers, who can we trust?"

"That's the question we need to answer. Not only that, but who can we deliver this information to in a way that actually promotes change? Someone with the authority to act. Someone we're certain isn't part of the network."

"The FBI?"

"Maybe. But we need to be strategic about it." Banks pulled out a notepad and started making a list.

"What about the USB drive?" I asked, looking at the chess piece sitting on her desk.

She handed it over to me. "You can work on the password later. But right now, we focus on what we can actually access and prove." Banks sat down and opened her laptop, then glanced at me over the top. "And Alex? Maybe you should talk to James. Feel him out about Chambers. See if he's picked up on anything that might tell us whether Chambers can be trusted with this information."

"How would James know that?"

"He's been working directly with Chambers on the Vance files. He might have noticed things. Heard things. Had conversations that would give us insight into where Chambers's loyalties lie." Banks started typing. "Just be careful about what you share. Just feel him out."

My head was spinning. We had found evidence of mass corruption within the federal judiciary, but we couldn't trust the people we were supposed to report to. We had proof of bribery and conspiracy but no clear path forward to utilize it.

"Banks," I said. "Pearce's confirmation is tomorrow. Even if we can't stop it, shouldn't we try? Shouldn't we go public with what we have?"

"And cause a media frenzy with incomplete evidence?" Banks shook her head. " His being sworn in does not mean game over. If we secure charges against him afterward, there are processes for removal. Judges have been impeached and removed before. It's not ideal, but it's not the end if we can't stop the confirmation itself."

"But—"

"We're not out of time," Banks interrupted, meeting my eyes. "But we need to be smart about how we bring charges. I need *you* to be smart about how we do this."

I nodded my head. "Okay."

A KNOCK on Banks's office door interrupted our conversation. Before either of us could respond, the door opened and James stepped inside.

"Marina told me you were in Banks's office," he said, looking at me with concern. "I've been trying to reach you all morning."

Banks turned to me with raised eyebrows. "I thought you didn't tell anyone about what we found."

"I didn't tell him yet," I said quickly.

Banks looked between us for a moment, then sighed. "Come in. Close the door."

James closed the door and moved into the office. His eyes landed on the documents spread across Banks's desk.

"What is all this?" he asked.

"Discovery from DataSecure," I said. "Corporate emails and financial records for Bayou Shipping and Gulf Coast Strategies."

"And?"

Banks gestured to the chair beside me. "Sit down. We'll bring you up to speed."

Over the next fifteen minutes we walked James through everything we had found. The email from Victor Ramsey to Carla Redmond explicitly discussing bribery. The $150,000 payment in exchange for federal earmarks. The reference to "the queen" asking questions about past projects, dated just two days before Eleanor Vance died. The mentions of "FP" and "TW" and how Pearce's move to the circuit court would lock in their interests.

James listened without interrupting. His expression grew darker as we explained each piece of evidence and how it all connected. When we finished, he sat back in his chair.

"This is ..." He ran a hand through his hair. "Evidence of bribery and wire fraud. More than enough to indict. You could take this to a grand jury right now."

"We could," Banks agreed. "But we were just discussing whether we should bring this to Chambers first."

James's response was immediate. "Don't."

I looked at him in surprise. "Why not?"

"Don't bring this to Chambers," James repeated. "I agree with Banks. I don't think we should involve him in this."

I stared at him. This was completely out of character for him. James was always the one advocating for following proper channels. For going through official procedures. For not breaking the rules.

"You're surprised," James said, reading my expression.

"Of course I am. You're Mr. By-The-Book. You're the one who always wants to follow protocol and get authorization before we do anything. Don't pretend that you're not."

"I know. But Chambers will try to block it." James leaned forward, his elbows on his knees. "Just like he did with the Vance research. Just like he's probably going to do with the indictment if you give him the chance."

Banks's eyes narrowed. "How do you know about the conversation I had with him about the indictment? That was private."

James paused, and I could see him weighing how much to say.

"We need to focus on getting these things into the right hands," he said finally, deflecting the question. "That's what matters right now."

Banks's nostrils flared, clearly dissatisfied with the answer, but she didn't push. "Okay. So, if we're not going to Chambers, where do we go?"

"I think we go straight to a senator," James said.

I couldn't stop the laugh from bubbling out of my throat. His suggestion seemed fantastical. "Are you serious?"

He looked at me, a serious expression in his eyes. "Yes. I think we bypass DOJ entirely. Take the evidence directly to someone on the Senate Judiciary Committee. Someone who has the authority to delay Pearce's confirmation and to demand an investigation into Redmond."

"And just what senator is actually going to help us with this?" Banks asked.

"I know exactly who." James stood up. "We should go now."

"Wait," I said, standing as well. "Right now, we'll just walk into a senator's office with a stack of documents and start making accusations?"

"Yes." James looked at me. "You should wait here. Let me handle this part."

"No way I'm staying behind."

James sighed. "Alex, this is delicate. We're going around official channels. If this goes wrong—"

"Then we both take the fall for it. But I'm not sitting here while you take *my* evidence to a senator without me." I crossed my arms. "There's no arguing with me on this. You've dated me long enough to know I'm not backing down on this."

"Fine." A small smile played at the corner of his mouth. James chuckled and turned to Banks. "Do you want to come?"

"Nah, I'll let you two lovebirds handle this political maneuvering." Banks waved us toward the door. "I'm going to stay here and work on what we need for the Redmond indictment. Get everything ready so when you come back with senatorial support, we can move immediately."

"I may be able to get this senator to help with that too," James said. "In a way that it doesn't land back on us directly. She has influence with the U.S. Attorney's office."

"Even better." Banks opened her laptop. "Alright then. Get going. And be careful. Once you hand this evidence to a senator, there's no taking it back. This becomes political very quickly."

I gathered up all the papers we had organized. The emails. The financial records. The timeline we had built connecting everything. Stuffing them into a folder, I tucked it under my arm.

James put his hand on the small of my back and guided me toward the door. "We need to move fast. Before anyone realizes where we're going."

We hurried out of Banks's office and down the hallway. The fifth floor was busier now. We kept our heads down, smiling as normally as possible to colleagues who said good morning, and moved quickly toward the elevators.

Outside the DOJ building, James flagged down a cab. "Hart Senate Office Building," he told the driver.

We climbed into the back seat, and the cab pulled into traffic. Government buildings and monuments passed by outside my window. The machinery of American democracy stretched out across the city. And somewhere in those buildings, corrupt officials were using that same machinery to protect a criminal network.

Facing James, I said, "I'm a little surprised that you're agreeing to help like this. Even though you agree about his involvement, it must be difficult to take active steps against him."

James was quiet for a moment. Staring out his own window before turning to face me.

"Alex, I'll always support you. I just want to make sure that we're going about things the right way. That we have real evidence and not just suspicions. That we're not destroying someone's career based on conspiracy theories."

"But—"

"Let me finish." He took my hand. "Yes, I had a relationship with the man. He was my mentor and I respected him. But if he did these things, if he really is part of this network, then he should have to answer for it. He should have a chance to clear his name if there's nothing to it. But that chance needs to be based on actual investigation, not just his being protected because of his position."

"And you think we have enough evidence now?" I asked.

"In this instance, yes. We have the right evidence. Direct communications linking him to the network. Financial records showing his family profited from those activities. Timing that's too coincidental to ignore." James squeezed my hand. "This isn't you being paranoid or seeing patterns that aren't there. This is real. And it needs to be investigated properly."

My chest loosened, relieving an ache I didn't even know I had. Having James fully on my side, not just tolerating my investigation but actively supporting it, meant more to me than I had realized.

"Banks talked to me about being a little too impulsive," I admitted. "About going all in and pointing fingers without being methodical. She's a good mentor. Maybe something I really needed all this time."

James chuckled. "It's such a hard thing because that's also one of the reasons I love you. You see injustice and you charge straight at it. You don't calculate the political costs or worry about your career. You just do what's right."

I shook my head but couldn't help smiling. "Okay, so who are we going to see? Which senator do you think will actually help us?"

"Senator Julia Collins," James lowered his voice. "She's been in the Senate for thirty years. She sits on the Judiciary Committee. And she's always had a bit of a rivalry with Redmond. They've clashed on policy issues for years. Plus, she already announced that she's retiring after this term. She's not going to worry about destroying her career or facing political backlash."

"Do you think she'll believe us?"

"I think she'll look at the evidence objectively. And when she sees what we have, she'll understand that this needs to be investigated." James looked out the window as the cab approached Capitol Hill. " Julia has a reputation for integrity. She's not going to cover this up or protect him just because he's a judicial nominee."

The cab arrived at the front of the Hart Senate Office Building. The massive white structure loomed over us. James paid the driver, and we climbed out.

We walked toward the entrance, my nerves buzzing more with each step. We were about to bypass the entire DOJ chain of command. We were about to hand evidence of a major corruption case directly to a United States Senator without authorization from our supervisors.

If this went wrong, our careers would be over, and I didn't have time to sort out whether I cared or not.

At the security checkpoint, James pulled out his wallet. But instead of showing his DOJ credentials, he flashed a different badge. One I didn't recognize. The security guards looked at it, nodded, and waved us through without question.

"They know you?" I asked as we moved past the metal detectors.

"Yeah," James said. "Sort of."

I snorted. "Sort of? What does that mean?"

He guided me toward the elevators. "It means I've done some work up here before. Consulting on judicial nominations. Advising senators on legal issues. You pick up access over time."

We rode the elevator up to the third floor. Congressional staffers hurried between offices while interns pushed mail carts down the hallway. Lobbyists clustered outside various doors, hoping to catch a moment with their target senator.

James led me down the corridor to an office with "Senator Julia Collins - Pennsylvania" on the placard. We pushed through the door and entered a reception area. A young woman sat at the desk, typing on her keyboard.

She looked up as we entered. "Can I help you?"

James stepped forward. "I'm James Holloway. I need to speak to Senator Collins. It's urgent."

The staffer's expression shifted to polite skepticism. "Do you have an appointment?"

"No. But she'll want to see me. Give her my name and tell her it's regarding Franklin Pearce's confirmation hearing and evidence of corruption related to Senator Carla Redmond."

The staffer's eyes widened. She picked up her phone. "Let me see if she's available. Please have a seat."

James and I moved to the waiting area, me clutching the folder of documents against my pounding chest. This was it. Once we handed this evidence to Collins, there was no going back. No walking away. No pretending we had followed proper channels.

We were committed.

The staffer hung up her phone and looked at us with surprise. "Senator Collins will see you now. Follow me."

We stood and followed her through a door into the back office area.

She led us down a short hallway to a corner office with windows over-looking the Capitol grounds.

Senator Julia Collins sat behind a large mahogany desk. She was in her early seventies with steel-gray hair pulled back in a neat bun. She wore a navy suit and pearls. Her expression was sharp and assessing as we entered.

"Mr. Holloway," she said, standing to shake his hand. "I wasn't expecting to see you today."

I frowned. James knew a Pennsylvania senator?

"I apologize for showing up without an appointment, Senator. But this couldn't wait." James gestured to me. "This is Alex Hayes. She's a federal prosecutor working on a public corruption case."

Collins shook my hand with a firm grip. "Please, sit. Tell me what's so urgent."

I looked at James and hHe nodded encouragement.

I set the folder on Collins's desk and opened it. Pulled out the email from Victor Ramsey.

"Senator, we have evidence that Carla Redmond has been taking bribes from Gulf Coast Strategies," I said. "And that Franklin Pearce's nomination to the Fifth Circuit is part of a larger pattern of corruption designed to protect a criminal network operating for decades."

Collins's expression didn't change. She picked up the email and started reading.

And so our gamble began.

CHAPTER
THIRTY

SENATOR COLLINS SAT BACK in her chair after reading through the email. She set it down on her desk carefully and looked between James and me.

"These are serious accusations," she said finally.

"Yes, they are," James said. "And we wouldn't be bringing them to you if we didn't have solid evidence to back them up."

"The email is explicit about Senator Redmond accepting payments in exchange for federal earmarks. That's bribery. That's a federal crime." Collins picked up the document again and scanned it. "But the references to Franklin Pearce are more oblique. FP and TW. Mentions of family support and contributions. His move to the circuit locking in interests."

"This email alone doesn't necessarily implicate Pearce in a criminal conspiracy," James said. "But it does show that his nomination serves the interests of a corrupt network. It shows that his family has received payments from the same organization that's bribing Redmond. And it establishes a pattern that needs to be investigated thoroughly."

Collins leaned forward. "So you're asking me to delay his confirmation hearing based on implications rather than direct evidence?"

"I'm asking you to ensure that Pearce is made to answer for these connections before he is elevated to an even more powerful position on the federal bench," James said. "If he's innocent, if there's an explanation for these financial ties and references, then he should have the opportunity to provide it. But that needs to happen before he's confirmed, not after."

Collins was quiet for a moment. Her expression suggested she was weighing something carefully. "James, you know Franklin personally, don't you? I seem to recall you clerked for him years ago."

"Yes, I did. Franklin was my professor in law school, and I clerked for him for two years after graduation. He's been a mentor to me for fifteen years."

"And yet you're here asking me to potentially derail his nomination to the appellate court."

"Yes, I am. Because that personal relationship doesn't change my professional responsibility."

Collins nodded slowly, seemingly satisfied with that answer. Then she turned her attention to me.

"Ms. Hayes, how exactly did you acquire these emails? Corporate communications between Gulf Coast Strategies and Senator Redmond would normally be protected by attorney-client privilege or executive privilege claims."

"By subpoenaing the data storage company that hosts Bayou Shipping's corporate email archives," I said, explaining the connection with DataSecure Solutions, how Banks and I had taken an unofficial trip there yesterday.

"You went to their facility in person?" Collins raised an eyebrow. "Rather than filing the paperwork through normal channels and waiting for a response?"

I nodded. "Franklin Pearce's confirmation hearing is scheduled for tomorrow. We couldn't afford to wait two weeks for a response through normal procedures."

Collins picked up another document from the stack I had brought. She studied it for a moment before looking back at me.

"That's very resourceful," she said. There was something like approval in her voice. "A lot of AUSAs would just file the paperwork and let chance decide their fate. Wait for the bureaucratic process to work itself out and accept whatever timeline resulted. But you went directly to the source and made it happen on your schedule."

"Alex doesn't wait for permission or accept artificial barriers," James said. "When she sees a path forward, she takes it. Even if there isn't one, she'll usually make one."

My face flushed slightly at the compliment.

"Yes ... I can see that," Collins said, the corner of her mouth quirking. "The Department of Justice is lucky to have prosecutors who are willing to be creative and aggressive in pursuing corruption cases."

She gathered the documents I had spread across her desk and tapped them into a neat stack.

"Thank you both for bringing this to my attention," Collins said. "I will take it from here. I'll speak with the other members of the Judiciary Committee."

Collins and I started to stand, but James paused and remained in his seat.

"Senator, if I may," he said. "There's one more thing we need to address."

Collins and I sat back down. She gestured for him to continue. "Go ahead."

"We need a way to be sure that Senator Redmond is implicated in a manner that prevents interference from supervisors who might not want to risk their careers on indicting a sitting senator." I could hear the caution in James's voice. "There are people at DOJ who will want to slow-walk this. Who will find reasons to delay or water down the charges. Who will protect Redmond because going after her is politically dangerous."

Collins studied him for a moment. Understanding dawned in her eyes. "You're concerned that your superiors will block the prosecution."

"I'm concerned that certain people will prioritize institutional protection over justice," James said.

Collins was quiet for a long moment, tapping her fingers on the closed folder.

"Okay, I understand," she said finally. "I'll make sure the evidence gets to the right people. And I'll make it clear that the Senate Judiciary Committee expects action. That will provide cover for prosecutors who want to move forward but are worried about pushback."

"Thank you, Senator," James said.

We both stood to leave. I gathered my bag and started toward the door. But something was nagging at me. A question I needed to ask before we left.

"I'm sorry to ask one more question," I said, turning back to Collins. She looked up from her desk. "Yes?"

"In the emails, there's a reference to a queen. Someone in D.C. who was asking questions about Gulf Coast's past projects. The timing of that reference coincides with Eleanor Vance's death." I pulled out the specific email and pointed to the relevant section. "You haven't heard that term used before, have you? Any idea who it could be referring to?"

Collins took the email from me and read through the section I had indicated. Her expression remained neutral but I thought I saw something flicker in her eyes.

"No, I can't say that I do." She handed the email back to me. "The reference is obviously coded language. But without more context, I couldn't tell you who they were discussing."

"Okay. Thank you anyway."

Collins walked us to her office door. "You've done good work here. Both of you. This took courage. Coming to me without authorization from your supervisors. Bypassing official channels. That's not an easy decision to make."

"It was the right decision," I said.

"I believe it was." Collins shook both our hands. "I'll be in touch as this moves forward. And please, be careful. If what you're saying is true, then you've made yourselves targets by bringing this to light."

"We understand the risks," James said.

We said our goodbyes and stepped out of Collins's office into the hallway. I let out a breath I hadn't realized I was holding.

"We did it. We actually did it," I said quietly.

"Yes, we did." James put his hand on the small of my back. "Now we just have to hope Collins follows through."

CHAPTER
THIRTY-ONE

WALKING down the hallway in silence, I got my phone out and checked the time. Almost eleven in the morning.

"I should get back to the office," I said. "I need to help Banks with drafting the indictment. I'm sure she'll want to get it filed as soon as possible. Especially with Collins putting pressure on DOJ."

"You can take an hour for yourself, Alex," James said, his voice gentle. "You've earned it. You've been up for almost thirty hours. You found the evidence. You brought it to a senator. You've done everything you can do for right now."

"But Banks is waiting—"

"Banks can handle drafting an indictment. She's been doing this longer than either of us." James steered me away from the exit. "Come on. Let me show you something."

"Where are we going?"

"You'll see."

Guiding me down the hallway and around a corner, we emerged into a larger corridor where a line of tourists had formed. They were waiting for the guided tour of the Hart Senate Office Building. Families with children. Students on school trips. People who had come to D.C. to see the inner workings of their government.

James ushered me into the line.

I looked at him incredulously. "Are you serious?"

"Why not? When's the last time you actually stopped and appreciated where you work? What you get to be part of?" James gestured around us. "You spend all day fighting corruption and chasing criminals. But you're doing it *here*. In the heart of American democracy. That's worth taking a moment to appreciate."

I wanted to argue, to insist that we needed to get back to work, that there was too much to do and not enough time. But James was right. I was exhausted. I had been running on adrenaline and caffeine for so long that I had forgotten what it felt like to just stop and breathe for a moment.

"Okay," I said. "One hour. Then we go back."

"One hour," James agreed.

The tour guide appeared at the front of the line. A young woman in a National Park Service uniform and with an enthusiastic smile. She started explaining the history of the Hart Building. How it had been constructed in the 1980s. How it was named after Senator Philip Hart from Michigan. How it housed fifty senators, their staff members, three committees and several subcommittees.

We shuffled along with the group. Through marble hallways with high ceilings. Past portraits of former senators. Into rooms where important committee hearings had taken place. The tour guide pointed out architectural details and shared anecdotes about famous moments in Senate history.

"And if you'll follow me this way," she said cheerfully, "we'll head through the underground tunnels to the Capitol building itself."

The group filed into an elevator that took us down to the subway system connecting the Senate office buildings to the Capitol. We boarded a small subway car that reminded me of an amusement park ride. James grinned at me as we sat down.

"This never gets old," he said.

The car whisked us through the tunnel and deposited us at the Capitol where we followed the tour guide up marble staircases and through grand corridors. The building was breathtaking. Frescoes covered the ceilings. Statues of historical figures lined the halls. Everything seemed to speak of history and power and the weight of democracy.

"Now we're approaching the rotunda," the tour guide announced. "The heart of the Capitol building. The dome you see above you was completed in 1866 and stands 288 feet tall."

We entered the circular room, and I tilted my head back to stare up at the painted ceiling. The Apotheosis of Washington stretched across the dome's interior. George Washington ascending to the heavens, surrounded by allegorical figures.

"Pretty incredible, right?" James said beside me.

"Yeah," I admitted. "I forget sometimes how beautiful these buildings are."

The tour guide was explaining the history of the Capitol dome when I felt it. That prickling sensation at the back of my neck. The feeling of being watched.

I turned slowly, scanning the crowd of tourists around me. Families taking photos. Students scribbling notes. An older couple holding hands. And there, at the edge of the group, a man in a dark coat. He was looking down at his phone, but something about his posture felt wrong. His body was angled towards me.

I fished out my phone and pretended to check something. Instead, I typed a message to James.

Me: *Don't look now, but I think someone's following us. Dark coat. Edge of the group by the statue.*

My phone buzzed almost immediately.

James: *You sure?*

Me: *No. But something feels off.*

James: *Let's watch. Not sure yet.*

The tour moved on, leading us down a corridor to show us the old Supreme Court chamber. I kept an eye on the man in the dark coat. He stayed with the group but always at the periphery. Never quite looking at me directly but always in position to see where we were going.

We reached Statuary Hall, and the tour guide launched into her explanation about the room's unique acoustics.

"This hall used to be the House of Representatives chamber," she said. "And it has a fascinating quirk. If you stand in certain spots, you can hear whispers from across the room perfectly clearly. John Quincy

Adams used to position his desk at one of these acoustic sweet spots so he could eavesdrop on his opponents."

She gestured to specific floor tiles. "If you want to try it, stand on these markers. Have someone whisper from the opposite side and you'll hear them as if they're standing right next to you."

Tourists scrambled to the marked spots, giggling as they tested it out. A little girl whispered "hello" from one side and her father heard it clearly from fifty feet away. The crowd applauded.

James pulled me to one of the marked spots. "Come on. We have to try it."

"This is ridiculous," I said, but I was smiling despite myself.

"Life needs ridiculous sometimes." James walked to the opposite marker and turned to face me. He mouthed something silently.

I shook my head to indicate I couldn't hear. He tried again, exaggerating his mouth movements.

A woman standing near him leaned over and whispered helpfully, "He said 'I love you.'"

I felt my face flush. James grinned from across the hall. I whispered back, "I love you too, you dork."

The words carried perfectly across the dome. James laughed.

But when I looked around the room, I saw the man in the dark coat again. He was standing near one of the pillars, still looking at his phone. Still too still. Still too aware.

I caught James's eye and tilted my head slightly toward the man. James's expression shifted. He had seen him too.

The tour continued through more rooms. The National Statuary Hall Collection. The Crypt beneath the rotunda. The guide shared stories and historical anecdotes while tourists took photos and asked questions, all the while we stayed at the back of the group, and the man in the dark coat stayed with us.

By the time the tour ended back at the Hart Building, I was certain we were being followed. But when we exited, the man had disappeared. I scanned the sidewalks and the steps of the building. He was nowhere to be seen.

"Do you see him?" I asked James quietly.

"No. He's gone." James took my arm. "Come on. Let's get out of the open."

As we walked quickly down the sidewalk away from the Capitol complex, my heart was racing. The exhaustion I had been feeling was mixed with fear now. Someone had been watching us. Did he know we had just met with Senator Collins?

"Food truck," James said, pointing ahead. "Let's grab something and sit down somewhere where we can see who's around us."

We reached a row of food trucks parked near the National Mall. The smell of fried food and coffee filled the air. We ordered hot dogs and coffee from a truck with a faded awning and a bored-looking vendor.

The coffee was terrible, all burned and bitter. The hot dogs were lukewarm, and the buns were stale. But I didn't care. I was too busy watching the crowd around us.

"I don't see him," I said after several minutes.

"Neither do I." James bit into his hot dog and made a face. "This is awful."

I sipped the bad coffee and grimaced. "Yeah, it really is."

We found a park bench overlooking the National Mall. The Washington Monument rose in the distance. Tourists walked along the beaten paths. Joggers passed by. Everything looked normal.

We sat down, and I set my coffee cup on the bench beside me. James finished his hot dog and crumpled the wrapper into a ball.

"So," I said. "What do you think is going to happen tomorrow?"

James was quiet for a moment. "I don't know. But whatever does or doesn't happen, it should at least shock some people. Collins isn't the type to sit on evidence like this. She'll make waves."

"Do you think she'll actually stop the confirmation?"

"I think she'll try. Whether she succeeds depends on how much political capital she's willing to spend and whether the other members of the Judiciary Committee take this seriously." James looked out at the Mall. "But even if Pearce gets confirmed tomorrow, we've started something. We've put evidence in the hands of someone who has the power to investigate. That matters."

I nodded. James was right. We had done all we could do. The rest was out of our control.

"I keep thinking about that man," I said. "The one who was following us during the tour."

"Could have been nothing. Could have been coincidence."

"Or it could have been the network watching us. Seeing who we were meeting with. Making sure we understood that they know what we're doing."

James turned to look at me. "If that's what it was, then they're getting nervous. They wouldn't be watching us if they felt secure. They wouldn't be trying to intimidate us if they thought they had this under control."

"That's either a good thing or a very bad thing."

"Probably both." James stood and held out his hand. "We should get back. Banks is waiting. And the longer we sit out here in the open, the more time we give whoever might be watching to track our movements."

I took his hand and let him pull me to my feet. We tossed our trash and started walking back toward the Metro station. I kept scanning the crowds around us for anyone who seemed to be paying too much attention.

But I saw nothing. Maybe the man really had been nothing. Maybe I was being paranoid after too many sleepless hours and too much caffeine.

We walked toward the Metro station. My phone vibrated with a text from Banks.

How did it go?

Senator Collins is on board.

Good work. Come back when you can. I've got the indictment drafted. Just needs your review.

"Banks has the indictment ready," I told James as we boarded the train.

James found us seats near the back of the car. "One step closer to taking them all down."

The train pulled out of the station, its rhythmic chugging against the tracks almost rocking me completely to sleep.

By the time we reached our stop, my eyes felt very heavy. The adrenaline from being followed had worn off. My body was reminding me that I had been awake for more than thirty hours. That I had consumed too much coffee and not enough food. That I needed to sleep soon or I would collapse.

"Are you okay?" James asked as we climbed the stairs out of the station.

"I will be. Just need to review the indictment with Banks, and then I'm going to find somewhere to take a nap. Even if it's under my desk."

James smiled. "That's probably a good plan."

CHAPTER THIRTY-TWO

JAMES TOOK me back to the DOJ building and walked me as far as the elevator bank.

"I have a meeting to get to," he said, checking his watch. "But I'll see you later?"

I nodded. "Yeah. I need to read through the indictment with Banks and then I'm heading home to sleep for about twelve hours."

He kissed my forehead. "Good plan. Text me when you get home safe."

"I will."

I rode the elevator up to the fifth floor and made my way to Banks's office. The door was open, and I could see her at her computer, typing rapidly. She looked up as I approached and smiled.

"Collins is on board?" she asked.

"Collins is on board," I confirmed, walking into her office. "She seemed genuinely concerned about what we showed her."

"That's good."

Banks hit a few more keys and then clicked her mouse. A printer on the credenza behind her desk came to life. She swiveled her chair around to collect the pages as they emerged.

"What's that?" I asked.

Banks handed me the document. "United States Attorney's Office for the District of Maryland filing charges against Senator Carla

Redmond. Bribery, wire fraud, honest services fraud, conspiracy. I structured it so we can file it through Maryland instead of D.C. Keeps it away from people here who might try to slow-walk it."

I scanned the indictment. It was thorough. Every charge was backed up with specific evidence from the emails we had found. The financial records showing the payments. The wiretaps discussing the arrangement. Everything we needed to put Redmond away.

I looked up at Banks. "I should have been here to help with this."

"It's okay. I want this ready to drop as soon as we get what we need from James's contact." Banks took the document back and set it on her desk. "Collins is going to make noise. That will provide the political cover we need. But we still need the actual indictment ready to file the moment we have clearance."

"Do you think Maryland will take it?"

"I think they won't have a choice once Collins starts asking questions publicly." Banks turned back to her computer. "And if they try to block it, we'll find another way. There's always another way."

Nodding, I sank into the chair across from her desk. The exhaustion was catching up with me fast now that the adrenaline had worn off completely.

"Any luck on the USB drive?" Banks asked without looking away from her screen.

"Honestly? I didn't try again. Spent all night looking at the documents from DataSecure." I rubbed my eyes. "The password is there somewhere. I just can't see it yet."

Banks looked back at me, her expression shifting to concern.

"Alex, why don't you go home and get some sleep? You're no good to anyone if you haven't slept. If things go the way we need it to, we'll be presenting to the grand jury by Monday. That means we have about ninety-six hours to make sure everything is airtight."

"No, it's okay. I can stay and help." The words came out through a yawn that I couldn't suppress.

Banks stood and came around her desk. She put her hand on my shoulder.

"As your supervisor, I'm ordering you to go home and eat a decent meal and get a proper amount of sleep. I will see you tomorrow morning. Fresh. Rested. Ready to work."

I wanted to argue. Wanted to insist that I could push through the exhaustion. But Banks was right. I was running on fumes. Another few hours and I would be useless.

"Okay," I said begrudgingly. "But call me if anything happens. If Collins makes a move. If Maryland responds. Anything."

"I will. Now get out of here."

Gathering my bag, I headed for the door. My legs were lead weights on my walk to the Metro, slowing me down more than usual. My thoughts were scattered. I kept seeing that man in the dark coat from the Capitol tour. Kept feeling like eyes were on me.

The Metro platform was crowded with other commuters and tourists. I found a spot near the wall and waited for my train. When it arrived, I found a corner seat to slump in and closed my eyes.

The swaying of the train was almost hypnotic. I felt myself starting to drift off but forced my eyes open. Not here. I needed to make it home first.

At my stop, I climbed the stairs to street level and walked the four blocks to my apartment building. The November air was cold, but it kept me awake.

Hair prickled at the back of my neck, and I turned to check over my shoulder. The street was empty. Just parked cars and bare trees and the distant sound of traffic.

At my building I fumbled with my keys. My hands were shaking from exhaustion and too much caffeine. Inside, I climbed the stairs to my floor and let myself into my apartment.

The silence was overwhelming after the constant noise of the city and the office. I dropped my bag by the door and stood in the entryway for a moment, not quite sure what to do first.

Food. Banks had said I needed to eat. But the thought of cooking anything made me want to cry. I opened the refrigerator and stared at the contents. Some leftover takeout from days ago. A carton of milk that might be expired. Condiments.

I closed the refrigerator and pulled out my phone. Ordered delivery from the Thai place down the street.

While I waited for the food, I called my dad.

On the third ring, he answered. "Alex? Everything okay?"

"Yeah, Dad. I'm fine. Just wanted to check in."

"At two-thirty on a Thursday? You must be exhausted if you're calling me during normal waking hours." I could hear the smile in his voice. "What's going on?"

"Big case. It's about to break wide open." I sat down on my couch and kicked off my shoes. "You should watch C-SPAN tomorrow. There's going to be some government drama going down."

"C-SPAN?" Dad laughed. "What kind of case are you working on that's going to be on C-SPAN?"

"The kind I can't really talk about yet. But trust me, it's big."

"Alright, kiddo. I'll tune in." There was a pause. " Are you taking care of yourself?"

"Trying to. My supervisor just ordered me to go home and sleep." I pulled a blanket off the back of the couch and wrapped it around myself. "Hey, Dad? Can I ask you a weird question?"

"Sure."

"If you had to pick a password, something that I would be able to guess, what would it be?"

The line was quiet for a moment. " I don't know, honestly. Why?"

"Just something I'm working through for the case." The blanket cocooned around me, warming from my body heat, and I yawned. "There's this encrypted file, and I need to figure out the password."

"And you think I might know it?" he asked.

"No, I just ... I'm trying to think about how people choose passwords. What would be meaningful enough to use but still something someone else could figure out if they were supposed to?"

Dad was quiet again. I could almost hear him thinking.

"I really don't know, Alex. That's tough. You'd have to know the person pretty well to guess something like that."

"Yeah." I yawned again. " Well, if you think of anything, text me."

"I will. Now get some sleep. You sound like you're about to fall over."

"I pretty much am. Love you, Dad."

"Love you too, kiddo. Watch yourself with this big case of yours."

"I will."

I hung up and let my head fall back against the couch. The conversation hadn't helped with the password, but it had been good to hear Dad's voice. To be reminded that there was life outside this investigation. Outside the corruption and conspiracy and constant fear.

The phone buzzed. The delivery driver was downstairs. I huffed and unraveled the blanket, dragged myself up, and went to collect the food. The smell of pad thai and curry made my stomach growl.

I took the food upstairs and ate directly from the containers while standing at my kitchen counter. It was delicious. Hot and spicy. I devoured the pad thai and half the curry before my stomach protested that I was eating too fast.

I put the rest in the refrigerator and headed for my bedroom. I forced myself to go through a normal routine of preparing for bed. Brushing my teeth, changing into pajamas. Because what I really wanted to do was just collapse onto the mattress and become dead to the world for the next twelve hours.

But when I finally lay down, my mind wouldn't shut off. It kept circling back to the password. To the folder labeled "To Alex" on the USB drive. Someone had created that specifically for me. Had hidden it in the chess piece and sent it to my apartment. Had wanted me to find it and open it.

So the password had to be something I could figure out. Something meaningful. Something connecting to me specifically.

But what?

I thought about my birthday. My mother's name. My father's name. The address of my childhood home. The name of my first pet. All the standard password options that people used.

I had already tried most of those. None had worked.

So it had to be something else. Something less obvious but still personal enough that I would eventually figure it out.

My eyes were getting heavy, exhaustion finally overwhelming the racing thoughts. I felt myself starting to drift off.

The password. I needed to figure out the password.

My body sank into the bed beneath me, like a cloud carrying me.

Tomorrow. I would work on the password tomorrow.

The phone buzzed as I started to drift. I checked it with one eye open.

James: *Made it home safe?*

Me: *Yeah. About to crash. See you tomorrow.*

James: *Sleep well. Love you.*

Me: *Love you too.*

I put my phone on the nightstand and closed my eyes. The bed was soft. The apartment was quiet. For the first time in more than thirty hours, I let myself fully relax.

CHAPTER
THIRTY-THREE

I WOKE up Friday morning feeling more human than I had in days. The exhaustion was still there but manageable. My body no longer felt like it was held together with caffeine and willpower alone.

I showered and put on a navy suit with a white blouse. Professional but not overdone. Today was important. Today was the confirmation hearing for Franklin Pearce. Today we would see if Senator Collins actually followed through on her promise to make waves.

From the moment I stepped onto the Metro platform, that sensation at the back of my neck returned. I scanned the crowd waiting for the train but saw nothing out of the ordinary. Just commuters in business attire checking their phones and drinking coffee.

The train arrived, and I found a seat near the middle of the car. Through the windows, I watched the tunnel walls blur past. At each stop, new passengers boarded and others departed. I kept checking to see if anyone was watching me too closely. But there was nothing. Just tired people heading to work. I shook it off. I was being paranoid. Too many sleepless nights and too much stress had me seeing threats that weren't there.

By the time I reached the DOJ building, I had almost convinced myself that the feeling was just residual anxiety from everything that had happened this week. Almost.

James was waiting in the lobby when I arrived. He smiled when he saw me.

"You look better," he said, falling into step beside me as we headed for the elevators.

"I feel better. Twelve hours of sleep will do that." I hit the button for the fifth floor. "Have you heard anything from Collins?"

"Not yet. But the hearing starts at ten. She'll make her move then if she's going to."

We rode the elevator up and made our way to Banks's office. She was already at her desk with her computer open and what looked like her third cup of coffee steaming beside her keyboard.

"Good morning," she said without looking up. "Are you both ready for the show?"

"As ready as we can be," James said.

Banks finally looked at us. "I got confirmation this morning that the Maryland U.S. Attorney's office is prepared to move forward with the Redmond indictment. They're just waiting for the political cover. Once Collins makes noise at the hearing, we file."

"How fast?" I asked.

"As fast as the paperwork allows. Could be this afternoon if everything goes our way."

James leaned against the door frame. "And if Collins doesn't make noise?"

"Then we wait and find another angle. But she will. I've dealt with Julia Collins before. She doesn't make promises she won't keep." Banks closed her laptop. "Now get out of here. Go watch the hearing. I want eyes on how this plays out so we know what we're dealing with."

"You're not coming?" I asked.

"Someone needs to be here to coordinate with Maryland. Besides, you two will give me a better read on the room than C-SPAN will." She shooed us toward the door. "Go on. Get good seats."

James and I left Banks's office and headed back to the elevators, riding back down to the lobby in silence.

"Are you nervous?" James asked as we exited the building and started walking toward Capitol Hill.

"Terrified," I admitted. "We're about to watch our evidence get used in a very public way. If this goes wrong, if Collins doesn't handle it right, we could end up exposed and vulnerable."

"She'll handle it right." James took my hand. "Trust me."

We reached the Hart Building and went through security. James flashed his badge again, and they waved us through. I narrowed my eyes at it but wasn't able to get a proper look before he tucked it away quickly. We took the elevator up to the hearing room and found seats in the public gallery.

The room was already filling up. Reporters clustered near the front. Congressional staffers occupied the seats behind the senators' dais. Members of the public who had come to watch the confirmation of a new circuit court of appeals judge filed into the gallery sections.

Franklin Pearce sat at the witness table facing the committee, projecting calm confidence. His suit was perfectly tailored, and his hair was neatly combed. As if this hearing wasn't about to go up in flames. As if he had already been confirmed and was just waiting for the paperwork to catch up.

Behind him sat what appeared to be his family. A woman I presumed to be his wife and his adult children. They were all dressed professionally and wearing supportive smiles.

My stomach twisted as familiar doubt crept in. Had I done enough? What if I had been wrong? I would ruin this man's reputation and career for nothing.

I tried to take a deep breath and calm my nerves. This time I had support. It wasn't just me that saw the connections. Banks and James, two extremely experienced prosecutors, saw the connections too. If I couldn't trust myself, maybe I could trust them.

The committee chairman, Senator Richard Brennan from Ohio, gaveled the hearing to order at exactly ten o'clock.

"This hearing of the Senate Judiciary Committee will come to order," Brennan announced in a deep voice. "We are here today to consider the nomination of Judge Franklin Pearce to the United States Court of Appeals for the Fifth Circuit. Judge Pearce has served with distinction on the federal bench for fifteen years and has an exemplary record of judicial temperament and legal scholarship."

He went on for several more minutes. Praising Pearce's qualifications. Noting his bipartisan support. Making it clear that this was expected to be a smooth confirmation.

I glanced at James. I couldn't read his expression as he watched Pearce.

"Opening statements will be brief," Brennan continued. "Then we'll move to questions from committee members. Judge Pearce, would you like to make an opening statement?"

Pearce leaned toward his microphone. "Thank you, Mr. Chairman. I'm honored to be here today and grateful for this committee's consideration of my nomination. I have devoted my career to the fair and impartial administration of justice. If confirmed, I will continue to serve with integrity and dedication to the Constitution and the rule of law."

It was a standard opening. Nothing controversial. Nothing that would raise any red flags.

The first round of questions came from Senator Michael Torres from Texas. He lobbed softballs that Pearce knocked out of the park. Questions about judicial philosophy. About precedent and stare decisis. About how Pearce would approach appellate review.

Pearce answered perfectly, citing cases, demonstrating his knowledge, showing the crowd why he had been nominated in the first place.

"Thank you, Judge Pearce," Torres said. "I have no further questions at this time."

The next senator was similarly friendly. Then another. Each one asking respectful questions that allowed Pearce to showcase his qualifications.

I was starting to worry that Collins had changed her mind. That she had decided not to rock the boat after all.

Then Chairman Brennan looked down at his list and said the words I had been waiting for.

"Senator Julia Collins from Pennsylvania, you have the floor."

Collins stood. She adjusted her microphone and looked directly at Pearce. Her expression was neutral, but I could see the calculation behind her eyes.

"Thank you, Mr. Chairman." Her strong voice carried through the hearing room. "Judge Pearce, I'd like to ask you about your financial disclosures."

Pearce's expression didn't change, but his shoulders tensed. "Of course, Senator."

"Your disclosure forms indicate that you served on the board of directors for Bayou Shipping Corporation from 2015 to 2018. Is that correct?"

"Yes, that's correct."

"And during that time, were you aware that Bayou Shipping was under investigation for potential involvement in human trafficking operations?"

The room went silent. Reporters started typing on keyboards, others' pens scratching paper. Some senators looked up from their notes with sudden interest.

Pearce's calm façade cracked slightly. "I was not aware of any such investigation, Senator."

"Really?" Collins pulled out a document. "Because I have here evidence suggesting that Bayou Shipping was connected to a dismissed trafficking case in Harris County, Texas, in 2003. A case where your brother-in-law, Thomas Whitaker, served on the company's board of directors. You weren't aware of that connection?"

"My brother-in-law's service on Bayou's board predated mine by more than a decade. I had no knowledge of any dismissed cases from that time period."

"But you did know that your brother-in-law had served on the board?"

"Yes, I knew that."

"And when you joined the board yourself in 2015, you didn't think to ask about the company's history? About why your brother-in-law had left the board in 2002, right before prosecutors filed trafficking charges?"

Chairman Brennan leaned toward his microphone. "Senator Collins, where is this line of questioning going?"

"I'm establishing Judge Pearce's connections to companies that have engaged in potentially criminal activities, Mr. Chairman. I think it's relevant to his fitness for a lifetime appointment to the federal bench."

Other senators were starting to pay attention now. Whispers rippled through the room.

Collins continued without waiting for Brennan's response. "Judge Pearce, I'd also like to ask about your financial relationship with Gulf Coast Strategies LLC."

Pearce's face went pale. "I don't have a financial relationship with Gulf Coast Strategies."

"No? Because here it shows that your family trust, which you control as trustee, received significant payments from entities connected to Gulf Coast. Payments that coincided with your nomination to this very position."

"Senator, I—" Pearce stopped, clearing his throat. "I manage a family trust on behalf of my late brother-in-law's estate. The trust has various investments. I don't personally oversee every transaction."

"But you do have discretionary authority over those investments. You can vote shares. Make corporate decisions. Isn't that correct?"

"Yes, but—"

"And during your time as trustee, did the trust hold shares in Bayou Shipping?"

Pearce was trapped. He couldn't lie under oath. But admitting the truth would confirm everything Collins was implying.

"Yes," he said finally. "The trust held shares in Bayou."

The room erupted. Reporters on their phones. Senators conferring with their staff. Chairman Brennan gaveled for order, but the noise level was only increasing.

Collins raised her voice to be heard over the commotion. "I also have information regarding Senator Carla Redmond's involvement with Gulf Coast Strategies. Information suggesting that she accepted bribes in exchange for federal earmarks that benefited Bayou Shipping. Information that implicates the network that Judge Pearce and his family have been financially connected to for decades."

"Senator Collins, that is a serious allegation!" Senator Douglas from Georgia stood. "You're accusing a sitting senator of bribery based on what evidence?"

Collins pulled out more documents. The emails in the DataSecure files. She held them up for the committee to see.

"Based on corporate communications obtained through a federal investigation. Communications that explicitly discuss payments to Senator Redmond in exchange for official acts. That reference Judge Pearce's nomination as serving the interests of this criminal network."

The hearing descended into chaos. Multiple senators were trying to speak at once. Chairman Brennan pounded his gavel, standing and opening his mouth to yell. Reporters were rushing toward the doors to file their stories.

Pearce sat frozen at the witness table. His face had gone from pale to gray. His family behind him looked equally stunned.

"Order!" Brennan shouted. "This committee will come to order!"

The noise gradually died down. Senators returned to their seats. The gallery quieted to whispers.

"Senator Collins." Brennan's voice was tight with barely controlled anger. "These are extraordinary allegations. I'm going to have to insist that you provide this committee with the evidence you claim to have. And I'm going to have to suspend this hearing until we can review that evidence and determine whether it's credible."

"I'm happy to provide everything to the committee, Mr. Chairman." Collins sat down. "In fact, I've already forwarded copies to the Judiciary Committee staff. I think you'll find the evidence quite compelling."

Brennan looked at his staff aide who nodded confirmation. The chairman's expression darkened.

"This hearing is suspended pending review of new evidence that has come to light." Brennan gaveled once. "We will reconvene when the committee has had adequate time to assess the situation. Judge Pearce, you are excused for now, but you should remain available for recall."

Pearce stood on shaky legs. His family was already standing, preparing to leave. The whole group looked shell-shocked.

The hearing room was still buzzing with activity. Reporters were interviewing senators. Staff members were clustering in urgent conferences. The public gallery was filing out with excited conversations about what they had just witnessed.

"She did it," I said quietly. "Collins actually did it."

"Yeah." James was watching as Pearce and his family made their way toward the exit. "She really did."

I looked down at my phone to see a text from Banks.

> Did you see that? Holy shit.

> Me: Saw it live. It was incredible.

> Get back here. Maryland is ready to file. We're moving on Redmond today.

I showed the texts to James. He nodded, and we stood to leave.

But as we made our way toward the exit, I stopped cold.

Standing near the back of the hearing room, watching the chaos, was the man in the dark coat.

He looked directly at me. Our eyes met.

And then he smiled.

Before I could react, before I could point him out to James, the man turned and disappeared into the crowd flowing out of the hearing room.

"Alex?" James touched my arm. "Are you okay?"

"He was here. The man from yesterday. He was watching the hearing."

James scanned the crowd. "Where?"

I looked at the spot he'd stood in, then to the crowd he'd vanished into. "He's gone now." I pulled out my phone. "We need to tell Banks. We need to document this. Someone in the network knows we're behind Collins's questions. They know we provided the evidence."

"Then we need to be careful." James placed his hand on my lower back, guiding me toward the exit. " Let's get back to DOJ. Let's finish this before they have a chance to regroup."

We pushed through the crowd and out of the hearing room. The hallways of the Hart Building were packed with people talking about what had just happened. About the scandal that had just erupted. About the confirmation hearing that had turned into an interrogation.

CHAPTER THIRTY-FOUR

BY THE TIME James and I made it back to the DOJ building, Banks's office had become command central. On her computer with multiple windows open, her phone was buzzing with texts, and there was someone I hadn't expected to see sitting in one of her chairs.

Chambers.

He looked up as we entered. "Well, that was quite the morning, wasn't it?"

I exchanged a glance with James. Since we hadn't told Chambers about going to Collins and we hadn't told him about the evidence we had handed over, how much did he know?

"It was certainly dramatic," Banks said. "Senator Collins made some serious allegations."

"Indeed she did." Chambers didn't look particularly pleased. He leaned back in his chair with his arms crossed. "Allegations that now have the entire country watching to see what the Justice Department does next."

Banks sat forward. "Which is exactly why we need to move on Redmond's indictment now. We have the evidence. We have a cooperating witness. And Collins just gave us all the political cover we could possibly need."

"Maybe." Chambers's tone was noncommittal. "Or maybe we

should take a step back and make sure we're not being rushed into something we're not ready for."

"Not ready?" Banks's voice had an edge to it. "We have emails showing explicit bribery. Financial records documenting the payments. A witness who can testify under oath about the scheme. What more do we need to be ready?"

Chambers was quiet for a moment. "What we need is to make sure we're not moving forward based on political pressure. Senator Collins just made a spectacle on national television. Every news outlet is going to be demanding action. But we don't indict people because it's good PR. We indict them because we have solid cases that can win at trial."

"We do have a solid case. Redmond accepted bribes in exchange for federal earmarks. That's textbook public corruption. We could present this to a grand jury tomorrow and get an indictment."

"We need to be strategic about timing. We need to make sure every element is airtight before we charge a sitting United States senator."

Banks stood and stared out at the city through the window, her jaw tight.

"With all due respect," she said without turning around, "this is exactly the kind of hesitation that lets corrupt officials think they're untouchable. We have the evidence. We have the authority. The only thing holding us back is fear of the political fallout."

"This isn't fear, Helen. It's caution." Chambers' voice had an edge now too. "There's a difference between being aggressive and being reckless."

"And there's a difference between being cautious and being complicit through inaction." Banks turned to face him. "Every day we wait is another day Redmond remains in office with the power to obstruct our investigation. Another day the network has to regroup and mount a defense. We need to strike while the iron is hot."

The tension in the room was thick. James and I stood near the door, silently witnessing the power struggle playing out between Banks and Chambers.

Chambers stood. "I'm not authorizing you to move forward today. I want more time to review the evidence and assess our position."

"How much time?" Banks asked.

"I'll let you know."

"That's not acceptable." Banks crossed her arms. "This case is ready. I'm ready. The team is ready. We need authorization to present to a grand jury by Monday."

Chambers moved toward the door. He paused when he reached it, clearly not having realized James and I had been standing there.

"You two did good work uncovering this evidence," he said. His tone was different now. "But you also went around the chain of command to get it. You handed evidence to a senator without authorization. That's not how we operate here."

"We did what was necessary to prevent a corrupt judge from being given even more power," I said. "And it worked. The confirmation hearing was suspended. The evidence is now public. Now we have an obligation to follow through."

"Your obligation is to follow proper procedures and respect the authority structure of this office." Chambers looked at Banks. "I'll review the materials over the weekend, and we'll discuss timing on Monday. Until then, no more moves without my authorization."

He left, pulling the door closed behind him with more force than necessary.

The silence that followed was heavy. Banks returned to her desk and sat down, opening her laptop but didn't start typing. She just stared at the screen.

"Chambers is going to slow-walk this," James said. "He's going to find reasons to delay until the political pressure dies down and then quietly shelve the whole thing."

"Not if I have anything to say about it." Banks's voice was determined. "I've been doing this job for fifteen years. I know when a case is ready. This case is ready."

"But we can't present to a grand jury without authorization from our supervisor," I said.

Banks didn't say anything right away. Then she picked up her phone and dialed.

"Who are you calling?" James asked.

Banks waited while the phone rang. "Clerk's office, Fourth Circuit." A few seconds passed and she didn't look at either of us. "Yes, this is

Helen Banks with the U.S. Attorney's Office. I need to schedule an emergency grand jury hearing for Monday morning."

I felt my eyes widen. She was doing it. She was going around Chambers entirely.

"I'm aware," Banks said in response to whatever was said on the other side. "But this is a matter of significant public interest. The target is a sitting United States senator, and the evidence just became public knowledge. We need to move quickly before the trail goes cold."

Banks put the phone on speaker and set it on her desk. The hold music played softly.

"Banks," James said carefully. "If you schedule this without Chambers's approval—"

"Then I'll deal with the consequences. But I'm not going to let bureaucratic hesitation kill a case this important." She looked at both of us. "Collins took a risk going public with that evidence. We owe it to her to follow through. And more importantly, we owe it to every victim of this network's corruption to see this through."

The hold music stopped. "Ms. Banks? I can give you Monday at nine a.m. Grand Jury Room B. You'll have two hours."

"That's perfect. Thank you." Banks made a note on her legal pad. "Who do I coordinate with for witness scheduling?"

"You'll need to contact the U.S. Marshals Service for any out-of-state witnesses who need transportation. And you'll need to file your witness list by today at five p.m."

"Understood. Thank you for accommodating the tight timeline." Banks ended the call and started typing on her computer.

I blinked while she remained silent, looking out the window, then back at her. "You just scheduled a grand jury presentation without authorization."

"No … I scheduled a presentation that I have every legal right to schedule as a senior prosecutor in this office." Banks didn't look up from her screen. "Whether Chambers agrees with the timing is a separate question. But the hearing is set. Monday morning. Nine a.m."

James whistled softly. "You're really doing this."

"We're really doing this." Banks finally looked up at us. "And Alex, I want you to present the evidence to the grand jury."

I felt my stomach drop as my eyes widened. "Me? Helen, I've never presented to a grand jury before. Shouldn't you—"

"You found the evidence. You built this case. You deserve to be the one who presents it." She closed her laptop. "Besides, you know this investigation better than anyone. You've been living and breathing it for weeks. You're the right person to walk the grand jury through what we've found."

"But what if I mess it up?" The words were out of my lips before I could stop them, that familiar self-doubt always creeping its way through. "What if I don't present it properly and they don't indict? What if—"

"You won't mess it up." Banks's voice was firm. "You're a good prosecutor, Alex. And you care about this case in a way that will come through when you're presenting. That matters more than experience sometimes."

I looked at James, and he nodded encouragingly.

"Okay," I said. "I'll do it. But if Chambers finds out we scheduled this without his approval—"

"Then I'll take responsibility." Banks stood. "This is my call. My career on the line. You two are just following orders from your supervisor."

"Orders that directly contradict what Chambers just told us," James said.

"Chambers told us not to move without his authorization. But I'm a senior prosecutor with independent authority to present cases to grand juries." Banks pulled out her phone. "Now we have seventy-two hours to prepare. Alex, I need you to draft your presentation outline. James, coordinate with Marina on getting Robert Kline here for Monday. I'll handle the witness list and evidence organization."

My phone buzzed.

MARINA

Have you seen the news? It's insane. Every channel is covering the hearing. Redmond's office just released a statement denying everything.

I showed the text to Banks and James.

"Of course she's denying it," Banks said. "But by Monday afternoon, denial won't matter. She'll be facing federal charges."

James nodded, checking his watch. "I'll get going and coordinate with Marina on Kline's transport." He looked at Banks. "You're sure about this? Going around Chambers?"

"I've never been more sure of anything," Banks said. "This case is righteous. The evidence is solid. And I'm not going to let political cowardice kill it before it even gets started."

James nodded and left. The door closed behind him, and it was just Banks and me.

"Alright." She pulled up a fresh document on her computer. "Let's start outlining your presentation. We need to tell the grand jury a clear, compelling story about how Carla Redmond betrayed her oath of office for personal financial gain. And we have seventy-two hours to make sure that story is airtight."

CHAPTER
THIRTY-FIVE

MONDAY MORNING CAME TOO QUICKLY. I stood at the base of the courthouse steps, looking up at the imposing federal building. The weekend had been a blur of preparation. Seventy-two hours of outlining presentations, organizing evidence, prepping witnesses, and running through every possible question the grand jury might ask.

I had barely slept. My apartment was covered in documents and sticky notes. I had practiced my presentation so many times that James finally told me to stop or I would sound robotic.

But now it was time. 9 a.m. Grand Jury Room B.

Banks appeared beside me, carrying a litigation bag stuffed with binders. "Ready?"

"No," I admitted. "But let's do it anyway."

We climbed the steps together. Through security. Up the elevator to the fourth floor. Down a hallway lined with courtrooms until we reached a door marked "Grand Jury Room B - Authorized Personnel Only."

Banks paused with her hand on the door handle. "Remember, this isn't a trial. There's no judge. No defense attorney. Just you, me, the grand jurors, and the witnesses. Our job is to present enough evidence to establish probable cause that Redmond committed the crimes we're alleging."

"Bribery and wire fraud," I said, reciting what we had practiced all weekend.

"And honest services fraud. Don't forget that count." Banks pushed open the door.

The grand jury room was smaller than I had expected. No elevated judge's bench. There was no jury box. Just a long conference table where twenty-three citizens sat with notepads and water bottles. They ranged in age from early twenties to late seventies.

At the front of the room was a small table for the prosecutors and a single chair where witnesses would sit. A court reporter sat in the corner, ready to transcribe everything.

The grand jurors looked up as we entered. Some were curious, whereas some were clearly bored. Most were just waiting to see what this emergency session was about.

Banks set her litigation bag on the prosecutor's table and pulled out her materials. I did the same, my hands shaking as I organized my notes.

"Good morning," Banks said to the room, her voice calm and authoritative. "I'm Helen Banks, Senior Assistant United States Attorney. This is Alex Hayes, also with the U.S. Attorney's Office. We're here this morning to present evidence regarding potential criminal activity by United States Senator Carla Redmond."

A few of the grand jurors sat up straighter. The mention of a sitting senator had their attention.

"Before we begin," Banks continued, "I want to explain how this process works for those of you who may be new to grand jury service. This is not a trial. There is no judge present. There is no defense attorney. Your role as grand jurors is to determine whether there is probable cause to believe that the target of this investigation committed the crimes we will outline for you today."

She gestured to the empty witness chair. "We will present testimony from witnesses. We will show you documentary evidence. And at the end of our presentation, you will vote on whether to return an indictment. That vote is secret. You need sixteen votes out of twenty-three to indict."

One of the grand jurors, a woman in her fifties, raised her hand.

"What's the difference between probable cause and beyond a reasonable doubt?"

"Excellent question." Banks smiled. "Probable cause is a much lower standard," Banks said. "At trial, the prosecution must prove guilt beyond a reasonable doubt. But here, you only need to find that there is probable cause to believe a crime was committed. Think of it as 'more likely than not' rather than 'certainty.'"

The woman nodded and jotted down a note.

"Now," Banks said, pulling out the first exhibit. "Let me outline the case we're presenting today. Senator Carla Redmond is charged with accepting bribes in exchange for official acts. Specifically, she accepted payments totaling at least $250,000 from an entity called Gulf Coast Strategies in exchange for securing federal earmarks for construction projects in Houston, Texas."

She displayed a chart on the screen at the front of the room. It showed the flow of money from Gulf Coast to Capitol Ventures to Redmond's campaign PAC.

"The scheme worked like this," Banks continued. "Gulf Coast Strategies, a consulting firm with ties to Bayou Shipping Corporation, needed federal funding for flood control projects in Houston. These projects would benefit Bayou's shipping operations. So they approached Senator Redmond, who sits on the Appropriations Committee, and offered her money in exchange for inserting earmarks into the federal budget."

Several grand jurors were taking notes. Others just watched the screen.

"To hide the bribery, Gulf Coast funneled the money through a shell company called Capitol Ventures LLC. This company then made donations to Redmond's political action committee. In exchange, Senator Redmond used her position on the Appropriations Committee to secure $60 million in federal funding for the Houston flood control bonds."

Banks clicked to the next slide. An email. The one we had found in the DataSecure files.

"This is a corporate email from Victor Ramsey, CEO of Gulf Coast Strategies, to Senator Redmond's private email address. It was sent in

May of 2023. In it, Ramsey explicitly discusses the payment arrangement and asks Redmond to confirm her 'committee vote' on the appropriations bill."

She let the grand jurors read the email on the screen. I watched their faces. Some looked shocked. Others looked disgusted. A few looked skeptical, as if they didn't quite believe a senator would be so blatant.

"Now," Banks said, "we're going to present testimony from a cooperating witness who can explain how this scheme worked from the inside. This witness is Robert Kline, former CFO of Bayou Shipping Corporation. Mr. Kline is currently in Houston, so we'll be taking his testimony via video conference."

She nodded to me. I stood and set up the laptop that would connect us to Kline's video feed. My hands were steadier now. The nerves were fading as the adrenaline kicked in.

The screen turned on, and Robert Kline appeared, sitting in what looked like a conference room with his attorney beside him.

"Mr. Kline," Banks said, "can you see and hear us?"

"Yes, I can." His voice came through clearly.

"Please raise your right hand." Banks waited while Kline complied. "Do you swear that the testimony you are about to give is the truth, the whole truth, and nothing but the truth?"

"I do."

"Thank you. Mr. Kline, can you please state your name and your former position for the record?"

"Robert Kline. I was Chief Financial Officer of Bayou Shipping Corporation from 2018 to 2024."

"And are you testifying today pursuant to a cooperation agreement with the United States Attorney's Office?"

"Yes, I am."

Banks pulled out her notes. "Mr. Kline, I want to direct your attention to May of 2023. Did there come a time when you became aware of payments being made from Gulf Coast Strategies to Senator Carla Redmond?"

Kline nodded. "Yes. Victor Ramsey, who ran Gulf Coast, sent me an email explaining that we needed to structure payments to Capitol

Ventures LLC. He said the money would ultimately go to Redmond's PAC, but we needed to keep it looking clean for FEC compliance."

"And how much money was discussed?"

"$250,000 total. Structured in installments over several months."

"What was the purpose of these payments?"

"To secure federal earmarks for the Houston flood control project. Ramsey was very explicit about that. He said Redmond had the votes to get $60 million approved, but she needed assurance that we would support her politically."

Banks displayed another email on the screen. "Is this the email you're referring to?"

Kline leaned forward to look. "Yes, that's it."

"Can you read the highlighted portion for the grand jury?"

Kline cleared his throat. "$250K via Capitol Ventures, structured per our discussion. Need assurance on appropriations vote before we transfer. Queen is making noise but we're managing. Pawns are in position."

One of the grand jurors, a younger man, raised his hand. "What does that mean? Queen and pawns?"

Banks turned to him. "We believe those are code words. 'Queen' appears to refer to someone who was asking questions about Gulf Coast's past activities. 'Pawns' likely refers to individuals who were positioned to help cover up the scheme."

"Do you know who the queen was?" the grand juror asked.

"We have theories," Banks said carefully. "But that's part of an ongoing investigation into related matters. For purposes of this indictment, what matters is the bribery scheme itself."

She turned back to the video screen. "Mr. Kline, did you have any other communications with Victor Ramsey or Senator Redmond regarding these payments?"

"Yes. I had several phone calls with Ramsey over the summer of 2023. He kept updating me on the status of the appropriations bill. And in July, after the bill passed with the Houston earmarks included, he sent me an email saying the payments could proceed."

"Do we have that email in evidence?"

"Yes, it's Exhibit 17." Banks pulled up the document. Another email from Ramsey's Gulf Coast account. This one was even more explicit: "Appropriations bill passed. Redmond delivered. Process the Capitol Ventures transfers as discussed."

The grand jurors were fully engaged now. This wasn't theoretical corruption. This was documented, timestamped evidence of a senator selling her vote.

Banks continued questioning Kline for another twenty minutes. Walking him through the financial records. The wire transfers. The dates that lined up perfectly with key votes in the Senate Appropriations Committee. Every answer built the case stronger.

Finally, Banks said, "Thank you, Mr. Kline. I have no further questions at this time. Grand jurors, do any of you have questions for this witness?"

A few hands went up. Banks called on them one by one. They asked clarifying questions about the timeline. About whether Kline had witnessed any direct communication between Ramsey and Redmond. About whether there were other similar schemes.

Kline answered patiently. His attorney occasionally leaned in to whisper something, but mostly Kline spoke freely. He had clearly decided that cooperation was his best path forward.

After the last question was answered, Banks thanked Kline and ended the video connection. The screen went dark.

"That concludes our witness testimony," Banks said to the grand jury. "Now we're going to present the documentary evidence that corroborates Mr. Kline's testimony. Ms. Hayes will walk you through the exhibits."

She looked at me and nodded.

This was it. My moment to present. To lay out the case we had built. To convince twenty-three strangers that a United States senator had betrayed her oath of office for money.

I stood and gathered my materials. My heart was pounding, but my mind was clear.

I had spent all weekend preparing for this. I knew this evidence inside and out. I knew every email, every financial record, every piece of the puzzle.

I could do this.

I had to do this.

"Good morning," I said to the grand jury, my voice steadier than my nerves. "I'm going to walk you through the documentary evidence that proves Senator Redmond accepted bribes in exchange for official acts. We'll start with the financial records showing the flow of money from Gulf Coast Strategies to her campaign PAC."

I pulled up the first exhibit on the screen.

And began to build the case that would bring down a United States senator.

CHAPTER THIRTY-SIX

THE FIRST EXHIBIT was a spreadsheet showing wire transfers from Gulf Coast Strategies to Capitol Ventures LLC. The dates. The amounts. The routing numbers that proved the money had crossed state lines.

"This is Exhibit 1," I said, my voice growing stronger as I settled into the presentation. "Financial records from SecureMail Communications, the banking platform used by Gulf Coast Strategies. These records span from May 2023 through December 2025 and show a pattern of payments structured to avoid detection."

I highlighted the relevant columns. "On November 25, 2023, Gulf Coast transferred $150,000 to Capitol Ventures. Then in August 2024, another $100,000. And in December 2025, a final payment of $50,000. Total: $300,000."

One of the grand jurors, an older man with glasses, leaned forward. "You said earlier the total was $250,000. Which is it?"

"Good catch," I said. "The initial agreement was for $250,000. But after the appropriations bill passed with even more favorable terms than expected, Gulf Coast sent a bonus payment of $50,000. Mr. Kline's testimony addresses this in his supplemental interview, which is part of Exhibit 3."

I clicked to the next exhibit. "This is a series of SEC filings from 2006 showing Gulf Coast Strategies' acquisition of a controlling interest in Bayou Shipping Corporation. These filings establish the corporate relationship between the two entities and show that they have been operating as essentially one organization for nearly twenty years."

More clicks. More exhibits. The wiretaps came next.

"These are transcripts from court-authorized wiretaps on Victor Ramsey's phone," I explained. "In this conversation from September 2025, Ramsey uses the phrase 'bishop's path' when discussing Franklin Pearce's nomination to the Fifth Circuit. He also references 'the queen's dead drop,' which we believe refers to evidence the late Deputy Attorney General Eleanor Vance had compiled before her death."

I paused to let them read the transcript on screen. I could almost hear Ramsey's voice as I looked at the text, using that arrogant tone as he discussed judges and senators and payments as casually as someone might discuss the weather.

"Now," I said, moving to the next section of evidence, "I want to show you how all of this connects to establish probable cause for the charges we're bringing."

I pulled up a timeline graphic that Banks and I had created over the weekend. It showed the key dates in parallel tracks: Redmond's committee votes, Gulf Coast's payments, and the federal earmarks that resulted.

"May 20, 2023: Ramsey emails Redmond proposing the payment scheme. May 25, 2023: First payment of $150,000 is transferred. June 15, 2023: Redmond votes in committee to advance the appropriations bill with Houston earmarks. July 28, 2023: The bill passes the full Senate with $60 million for Houston flood control. August 3, 2023: Second payment of $100,000 is transferred."

I let the timeline speak for itself.

"This establishes the quid pro quo," I said. "Senator Redmond received money and in exchange she used her official position to secure federal funding that benefited the entities paying her. That's bribery under 18 U.S.C. Section 201."

I moved through more exhibits. More emails showing Ramsey coordinating with Redmond. More financial records showing the money flowing through shell companies. More evidence of a systematic scheme to corrupt the federal appropriations process.

By the time I finished presenting the documentary evidence, forty-five minutes had passed. My throat was dry, but I felt energized rather than exhausted.

"That concludes the documentary evidence," I said. "Do any of the grand jurors have questions?"

Nearly half the hands in the room went up.

I called on them one by one. A woman in her thirties wanted to know how we could prove the payments to Capitol Ventures were actually intended for Redmond. I walked her through the corporate structure, showing that Capitol Ventures was a shell company with no legitimate business purpose other than to funnel political donations.

A man in his forties asked about the legal standard for bribery. Did we need to prove that Redmond wouldn't have voted for the earmarks without the payments? Or just that she received payment in connection with her official acts?

"The latter," I explained. "Under federal bribery law, we don't need to prove that the official wouldn't have acted without the bribe. We only need to prove that they received something of value in exchange for or because of their official acts. The statute uses the phrase 'in return for being influenced' or 'for or because of any official act.' The causation runs both ways."

More questions followed. About the timing of payments. About whether there were other similar schemes we were investigating. About the wire fraud charges and how those differed from straight bribery.

"Wire fraud is charged because the scheme involved interstate wire communications," I explained. "The emails crossed state lines. The wire transfers moved money between states. That gives us federal jurisdiction even if the underlying fraud wouldn't otherwise be a federal crime."

A younger woman asked about the honest services fraud charges. "What does that mean exactly?"

"Honest services fraud is a specific type of wire fraud," I said. "It applies when a public official deprives citizens of their right to honest services. Senator Redmond took an oath to serve the public interest. But instead, she used her position to serve her own financial interests and those of her co-conspirators. That's a breach of her duty to provide honest services, and when that breach is carried out through interstate communications, it becomes federal wire fraud."

Banks stood up. "If I may add to that explanation," she said. "The honest services fraud statute was specifically designed to address public corruption. It recognizes that when elected officials sell their offices, they're not just taking bribes—they're depriving every citizen of the honest government they're entitled to. That's why we charge it as fraud rather than just bribery. It captures the full scope of the harm."

The grand jurors nodded. They seemed to understand.

Banks moved to the front of the room beside me. "Now, I want to walk you through the specific charges we're asking you to consider. We've prepared a draft indictment that breaks down each count and the elements we need to prove."

She pulled up the indictment on the screen. Six counts total.

"Count One: Bribery under 18 U.S.C. Section 201. This requires proof that Senator Redmond, a public official, corruptly demanded, sought, received, accepted, or agreed to receive or accept something of value in return for being influenced in the performance of an official act. The 'something of value' is the $300,000 in payments. The 'official act' is her vote and advocacy for the Houston earmarks."

She scrolled to the next count. "Count Two: Wire fraud under 18 U.S.C. Section 1343. This requires proof of a scheme to defraud and use of interstate wire communications in furtherance of that scheme. The emails and wire transfers we've shown you satisfy both elements."

"Count Three: Honest services wire fraud under 18 U.S.C. Sections 1343 and 1346. Same as Count Two but specifically focused on Redmond's breach of her duty to provide honest services to her constituents."

Banks continued through the remaining counts. Two more counts of bribery for earlier, smaller payments we had uncovered. Two more counts of wire fraud tied to those earlier schemes. And a final honest services fraud count that encompassed the full scope of Redmond's corruption from 2022 through 2025.

"To indict on any count, you need to find probable cause," Banks emphasized. "Not proof beyond a reasonable doubt. If you believe the evidence we've presented establishes probable cause for these charges, you vote to indict. If you don't believe we've met that burden, you vote not to indict."

She paused and looked around the room. "This is an important decision. We're asking you to charge a sitting United States senator with betraying her oath of office. That's not something to be taken lightly. But we believe that the evidence speaks for itself. Senator Carla Redmond sold her office for personal gain. She deprived you—all of you—of the honest government you deserve. And she broke federal law in doing so."

Banks let that statement hang in the air for a moment. Then she clicked to the final slide. A summary of the evidence tying Redmond to each count.

She went through each count methodically. Summarizing the evidence. Connecting the dots. Making it clear that this wasn't a close case. This was overwhelming evidence of systematic corruption.

When she finished, Banks closed her laptop. "That concludes our presentation. Ms. Hayes and I will now leave so you can deliberate in private. A foreperson will be appointed to oversee your discussion and conduct the vote. You need at least twelve votes on each count to return a true bill—that's what we call an indictment. If you don't reach twelve votes, that count fails and no charges are filed on that count."

"Any final questions before we leave?" I asked.

Silence. The grand jurors looked at each other. A few were already pulling their notepads closer, ready to start deliberating.

"Alright then," Banks said. "Take your time and deliberate thoroughly. Thank you for your service."

We gathered our materials and headed for the door. As we stepped into the hallway, I felt the gravity of what we had just done.

We had presented charges against a United States senator. We had laid out evidence of corruption that reached into the highest levels of government. And now, twenty-three ordinary citizens were going to decide whether that evidence was enough to move forward.

Banks set her litigation bag on a bench in the hallway and sat down beside it. "Now we wait."

"How long does it usually take?" I asked.

"Depends. Sometimes fifteen minutes if the case is overwhelming. Sometimes hours if there's disagreement." She pulled out her phone. "But given the profile of this target and the amount of evidence we presented, I'd guess at least an hour. Maybe two."

I sat down beside her. My hands were shaking now that the adrenaline was fading. "Did we do enough? Did I present it well enough?"

"You did great, Alex. Better than great." Banks smiled. "You were clear, confident, and thorough. The grand jurors understood the evidence because you explained it well. Now we just have to trust that they'll do the right thing."

We sat in silence for a few minutes. Other prosecutors and court staff passed by in the hallway. A few gave us curious looks, clearly wondering what case was important enough for an emergency Monday morning grand jury session.

My phone buzzed.

James: *How's it going?*

Me*: Presentation done. Grand jury is deliberating now.*

James*: You did great. I know you did. Call me when you have news.*

I put my phone away and leaned my head back against the wall.

Somewhere in that room, twenty-three people were deciding whether a United States senator would face criminal charges.

And all Banks and I could do was wait.

CHAPTER
THIRTY-SEVEN

AFTER ABOUT TWENTY minutes of sitting in the hallway, Banks stood and stretched. "There's a conference room down the hall we can use. No point in sitting out here on uncomfortable benches for what could be hours."

I agreed and followed her down the corridor to a small conference room with a table, six chairs, and a window overlooking the city. Banks dropped her litigation bag on the table and pulled out her phone to check messages.

I couldn't sit still. I paced to the window and stared out at the buildings below. Somewhere in this city, Senator Carla Redmond was going about her day, possibly unaware that a grand jury was deciding whether to charge her with federal crimes.

"You need to relax," Banks said without looking up from her phone. "Pacing isn't going to make them deliberate faster."

"I know. I just—" I turned away from the window. "What if we didn't present enough? What if they don't think the evidence is sufficient?"

"Then we didn't do our jobs correctly, and we deserve the no bill." Banks finally looked at me. "But we did do our jobs correctly. Try to think about something other than what's happening in that room."

I nodded and sat down, opening my laptop with the intention of checking emails. But my mind kept replaying the presentation. Had I explained the financial records clearly enough? Had I connected the dots between the payments and Redmond's votes? Had I —

"Stop second-guessing yourself," Banks said. "I can literally hear you spiraling from over here."

I smiled despite my anxiety. "Am I that obvious?"

She let out a breath. "You're chewing your thumbnail. You only do that when you're overthinking."

My phone lit up with a news alert. I glanced at the screen.

The contents had my stomach roiling.

"Helen," I said quietly. "You need to see this."

I turned my phone so she could read the notification: "BREAKING NEWS: Senate Judiciary Committee Votes to Advance Pearce Nomination Despite Corruption Allegations."

Banks took my phone and read the full article. Her features darkened as her eyes moved across the screen. " Collins presented all that evidence, and they're still moving forward with his confirmation."

"How is that possible?" I stood and moved to look over her shoulder at the screen. "We gave her proof that Pearce is connected to Gulf Coast. That his family profited from the same network that was bribing Redmond. How can they just ignore that?"

Banks handed my phone back. "Because the evidence against Pearce is circumstantial. It shows connections and financial ties, but it doesn't show him directly participating in criminal activity. The committee can claim they're evaluating his judicial qualifications, not his family's business dealings."

"That's bullshit. This is exactly what we were worried about. The network protecting its own."

"Maybe. Or maybe it's just politics." Banks rubbed her eyes. "The committee is majority Republican. Pearce is a conservative judge. They're not going to torpedo his nomination based on implications and suspicious timing. They want another conservative on the Fifth Circuit, and they're willing to overlook questionable connections to get it. We've watched Supreme Court justices get appointed with far worse allegations."

I slumped back in my seat. "So, after everything we did. None of it mattered?"

"It mattered. We made it a lot harder for Pearce to operate, even if he does get confirmed. And we laid groundwork for future charges if we can develop more direct evidence."

"But he's going to be a federal appellate judge."

"Probably, yes." Banks looked at the article again. "The committee vote was 12-10. Strictly along party lines. It'll go to the full Senate for a vote, and unless something dramatic changes, he'll be confirmed within the week."

I felt sick. All that work. All that risk. Going around Chambers. Defying orders. Giving evidence to Collins. And Pearce was still going to get exactly what he wanted.

"How could they confirm someone like that?" I asked. "After everything we uncovered? How could they possibly justify putting someone with his connections into a circuit court seat?"

"Because the evidence doesn't directly implicate him in crimes," Banks said. "It implicates his brother-in-law. His family trust. Companies he had financial ties to. But not Pearce himself, acting with corrupt intent. That's the line the committee is drawing. They're saying his judicial record is excellent and his personal conduct has been above reproach, so they're separating him from the alleged criminal activity of people and entities around him."

"That's incredibly convenient for him."

"It is. But it's also technically defensible from their perspective." Banks closed her laptop. "Politics isn't about truth, Alex. It's about what you can prove and what you can spin. The committee is spinning this as an attack on a qualified nominee by partisan opponents. They're accusing Collins of political theater. And half the country will believe them."

There was a knock on the conference room door. We both jumped.

"Ms. Banks?" A clerk poked her head in. "The grand jury has reached their decision. They're ready for you."

My heart started racing again. Banks gathered her materials and stood. "Alright. This is it."

We walked back down the hall to Grand Jury Room B. The door was closed. The clerk gestured for us to wait.

"How does this work?" I whispered to Banks. "Do they announce the decision in front of us?"

"The foreperson will hand me the decision form," Banks explained quietly. "It'll show whether they voted to indict on each count. If they returned a true bill, meaning they voted to indict, I'll read it aloud and thank them for their service. If they returned a no bill, meaning they declined to indict, I'll accept their decision and we're done."

"And if it's a no bill?"

"Then we go back to the drawing board. Figure out what evidence we didn't present effectively or what elements we failed to prove. And decide whether to try again with a different grand jury or drop the case entirely."

"But the evidence is overwhelming," I said. "There's no way they vote not to indict."

"Don't assume anything." Banks's voice was firm. "Grand juries are unpredictable. They're ordinary citizens, not lawyers. They might not understand all the legal nuances. They might be uncomfortable charging a senator even when the evidence is clear. They might just fuck up the vote count. Anything can happen."

The door opened. The foreperson, a woman in her sixties wearing a navy cardigan, stepped out, a folder tight against her ribcage.

"The grand jury has completed its deliberations," she said. "We're ready to deliver our decision."

Banks and I followed her back into the grand jury room. The twenty-three jurors sat at the long table. Some looked relieved that the process was over. Others looked troubled. A few wouldn't meet our eyes.

The foreperson walked to the front of the room and handed the folder to Banks. "This is the grand jury's decision on all counts presented."

Banks opened the folder. I watched her face, looking for any sign of what the decision was.

Her expression went blank, then her features tightened. Finally, something that looked like controlled anger appeared.

She closed the folder slowly and looked at the foreperson. "The grand jury has declined to return a true bill on all counts?"

"That's correct."

My brain struggled to process those words. Declined to return a true bill. On *all* counts? That meant no indictment. That meant the grand jury had looked at all our evidence—the emails, the financial records, Kline's testimony, everything—and decided it wasn't enough.

Banks kept her voice neutral. "May I ask how the votes broke down?"

"The votes were close on most counts," the foreperson said. "But we did not reach the twelve votes required on any single count. The closest was Count One, which received eleven votes to indict."

Eleven votes. One vote short. One single person had stood between us and an indictment of Senator Carla Redmond.

Banks nodded once. "Thank you for your service and your careful consideration of the evidence. This grand jury is dismissed."

The jurors began gathering their things. Banks and I walked out of the room in silence. In the hallway, she set down her bag and just stood there, staring at the wall.

"How?" I finally managed to ask. "How did we not get twelve votes?"

"I don't know." Banks's voice was flat. "I know what I said to you just moments before, but realistically, I didn't think we wouldn't even get one count. The evidence was solid. The testimony was clear. I don't understand how they couldn't see it."

"Can we try again? Present to a different grand jury?"

"Technically, yes. But it would look desperate. Like we're shopping for a grand jury that will give us the result we want." Banks picked up her bag. "And Chambers is going to lose his mind when he finds out we presented without his authorization and came back with a no bill."

I had been so focused on the presentation and the deliberation that I had almost forgotten we had gone around Chambers to be here.

And now we had nothing to show for our insubordination.

"What do we do now?" I asked.

Banks went quiet. When she finally spoke, her voice was tired. "We go back to the office. We figure out what went wrong. We decide if there's enough evidence to try again or if we need to drop the case."

"Drop the case? After everything we found?"

"A no bill from a grand jury is a pretty clear signal, Alex." Banks started walking toward the elevator. "It means either our evidence isn't as strong as we thought, or we didn't present it effectively, or the grand jurors just weren't willing to indict a sitting senator regardless of the evidence. Any of those scenarios is a problem for moving forward."

We rode the elevator down in silence.

I looked down at my phone.

James: *How did it go?*

I stared at the message.

Me: *No bill. Grand jury declined to indict.*

The three dots appeared immediately, then disappeared, then appeared again.

James: *What? How is that possible?*

Me: *We don't know. Heading back to office now.]]*

Banks and I descended into the Metro station and found a spot against the northernmost wall to wait for the train.

"You know what the worst part is?" I said quietly. "Pearce is about to be confirmed to the Fifth Circuit. Redmond is going to remain in the Senate. The network wins. Everything we did was for nothing."

"It's not for nothing." Banks's voice was firm despite her obvious disappointment. "We exposed connections. We gathered evidence. We made it harder for them to operate in the shadows. That matters even if we didn't get the outcome we wanted today."

The train arrived. We boarded and found seats near the back of the car. I stared out the window as the tunnel walls blurred past.

One vote. We had been one vote short of indicting a corrupt senator. One person out of twenty-three had looked at all that evidence and decided it wasn't enough.

And now we had to go back to the office and explain to Chambers why we had defied his direct order and ended up with nothing.

BANKS and I returned to the DOJ building in silence. The defeat was crushing. We had presented overwhelming evidence—emails, financial records, witness testimony—and still come away with nothing. A no bill from the grand jury felt like a referendum not just on our case, but on our competence as prosecutors.

We took the elevator to the fifth floor and walked down the hall to Banks's office. Banks dropped her bag on her desk and sank into her chair. She stared at her computer screen without turning it on.

I stood still, frozen in front of the door. "How do twenty-three people look at all that explicit evidence and decide it's not enough?"

"Hell, I don't know." Banks's voice was hollow. "Maybe we didn't present it well enough. Maybe the jurors didn't understand the legal standards. Maybe—"

"Maybe someone got to them."

Banks glared at me. "We can't start assuming grand jury corruption just because we didn't get the win we wanted."

"But what if it's true? What if the network has reach even into grand jury rooms? What if they knew exactly which juror to pressure or threaten or—"

"Stop." Banks held up her hand. "That's conspiracy thinking. That's how you lose perspective and start seeing patterns that aren't there."

Wanting to argue, something in her tone made me pause. She was right. I was spiraling. Looking for explanations that fit my narrative rather than accepting the simple truth that sometimes prosecutors lose even when they have strong evidence.

But this didn't feel like a normal loss.

"You told me earlier to let the outcomes play out," I said. "To see what happens and adjust accordingly. So what does this outcome tell us?"

Banks was quiet for a moment. "It tells us that either our evidence wasn't as strong as we thought, or that there are factors at play we don't fully understand."

"Factors like someone protecting someone," I said. "Think about it. We've been hitting wall after wall on this investigation. Chambers trying to slow us down. The confirmation hearing getting suspended, but Pearce still advancing. And now a grand jury declining to indict despite overwhelming evidence. What if it's all connected? What if there's a single thread running through all of this?"

"A single thread implying what? That Chambers is part of the network? That federal grand jurors are being corrupted? That goes beyond—"

A knock on the door interrupted her. We both turned to see Chambers standing in the doorway. His expression was unreadable.

"Helen, can I speak with you for a moment?"

Banks stood. "Of course."

"Actually," Chambers said, looking at me, "Alex should go home for the day. You both look exhausted, and I think some rest would do everyone good."

"I'm fine," I said. "If this is about the grand jury presentation, I want to be part of the conversation."

"It's not about that. Not directly." Chambers stepped into the office. "Alex, you've been working nonstop for weeks. You were up all night this weekend prepping. You just spent three hours presenting to a grand jury. Go home. Get some rest. We'll regroup tomorrow."

There was something in his tone that wasn't quite a suggestion. More like an order dressed up as concern.

Banks nodded at me. "He's right. You should go home. I'll call you later, and we can discuss next steps."

I wanted to protest, to insist on being part of whatever conversation they were about to have. But the look Banks gave me said, *Don't fight this right now.*

"Okay," I said, gathering my bag. "I'll be available if you need anything."

Chambers stepped aside to let me pass. As I walked out of the office, I heard him close the door behind me. Through the frosted glass, I could see their silhouettes. Chambers's voice was low, and I couldn't make out the words, but his body language was tense.

I walked away feeling like I was being dismissed. Sent away so the adults could talk. It rankled, but I was too exhausted to fight it.

The Metro ride home felt longer than usual. I kept replaying the grand jury presentation in my mind. Looking for mistakes. For moments where I could have been clearer or more persuasive. For the point where I lost that one crucial vote.

But I couldn't find it. The presentation had been solid. The evidence had been clear. There was no obvious mistake that explained the no bill.

Which left only the uncomfortable possibility that Banks was right —that sometimes you just lose even when you shouldn't.

Or the even more uncomfortable possibility that I was right, despite what she had said, and someone had interfered.

At my apartment building I wearily climbed the stairs to my floor. The corridor was empty. I unlocked my door and stepped inside.

I set my bag by the door and pulled out my phone and called James.

He answered on the second ring. "Hey. Are you okay?"

"Not really." I walked to my couch and collapsed onto it. "I don't understand how this happened, James. The evidence was there."

" I've been wracking my brain about it too." There was noise in the background. Traffic. "Listen, I'm going to come over. I'll bring food. You shouldn't be alone right now."

"You don't have to—"

"I want to. Besides, you probably haven't eaten all day." A horn honked on his end. "I'll be there in thirty minutes. Okay?"

"Actually, wait," I said. "Can I ask you something? About the USB drive?"

"The chess piece?" he asked. "Yeah, of course."

"I've been trying to guess the password for days. It has to be something I know, but I've tried birthdays, addresses, dates that mean something in my life. Nothing's worked. But you know me better than almost anyone. If you had to pick a password that I could guess, what would it be?"

James was quiet for a moment. "What drives you, Alex? What's always on your mind? That would be the natural thing for you to choose, right?"

"I've tried Eleanor Vance's name and date of death. I've tried the word 'justice.' I've tried the names of every case I've worked on. Nothing."

"Maybe it's not what drives you. Maybe it's what drives whoever created the password." James paused. "Someone sent you that chess piece, labeled a folder on the drive 'To Alex.' They wanted you specifically to find this. So what would they think is important to you? What would they assume you'd never forget?"

I thought about what he said for a moment.

"I'm at the counter. Gotta grab the food. I'll be there in a minute."

"Of course. See you soon."

Hanging up, I set the phone on the coffee table, the noise almost echoed through my empty apartment. I grabbed the remote and turned on the TV just for the background noise. A news channel was covering the Pearce nomination. Talking heads debating whether the corruption allegations should disqualify him or whether his judicial record should be the only consideration.

I turned the TV back off.

Instead, I went to my bedroom and changed out of my suit into sweatpants and a t-shirt. My body settled into the fabric, warming against the soft cotton.

Back in the living room, I stood in front of my bookshelf where I had placed the antique chess piece disguising the USB drive. I picked it up and turned it over in my palm as I walked out of the room.

I sat down at my kitchen table, opened my laptop, inserted the chess piece drive, and double-clicked on the "To Alex" folder. The password prompt mocked me.

"You had to pick out a password that I could guess, right?" I said aloud, as if whoever had created this folder could hear me. "You wanted me to find this. You wanted me to see whatever's inside. So what would you choose?"

I thought about my mother. About the things that drove her. The cases she'd worked on. The causes she'd believed in. The people she'd tried to protect.

Justice. Truth. Protecting the vulnerable.

But those were abstract concepts. Not passwords.

What would be the natural thing for me to choose? What was always on my mind? What drove everything I did?

My mother's death.

The date I lost her. The day that defined my entire childhood and set me on this path.

I double-clicked on the "To Alex" folder. The password prompt appeared.

My fingers hovered over the keyboard. My mother had been declared a missing person on April 15, 2003. I had been eight years old. The date was seared into my memory. Every year on that day, I thought about her. Wondered what had really happened. Who had killed her and why?

I typed: 04152003

Hit enter.

The password prompt disappeared.

And the folder opened.

My breath caught in my throat. For a moment I stared at the screen, unable to move.

My hands started trembling. I pressed them flat against the table to steady them, but it didn't help. The shaking spread through my whole body.

Inside the folder were dozens of files. Documents. Audio recordings. Video files. A comprehensive archive.

Tears welled in the corners of my eyes, but I blinked them back. Not yet. I needed to see what was here first, to understand what this was.

I started clicking through files at random, my hands still shaking so badly that I could barely control the mouse. My heart was pounding, vision blurred as I tried to focus on the screen.

The first document I opened was entitled "To Alex Hayes - Read This First."

I opened it and started reading.

Alex,

If you're reading this, then I'm dead and you've figured out the password. I'm sorry to be so morbid, but we both know the people I'm investigating don't leave loose ends.

I know about your mother. I know what happened to her in 2003 when she got too close to exposing this network. And I know you're the only person I can trust with this information.

I've been investigating a corruption network that operates through Gulf Coast Strategies, Bayou Shipping, and a web of shell companies. This network has been active for decades. It reaches into the Senate, the federal judiciary, and the Department of Justice itself. Your mother discovered it twenty-two years ago. They silenced her for it.

Now I've uncovered the same thing. And I'm documenting everything before they do to me what they did to her.

In these files, you'll find evidence of bribery, conspiracy, and obstruction of justice. You'll find proof that Senator Carla Redmond has been taking payments for years. You'll find documentation of Franklin Pearce's involvement in protecting the network. And you'll find something else, something I haven't been able to fully verify but that I believe to be true.

There is someone higher than all of them. Someone who sits above even the operational leaders like Victor Ramsey. Someone in a position of significant authority who has been orchestrating this for decades. I don't know who it is. But the clues are in these files.

I'm leaving this for you because you have every reason to see this through. Because you lost your mother to these people. Because you're a federal prose-

cutor who can actually do something with this evidence. And because I believe you won't stop until you bring them all down.

Be careful, Alex. Trust no one in positions of power until you're certain of their loyalty. The network's reach is wider than you can imagine.

Finish what your mother started. Finish what I couldn't.

—Eleanor Vance

I sat back from the computer, my whole body vibrating, breaths shallow. Eleanor Vance had left this for me. Had compiled evidence knowing she was going to die. Had hidden it in a chess piece with my mother's supposed death date as the password because she knew I would be the one to figure it out.

She had known about my mother and about the network. She'd investigated the same conspiracy that had gotten Katherine Hayes killed twenty-two years earlier.

And now she was dead too.

There was a knock at my apartment door. I wiped my eyes quickly and stood. James was here with food like he had promised.

I walked to the door, my mind still reeling from what I had just read.

"James, you have to see this," I said as I pulled open the door. "The USB drive unlocked. Vance left me—"

I stopped.

The person standing in my doorway wasn't James.

It was a man I didn't recognize at first. Until I did.

Tall. Dark coat. Cold eyes.

He held a cloth in his hand. Before I could scream, could move, he lunged forward and pressed the cloth over my mouth and nose.

The smell was chemical. I tried to fight back, to pull away, but his grip was like iron. His other arm wrapped around me, pinning my arms to my sides.

The world started to blur. My legs went weak.

I tried to hold my breath, but my lungs burned. I gasped involuntarily, and the chemical smell flooded my system.

The edges of my vision darkened.

My laptop. The files. Vance's letter. James was coming. Someone would find —

The thought dissolved as consciousness slipped away.

The last thing I saw was the man's cold eyes watching me collapse.

Then nothing.

CHAPTER
THIRTY-NINE

I WOKE to the sound of voices. Low. Male. I couldn't make out their discussion through the fog in my head.

My mouth tasted like chemicals. My head pounded. I tried to move and realized my hands were zip-tied behind me. I was slumped in a wooden chair. I blinked away the fog and tried to lift my head up. It was heavy on my neck. I swiveled to look left and right until my surroundings became clear. The space had concrete floors, high ceilings, and harsh industrial lighting. Some kind of warehouse.

The voices were getting clearer now. I forced myself to keep my breathing slow and steady. I closed my eyes, pretending I was still unconscious.

"—should have just taken the laptop," one man said. "This is messy."

"We needed to know what she read first," the other replied. "What she knows."

Footsteps approached. I couldn't pretend anymore. I opened my eyes fully.

Three men stood in front of me. The man in the dark coat who had grabbed me stood next to another I didn't recognize. Franklin Pearce stood in the center.

"Ms. Hayes." Pearce's voice was calm, almost pleasant. "I admit, you're a very resourceful woman. You really tried to mess things up for us, didn't you?"

I didn't respond, schooling my expression against my racing heart.

Pearce walked closer. "All this time I thought James was on our side. Thought he was keeping us informed about your investigation like he was supposed to." He gestured to the man in the dark coat. "And then Shaw here goes and sees James helping you."

My stomach dropped. James? He was working with them?

"He'll have his deeds to answer for," Pearce continued. "Betraying the network after everything we've done for him. After all the years he's been part of this."

The words came out before I could stop them. "James was part of your network?"

"The past tense is important there. Apparently, he developed feelings for you. Let those feelings compromise his judgment." Pearce shook his head. "Very disappointing. We had such high hopes for him."

My mind was reeling. James had been part of this? Part of the network that killed my mother and Vance? But then he'd helped me? Turned against them?

"Eleanor Vance made the same mistake many people do," Pearce said, his tone almost conversational. "She thought she could turn against us and live to tell about it. But the irony is that Vance had been one of us for years."

"What?" I stared at him. "Vance was part of the network?"

"Oh yes. Eleanor was quite helpful, actually. She understood how the system worked. Helped us identify problems before they became threats. Told us which investigations to worry about and which would fizzle out on their own." Pearce pulled over a crate and sat down, resting his elbows on his knees like we were having a casual conversation. "Eleanor took payments just like Redmond does now. She had her own role to play in the conspiracy."

My wrists ached against the zip-ties. "You're lying."

"I'm really not. It's all documented. Eleanor was complicit for years. She helped us operate in the shadows. Helped us avoid scrutiny." Pearce's expression hardened. "And then she tried to flip. Tried to broker a deal with the feds. Bring down the network in exchange for immunity for her own crimes."

"That's why you killed her."

"Let's say we cleaned up a problem. Just like we did with your mother twenty-two years ago." He watched my reaction carefully.

"Vance had access to a lot of problematic files," Pearce continued. "And then she tried to flip to bring us down, well. That's when she became a liability we couldn't afford."

"So you murdered her."

"We eliminated a threat. And we thought we'd recovered all the evidence she'd compiled. But apparently she was smarter than we gave her credit for. She hid copies. Put them in that chess piece and had it delivered to you specifically."

There was a crash from somewhere in the warehouse. Glass shattering. All three men turned toward the sound.

"Check it out," Pearce ordered.

The other two men moved toward the noise, pulling weapons from their waistbands. Pearce remained focused on me, his hand moving to his jacket where I could see the outline of a gun.

There was more crashing followed by shouting. Then the sound of doors being kicked in from multiple directions.

"FBI! Hands in the air!"

The warehouse exploded with activity. Tactical teams poured in from every entrance. Red laser sights cut through the dim lighting. Agents in tactical gear surrounded us with weapons raised.

James stood at the front of the team, leading the breach. He had his gun drawn. FBI credentials hung around his neck. His expression was hard and focused as he aimed directly at Pearce.

"Hands in the air! Now!" James's voice carried command authority I'd never heard from him before. "Drop any weapons and get on the ground!"

Pearce's hand had been moving toward his jacket. He froze now. Slowly raised his hands.

Agents swarmed forward. Within seconds, they had Pearce face down on the ground, cuffing him.

James ran to me, holstering his weapon. He pulled a knife and cut through the zip ties on my wrists.

"Are you okay?" He took my hands in his, helping me to my feet. "Did they hurt you?"

I stared at him. Trying to process what I was seeing. James was FBI? James had just led a tactical team to rescue me?

"I don't understand," I managed to say. "Pearce said you were part of the network. That you'd been working for them. That you—"

"I'll explain everything," James said. "But first, let's get you out of here and to a hospital. You've been exposed to chloroform. You need to be checked out."

He wrapped an arm around me as my legs threatened to give out. Led me toward the warehouse exit where more emergency vehicles were pulling up.

I looked back at Pearce being hauled away in handcuffs.

He had confessed. Admitted to killing Vance. Told me about the network. Revealed that Vance had been corrupt before trying to flip.

And now he was in custody.

But I still had so many questions.

Starting with: who the hell was James Holloway, really?

CHAPTER
FORTY

THE HOSPITAL ROOM was too bright. White walls. White sheets. White ceiling tiles with fluorescent lights that made my head throb worse than it already did.

I lay in the bed with an IV in my arm and monitors chirping beside me. The doctors had said I was lucky. Just a bad bruise on my head where I'd hit something when Shaw grabbed me. They wanted to keep me overnight to be safe.

Staring at the ceiling, I tried not to think about everything that had happened. Pearce's confession. The revelation about Vance's corruption. James leading an FBI tactical team to rescue me.

James.

There was a soft knock on the door and I turned my head to see him standing in the doorway holding a bouquet of flowers. Yellow roses. My favorite, though I couldn't remember ever telling him that.

"Can I come in?" he asked, his voice low.

I wanted to say no. Wanted to tell him to leave and never come back. But I also desperately needed answers.

I swallowed against my dry throat. "Yeah."

He entered, set the flowers on the table beside my bed, pulled a chair close and sat down. For a long moment, neither of us spoke.

"How are you feeling?" he finally asked.

"Like I was kidnapped and drugged and then told by my kidnappers that my boyfriend and man that I loved was part of a criminal network that killed my mother." My voice came out flat. "How do you think I'm feeling?"

"Fair enough." He looked down at his hands. "Alex, I need to explain. I need you to understand—"

"And you're FBI."

He took a breath in and exhaled. "Yes. I'm an FBI agent. I've been working to uncover the network for the last five years." He met my eyes. "I was assigned to get close to you. To monitor your investigation into the network. The Bureau thought you might be able to get information on the trafficking ring that we couldn't access through traditional channels."

A deep pang hit my chest, distracting me from any pain that lingered in my body. "The FBI informant from the Torres trial. The one who leaked all of this in the first place. Was that you?"

He nodded. "A well-placed anonymous tip was what set this into motion, yes."

"So everything between us. Everything we had. It was an assignment?"

"It started that way," James admitted. His voice was raw. "I was told to establish a relationship with you. To gain your trust. See what you uncovered in your investigation. That was the job."

"And you did your job so well." Bitterness crept into my tone.

"Alex, please listen. Yes, you were a target for the FBI. But my feelings for you developed, and they were real. They *are* real. What we have isn't fake. I swear to you."

I wanted to believe him. God, I wanted to believe him so badly it hurt. But how could I trust anything he said now?

I couldn't look him in the eye. "James, you've been lying to me for months."

"I did. And I'm sorry. But I also helped you. I encouraged your investigation. I went with you to Senator Collins. I helped you crack the USB drive password." He leaned forward. "If I was really just working for the Bureau, I would have tried to slow you down. To keep you from getting too close. But I didn't do that. I helped you because I believed in what you were doing."

"All while making me feel insane for thinking there was a conspiracy in the first place. You used me to uncover evidence they could use."

"Maybe at first. But not when I realized how deep this conspiracy went." His hands clenched into fists. "When I found your apartment empty tonight, when I realized they'd taken you, I thought I was going to lose you. I pulled every string I had. Called in every favor. Got a tactical team mobilized in under an hour. That wasn't the Bureau directing me. That was me trying to save the woman I love."

Closing my eyes, I felt tears slip out. I felt very betrayed. Very shaken. I didn't know how to process any of this.

"I don't know how I feel about this," I said quietly. "Don't know what to think. I need time and space to figure this out."

"I understand." James's voice was heavy with his own pain. "Take all the time you need. I'll wait."

"What will you do?" I opened my eyes to look at him. "Will you go back to Texas? Back to your normal FBI work?"

"I don't know." He rubbed his face, his eyes rimmed with dark circles. "This case is still open. Pearce is in custody, but there are others involved. Redmond. Chambers potentially. The whole network."

"Chambers?" The name made me sit up a little straighter in the bed. "Do you think Chambers is part of this?"

"I don't know. But his behavior has been suspicious. The way he tried to slow down your investigation. The way he hesitated on the Redmond indictment. It's worth looking into."

I thought about that. About how Chambers had been reluctant to move forward. How he'd sent me home right after the grand jury no bill only for me to be kidnapped. How he'd tried to keep us from presenting.

"Alex, you should embrace this," James said. "This opportunity. You could be an informant officially. Work with the FBI to bring down the rest of the network. It's what you wanted to investigate anyway."

I stared at him. "You're asking me to become an FBI informant?"

"I'm saying you have a chance to finish what your mother started. What Vance tried to do. You could work with us to expose everyone involved and bring them to justice."

"I don't know." The words didn't feel like enough in this moment, but they were all I had. "I need to figure it out. I need time to think about whether I want to be part of this anymore. Any of this."

"Any of this meaning the investigation?" he asked, his eyes boring into me. "Or us?"

"Both. All of it." I turned away from him. "I'm tired, James. So tired of not knowing who to trust. Of feeling like everyone around me has secrets. Of being hurt by the people I thought loved me. I just need time."

"Okay." He stood up. "I'll give you time."

The door opened, and Banks walked in. She looked exhausted but relieved when she saw I was awake.

"How are you doing?" she asked, coming to stand on the other side of my bed.

"I've been better." I managed a weak smile.

Banks glanced at James, then back at me. "Can I have a minute alone with Alex?"

James nodded. "Of course. I should go check in with my team anyway. Make sure all the reports are being filed correctly." He looked at me. "I'll be around if you need anything. Just call."

He left, closing the door quietly behind him.

Banks sat in the chair James had just left. She took my hand and squeezed.

"He told you," she said. It wasn't a question.

I recoiled, my heart stopping. "You knew? You knew he was FBI?"

She placed her hand back in her lap. "I suspected. Some of his behavior didn't add up. The way he always seemed to know things before we told him. The way he had access to resources that didn't make sense for his position." Banks sighed. "But I didn't know for sure until tonight."

I shook my head. "He says his feelings for me are real. That it wasn't all an act."

"Do you believe him?"

"I don't know what to believe anymore." I closed my eyes, almost unable to open them from exhaustion. "I just want to sleep. I want to wake up and have this all be over."

"Sleep, then," Banks said softly. "I'll be here when you wake up. We can figure everything out then."

My body began to sink into the bed, my mind drifting to somewhere outside the room.

Before I let it take over completely, I mumbled, "Helen?"

"Yeah?"

"Thank you. For believing me. For helping me investigate even when everyone else thought I was crazy."

"Always, Alex. Always."

I heard footsteps. The door opening. A nurse's voice.

"I'm sorry, but visiting hours are over. You'll need to leave now."

"Of course." Banks squeezed my hand one more time. "Get some rest. I'll see you in the morning."

I drifted off before I heard the door close. Into darkness. Into sleep I desperately needed. Into dreams where nothing was as it seemed and everyone wore masks I couldn't see through. And into a nightmare where they pulled them off and weren't who I thought they were.

CHAPTER FORTY-ONE

I WOKE to sunlight streaming through the hospital window and the sound of someone snoring softly beside my bed. I opened my eyes to see my dad sitting in the chair next to me. He was leaning back with his arms crossed, head tilted to one side, clearly having fallen asleep while keeping watch.

"Dad?" My voice was hoarse.

His eyes opened. He straightened in the chair and cleared his throat. "Hey, kiddo. How are you feeling?"

"Like I got kidnapped and chloroformed." I tried to sit up. My head still throbbed, but the fluids in my IV aided any lingering discomfort. "What are you doing here?"

"James called me last night. Told me what happened. I took a red-eye to get here as fast as I could." Dad reached over and took my hand, his grip warm, solid, and familiar. I almost cried at his touch. "I was scared as hell, Alex."

"I'm okay. Really. Just a little banged up."

"The doctors said you can check out this morning. They want you to rest, but they don't think you need to stay here." Another squeeze of my hand again. "I figured you'd want to go back to your apartment. Get some real sleep in your own bed."

"Yeah, that does sound good."

James must have brought clothes from my apartment, because

there was a duffle bag in the corner of the room with a fresh outfit. Once I was out of bed and changed, a nurse came in with discharge paperwork and instructions about monitoring for concussion symptoms.

Twenty minutes later, we were in a cab heading back to my apartment, slowly navigating through morning rush hour traffic. The sidewalks were filled with pedestrians going about their daily lives, unaware that a federal judge had just been arrested for kidnapping and murder.

"James explained everything to me," Dad said, keeping his voice down. "About being FBI."

That surprised me. I wasn't sure how to process how open James was being with all of this; with how many secrets he'd kept from me since the first day we met.

I toyed with the fabric on my pants. "What did you think? About him telling you that?"

"Honestly? I wanted to punch him. Still kind of do." Dad's jaw was tight. "But he saved your life last night. Led that tactical team straight to you. So I'm conflicted."

"Me too," I said softly.

At my apartment building, yellow crime scene tape stretched across my doorway, but the door itself was unlocked. We ducked under the tape and went inside.

The apartment looked like it had been ransacked. Drawers pulled open. Couch cushions askew. Books knocked off shelves. The FBI had clearly searched for evidence after I was taken.

But what made my stomach drop was the kitchen table.

It was empty.

The white chess piece USB drive was gone. My laptop was gone. All the files I had opened. All the evidence Vance had compiled. Everything.

"No." I rushed to the table as if looking closer would somehow make the items reappear. "No, no, no. It was right here. The USB drive. My laptop. All of it."

Dad came up behind me. "What's missing?"

"Everything. The chess piece with all of Vance's evidence. My computer that had the files open. They took it all." I spun around, looking at the rest of the apartment. "Did I have a backup? Did I save anything to the cloud?"

But I knew the answer. I had just opened the drive. Had just read Vance's letter. Had been about to start going through the other files when Shaw showed up at my door.

I hadn't managed to make a backup. Hadn't copied anything. Hadn't done anything to preserve the evidence before it was stolen.

"Could the FBI have taken it?" Dad asked. "As evidence?"

" James would have told me if they had it. He would have mentioned it at the hospital." I gripped the edge of my kitchen table. "Someone took it. Either while I was being held or right after. Someone who wanted to make sure that evidence never saw the light of day."

Dad rested a hand on my shoulder. "What was on it? What did this Vance person document?"

I didn't turn to look at him. "I don't know. I only read one file. A letter explaining that she had been part of the network. That she tried to flip." The next words caught in my throat. "And she knew Mom had been investigating them and was killed for it."

"Alex, I know this is devastating. But you're alive. That's what matters. Evidence can be recreated. Files can be recovered. But I can't get my daughter back if something happens to her."

"I know. You're right. I just …" I put my head in my hands. "I was so close. Vance left that evidence specifically for me. Used Mom's disappearance as the password because she knew I would figure it out. And now it's gone." He took me into a hug and I let the tears fall, wetting his shirt. I'd missed him so much.

"I don't know what to do, Dad." I looked up at him. "James says I should become an official FBI informant. Work with them to bring down the network. But I don't know if I can trust him anymore. I don't know if I can trust anyone."

He looked away from me as if searching for something. "Do you think he was lying about his feelings for you?"

"I … I don't know. He says they're real. That it started as an assignment but became something more. But how do I know that's true? How do I know he's not still playing a role?" I shook my head, pulling back to wrap my arms around myself. "And, even if it is true, will I ever be able to move past the fact that that's how we met? That our entire relationship was based on a lie? I don't know if I'll ever be able to fully move past that fact. And is it really fair to be in a relationship with him if I can't forgive him?"

"I can't answer that for you, kiddo. Only you can decide whether to trust him." Dad wrapped an arm around me, squeezing. "But I will say this. The way he looked at you in that hospital room last night. The fear in his voice when he called to tell me what happened. That wasn't an act. That man was terrified at the thought of losing you."

I wanted to believe that. Wanted to think that at least some of what James and I had was genuine.

My phone rang. I pulled it out and saw Banks's name on the screen. "Hey," I answered.

"How are you feeling today? Are you home?"

"Better," I said, trying to hold back a bit of a sigh. "I'm at my apartment with my dad."

"I'm glad you're safe." She paused. "I hate to do this right now, but I wanted to talk to you about the Redmond case."

My body buzzed, back straightening on its own. "What about it?"

"I still think we have enough evidence to retry. The Maryland U.S. Attorney's office is willing to present to another different grand jury if we want to move forward."

"You want to retry after what happened?"

"I think the evidence is solid. I think we were unlucky with our jury composition. And with everything that happened to you yesterday, well … maybe I should have taken your point about interference more seriously. I'm not saying it did happen. I'm just saying it seems like more of a possibility against the backdrop of what just happened. And I think if we present again, we'll get an indictment." Banks's voice softened. "But I also understand if you don't want to. If you want to step back from this case after everything that's happened. I can handle it myself if you need me to."

I looked at my dad. He was watching me with concern but also with a look that said he believed I could handle whatever decision I made.

"Can you give me a few days to give you a decision?" I asked Banks. "I just need some time to think about whether I want to keep going with this. Whether I can keep going."

"Of course. We weren't planning to present immediately anyways. Well, call me if you need anything. Day or night. I'm here for you."

"Thank you, Helen. I appreciate it."

The call ended, and I tossed the phone on the table and slumped into a chair.

"She wants you to keep working the case," Dad said, taking the chair opposite me.

"Yeah. Wants to retry the Redmond indictment with a different grand jury."

He nodded, letting the implication settle for a moment. "What do you want to do?"

"I don't know." I stared at my phone. "I want to finish this. Want to see it through and bring down everyone involved. But …"

He nodded at me, gesturing to go on.

"I am just so tired, Dad. So done with all the lies and danger. Of feeling like I have to look over my shoulder everywhere I go."

He made a noncommittal noise. Then said, "My two cents? You need to do what feels right. Not what other people think you should do. Not what would make the best career move or the most dramatic story. What feels right to you in your gut."

"And what if I don't know what feels right?"

"Take the time you need to figure it out. You've got a few days. Time to think. To rest. To decide who you are and what you want. But whatever you decide, about the case, about James, I'm proud of you. You exposed corruption at the highest levels. You survived a kidnapping. You solved what your mother didn't get to. That matters, Alex. Even if the evidence is gone. Even if the case doesn't move forward. What you did matters."

We looked at each other for a long moment. "Thanks, Dad."

He stood and walked over to the sink, reaching in the cabinet underneath for cleaning wipes. "Let's get this place cleaned up and then make some food. When's the last time you ate something that wasn't hospital food or takeout?"

I chuckled. "I honestly can't remember."

"That's what I thought. I'm making you a proper meal. And you're going to rest. And we're not going to talk about federal cases or FBI informants or criminal networks for at least the next twelve hours. Deal?"

"Deal."

We spent the rest of the morning and early afternoon cleaning up my apartment. Putting books back on shelves. Organizing the papers the FBI had scattered. Making the space feel like home again instead of a crime scene.

Dad cooked lunch. Grilled cheese sandwiches and tomato soup. Simple comfort food that reminded me of being a kid. Of a time before my mother died. Before I learned about corruption and conspiracies. Before everything got so complicated.

By mid-afternoon, I was exhausted again. Dad set me up on the couch with blankets and pillows and turned on a mindless movie. I fell asleep within minutes.

When I woke up, it was dark outside. Dad was sitting in the chair across from me, reading a book. He looked up and smiled when he saw I was awake.

"Feel better?"

"Yeah. A lot better." I sat up and rubbed my eyes. "What time is it?"

"Almost eight. You slept for about four hours."

My phone buzzed with a text.

JAMES

I know you need space. Just wanted to make sure you're okay. Let me know if you need anything.

I stared at the message. Not sure how to respond. Not sure what I even wanted to say to him.

"Is that James?" Dad asked.

I nodded. "Yeah."

"You don't have to answer if you're not ready."

"I know."

But I typed out a response, anyway.

> I'm okay. At my apartment with my dad. Thanks for checking in.

> Good. Get some rest. We can talk when you're ready.

I set the phone down and looked at my dad. "I think I need time to figure this out."

"That's fair. And I'll be here if you want me to be."

"You don't have to stay that long."

"I'm retired," he said with a chuckle as he closed his book. "And even if I weren't, you're my priority right now, kiddo. Everything else can wait."

I felt a surge of gratitude for my dad. For his steady presence. For the way he showed up when I needed him without making me feel weak or incapable. It made me sad for all of the time that we lost when he was in prison.

"Thank you," I said. "For being here. For everything."

"Always."

We ordered dinner. Watched more mindless TV. Talked about anything except the case. It was exactly what I needed.

By the time I went to bed that night, I still didn't have answers. Didn't know what I was going to tell Banks, nor if I could trust James or if our relationship could survive what I'd learned.

But whatever I decided, my dad would support me, and that was enough for right now.

EPILOGUE

I'D TAKEN an entire week off from work. Banks checked in daily, and each time I'd told her that I didn't have an answer for her yet, but that I would soon. Dad had flown back to Texas after spending the week with me, satisfied that I was physically okay even if I was still emotionally processing everything. Hugging me tight at the airport, he'd made me promise to call him every day. I'd promised.

Now I had one day left before I needed to give Banks an answer about whether I was coming back to work. She was moving forward with the Redmond indictment tomorrow with or without me.

I hadn't spoken to James the whole week. He'd called twice. Left messages. Sent a few texts. But I'd ignored all of them, still unsure of what to say. I didn't know if I could trust my own judgment when it came to him.

I hadn't left my apartment since coming home from the airport. The walls felt like they were closing in. So I pulled on a jacket and walked to the National Mall.

The Mall was quiet this early on a Sunday morning. A few joggers passed by. Some tourists took photos. But it was mostly empty. I took a deep breath, inhaling the crisp winter air.

I bought a hot coffee from a vendor near the Washington Monument and found an empty bench to sit down to sip it. The coffee was terrible. Bitter and lukewarm. But I drank it anyways because I needed to do something normal. Something that had nothing to do with conspiracies or corruption or lies.

A man sat down on the other end of my bench. I glanced at him briefly. Middle-aged. Nondescript features. Dark coat. Nothing remarkable or memorable about him. There were dozens of empty benches along this stretch of the Mall. Why sit on the one I was occupying?

Pulling a bag of seed from his pocket, he started tossing it to the pigeons that swarmed around the bench.

I said nothing. Just watched the pigeons fight over the scattered seeds.

The man didn't speak. Didn't look at me. Just fed the birds with a distant expression on his face. Like he was somewhere else entirely. Thinking about something far away.

After a few minutes, he stood, brushed crumbs off his coat, and walked away without a word.

I tried to turn back to my own thoughts. Watching him had given me momentary reprieve from my swirling thoughts about the decision I needed to make tomorrow. To whether I had the strength to keep fighting.

Where the man had been sitting, something caught my eye on the bench. A small object left behind on the weathered wood.

It was a chess piece. A black knight.

I picked it up, feeling its weight in my hand. It looked like it was carved from the same material as the white queen flash drive. Had the same worn porcelain surface, albeit a different color.

My heart started racing. I turned the piece over, examining it. I started looking for seams, for a way to open it like the white queen had opened.

I gripped the horse's head and the base and twisted.

A soft click, and the piece came apart in my hands. But instead of an integrated USB drive, it was hollow. I peered inside and could see something stuffed at the bottom. I tapped it on the bench, and a small slip of paper fluttered onto the worn wood of the bench.

I smoothed it out with shaking fingers.

Written in messy scrawl was a phone number.

I looked up. Scanned the Mall for the man who had left it. But he was gone.

I stared at the phone number — ten digits with no name attached to it.

The black knight meant someone out there knew the game was still being played.

And they wanted me back on the board.

————

The story continues in *Improper Influence*
Grab your copy on Amazon:
https://a.co/d/4d1s6L6

THE ALEX HAYES SERIES

ALSO BY L.T. RYAN

Find All of L.T. Ryan's Books on Amazon Today!

The Jack Noble Series

The Recruit (free)

The First Deception (Prequel 1)

Noble Beginnings

A Deadly Distance

Ripple Effect (Bear Logan)

Thin Line

Noble Intentions

When Dead in Greece

Noble Retribution

Noble Betrayal

Never Go Home

Beyond Betrayal (Clarissa Abbot)

Noble Judgment

Never Cry Mercy

Deadline

End Game

Noble Ultimatum

Noble Legend

Noble Revenge

Never Look Back

Bear Logan Series

Ripple Effect

Blowback

Take Down

Deep State

Bear & Mandy Logan Series

Close to Home

Under the Surface

The Last Stop

Over the Edge

Between the Lies

Caught in the Web

The Marked Daughter

Beneath the Frozen Sky

Rachel Hatch Series

Drift

Downburst

Fever Burn

Smoke Signal

Firewalk

Whitewater

Aftershock

Whirlwind

Tsunami

Fastrope

Sidewinder

Redaction

Mirage

Faultline

Switchback

Mitch Tanner Series

The Depth of Darkness

Into The Darkness

Deliver Us From Darkness

Cassie Quinn Series

Path of Bones

Whisper of Bones

Symphony of Bones

Etched in Shadow

Concealed in Shadow

Betrayed in Shadow

Born from Ashes

Return to Ashes

Risen from Ashes

Into the Light

Blake Brier Series

Unmasked

Unleashed

Uncharted

Drawpoint

Contrail

Detachment

Clear

Quarry

Dalton Savage Series

Savage Grounds

Scorched Earth

Cold Sky

The Frost Killer

Crimson Moon

Dust Devil

Savage Season

Maddie Castle Series

The Handler

Tracking Justice

Hunting Grounds

Vanished Trails

Smoldering Lies

Field of Bones

Beneath the Grove

Disappearing Act

Silent Witness

Affliction Z Series

Affliction Z: Patient Zero

Affliction Z: Abandoned Hope

Affliction Z: Descended in Blood

Affliction Z : Fractured Part 1

Affliction Z: Fractured Part 2 (Coming Soon)

Alex Hayes Series

Trial By Fire (Prequel)

Fractured Verdict

11th Hour Witness

Buried Testimony

The Bishop's Recusal

The Silent Gavel

Improper Influence

Stella LaRosa Series

Black Rose

Red Ink

Black Gold

White Lies

Silver Bullet

Avril Dahl Series

Cold Reckoning

Cold Legacy

Cold Mercy

Savannah Shadows Series

Echoes of Guilt

The Silence Before

Dead Air

———

Receive a free copy of The Recruit. Visit:

https://ltryan.com/jack-noble-newsletter-signup-1

ABOUT THE AUTHORS

L.T. RYAN is a *Wall Street Journal* and *USA Today* bestselling author, renowned for crafting pulse-pounding thrillers that keep readers on the edge of their seats. Known for creating gripping, character-driven stories, Ryan is the author of the *Jack Noble* series, the *Rachel Hatch* series, and more. With a knack for blending action, intrigue, and emotional depth, Ryan's books have captivated millions of fans worldwide.

Whether it's the shadowy world of covert operatives or the relentless pursuit of justice, Ryan's stories feature unforgettable characters and high-stakes plots that resonate with fans of Lee Child, Robert Ludlum, and Michael Connelly.

When not writing, Ryan enjoys crafting new ideas with coauthors, running a thriving publishing company, and connecting with readers. Discover the next story that will keep you turning pages late into the night.

Connect with L.T. Ryan
Sign up for his newsletter to hear the latest goings on and receive some free content
➜ https://ltryan.com/jack-noble-newsletter-signup-1

Join the private readers' group
➜ https://www.facebook.com/groups/1727449564174357

Instagram ➜ @ltryanauthor

Visit the website ➜ https://ltryan.com
Send an email ➜ contact@ltryan.com

————

LAURA CHASE is a corporate attorney-turned-author who brings her courtroom experience to the page in her gripping legal and psychological thrillers. Chase draws on her real-life experience to draw readers into the high-stakes world of courtroom drama and moral ambiguity.

After earning her JD, Chase clerked for a federal judge and thereafter transitioned to big law, where she honed her skills in high-pressure legal environments. Her passion for exploring the darker side of human nature and the gray areas of justice fuels her writing.

Chase lives with her husband, their two sons, a dog and a cat in Northern Florida. When she's not writing or working, she enjoys spending time with her family, traveling, and bingeing true crime shows.

Connect with Laura:

Sign up for her newsletter: www.laurachaseauthor.com/

Follow her on tiktok: @lawyerlaura

Send an email: info@laurachase.com

Made in the USA
Middletown, DE
13 January 2026

26987713R00152